To

Enjoy this book as much as I enjoyed your company. Till we meet again.

Natasha Jacques

Author of

Chasing Rainbows

Natasha Jacques.

x .

NATASHA JACQUES

To My Beloved Children and Grandchildren,
I am so blessed to have you in my life.
Love you forever xxx

To My Husband Peter,
Thank you for always believing in me. Love you xxx

Natasha Jacques

NATASHA JACQUES

Chasing Rainbows

Chapter 1

The sun rose high in the sky lighting up my bedroom as though a halogen bulb had been switched on. It was Monday and I knew as I turned over and buried my head deeper under the covers the sleep and solitude I sought was not mine for the taking. I was tired of waking up every morning with the heavy weight of my unhappiness totally encompassing me and not being able to do anything about it. It was totally consuming and though aware of my withdrawal to other people around me, I still robotically went through the motions.

"Do you realise what time it is Grace, you'll be late if you don't get up. Are you listening to me or do I have to come up there and pull you out of bed?"

"Yeah whatever," I grumbled sinking deeper beneath the duvet. Just sleep I kept telling myself. It was so much easier, enabling me the release and peacefulness I so desperately craved. What did it matter anymore if I didn't get up? "He doesn't care about you anymore," my head kept taunting me, "There will be no text messages from you to him or visa versa with 'Hi baby miss you."

"Gracie do I have to keep repeating myself, I'm not a parrot. Get yourself out of bed before I do it for you."

"Alright" I shouted, kicking back the covers in sudden irritation. Reluctantly I looked back at my bed grimacing as I walked sleepily into the wardrobe.

"Ouch for God's sake."

I stopped, catching a glance of myself in the door mirror, I wanted to walk away. The black cloud inside of me made me remain. I needed the torment for nourishment which now felt so familiar to me. I stepped back breathing deeply as my eyes a duller version of hazel stared back. . I didn't look physically different than the previous day, but somehow I knew that I'd changed. I leaned in more closely frowning at my reflection. Was that an extra line on my forehead that hadn't been there yesterday or had I just had more nightmares I was unaware of? The way I was feeling now I puckered my mouth not caring either way.

The bedroom door opened behind me revealing the indignant hands on hips plump statuesque form formerly known as my mother.

"Oh, so you decided to honour us with your presence then?"

"Mum, please don't, not today."

Whether she had noticed the pleading in my voice, or the dejected form I was inadvertently presenting she pressed her lips together before coming over to me wrapping her arms tightly around my dishevelled pyjama clothed frame.

"I know love, but you'll be fine, you know that, don't you?"

Her eyes met mine in the mirror's reflection.

"Yes mum I know, but it still hurts so much."

"Don't you worry your pretty little head about the likes of him my girl. You know what they say Grace, there's plenty more fish in the sea."

But I wasn't interested in the rest of the fish I wanted my fish, the one I had loved and cherished and been married to for over five years. As if my mother was able to tune in to my thoughts I hung my head not voicing the protestations of love swirling around my stricken and incapacitated brain.

"I know mum, what you're saying is right, but I don't want anybody else?"

Sighing deeply Esther Fairfax bit her lip again, her eyes caressing her young daughter in front of her.

"It's bound to hurt love, your healing. In time it will eventually fade."

Whether it was her words or her expression I didn't want to stand there anymore feeling her pity, or listening to her empty words of wisdom.

"Mum, how would you know? You and dad have always been together, what would you know about heartbreak?"

"You don't have to put your finger in a pan of boiling water Grace to know it's going to hurt. Just because your dad and I have been together for more years than I can comfortably count, it doesn't mean I don't feel what my daughter feels."

"Oh mum, I hate him so much for hurting me, why did he do it, why?"

Burying my head in her shoulder not bothering to fight back the tears any longer I cried as helplessly as I had when I been hurt as a small child. Now, as then, she held me close stroking my tousled hair softly, all the while whispering words of comfort as she soothed and calmed me.

"My dearest darling it will all sort itself out don't you worry. You are still only young; you have the whole world in front of you. Don't pin all your dreams on a lowlife like Dylan. You are worth ten of him, you know that don't you?"

She held me at arm's length studying my face closely. Seeing no change in my expression, she ran her forefinger gently over my cheek whispering gently,

"Don't give in Gracie, I've brought you up to be tougher than that."

Nodding in reply I forced back the tears still erupting from my eyes, I swore to myself there and then that Dylan Hunt would pay dearly for every tear drop I spent on his behalf.

As if understanding my rigid pose, I stood away from her my head held high my shoulders straight. She smiled back at me nodding her head in agreement.

"That's my girl. Twenty minutes Gracie then your breakfast will be on the table."

"But I'm not..."

" If you're about to say you're not hungry then you can think again my girl."

Sighing despondently spouting out 'fine,' before she closed the door gently behind her, I spun round to stare once more at my reflection. Unlike earlier that morning when I was faced with self-pity and rejection, mum's words as usual had had a calming effect. I now stared back at my image with renewed confidence, and something else. Something else, that hadn't been evident twenty minutes before. Perhaps, just perhaps I could get through this, fed up with my pity party I made myself a promise. I was done with my wallowing, time to turn over a new leaf.

I knew I was looking as good as I felt, not because of all the admiring comments I had received throughout the day, which though making me smile had also contributed in reinforcing my new found resolve. I hurriedly left the office running blindly through the after work crowd to catch the bus home. I had taken extra time that morning after the tete a tete with my mother. She was right of course she always was. Just because the one man I loved beyond anyone else didn't want me anymore didn't mean I had to look like the cast off Dylan had made me feel.

Smiling warmly at the young guy who had stood up to let me have his seat I pondered as the bus lurched forward, what was I going to do with the empty evening ahead of me? I had two choices I realised. One was to go home to spend an evening of television with my parents who now were settled in a happy and predictable routine, or I could do something different. I was fed up with shutting myself away all the time, pretending to the outside world that I was fine, handling everything in my stride with a permanent smile etched on my face. I wanted to be me again. The anger I felt was not with myself, It was all connected to my soon to be ex-husband. Dylan Hunt.

As I settled more comfortably in the uncomfortable seat I ignored the irritated glance of my fellow passenger as my arm accidentally knocked hers. Whereas normally I would have apologised, I didn't on this occasion, choosing instead to look straight-ahead, my eyes blinded by the shaggy hair-do of the guy in front of me. I had thought long and hard throughout the day, what my next point of action would be. I had received the object of my denial through the post, my denial being my decree nisi. I could recall the jolt of pain when I recognized the solicitor's name stamped on the front of the envelope. My mother who also noticed it, said nothing as she silently placed the eggs and bacon on my plate. I had fully intended not to eat anything but suddenly the pain I was feeling inside was so monumental, that I ate just to occupy my mind and hands. Now, I didn't have that distraction so I looked out of the window suddenly noticing the rain, as it splattered against the steamy glass.

When the bus shuddered to a halt six stops later I stared absently out of the window again. My heart started beating erratically when I realised where I was. If I got off the bus now I would be a couple of doors away from the life that had been ours twenty-five weeks before. It was only when feeling the rain on my face and the pavement beneath my feet did I realise what I had compulsively done. Why had I done that? Feeling completely out of place I looked around me, feeling sudden guilt at my actions. Nervous about my intentions I looked hurriedly around for witnesses. Seeing no one, I cast off my spur of the moment insanity and walked hesitantly towards the brightly coloured red front door with its brass letterbox of number twenty two Lansdale Avenue.

The house was in darkness, its bay fronted windows staring back at me with their dark soulless eyes. The narrow walled front garden reminded me of the summer previously, when we had planted miniature box hedges, separating the tiled brick path from the small handkerchief lawn, with its miniscule array of flowers. Only now, like me the flowers were no longer there. Died and forgotten like Dylan had forgotten me. Okay Grace, breathe in and deal with it. I told myself repeatedly, don't give in and don't walk away. Fishing around in my handbag my fingers enclosed around the keys. I felt like an intruder as I slipped the key into the lock and looked pensively around me to see whether I was being observed. I opened the door and closed it gently behind me. The first thing that hit me was the stale air and mustiness, which told me the house hadn't had its occupant home for a while. So if he wasn't staying here, where the hell was he staying?

I should have felt empowered at having achieved the strength to step over the threshold after such a long time away. But I didn't. Instead I felt hurt, lost and abandoned all over again. My fingers lightly touched the glass vase with its dead remains of tiger lilies and fetid water fumigating the air. The glass console table was covered in dust so deep I was tempted to write my initials in it, but I refrained, opting instead to step further into the sleeping house unsure of every step I took.

This house once had been a home of love and laughter. I thrust back the immediate memory that sprang to mind of when Dylan had carried me over the threshold to our new home. My heart had been fit to bursting with love for him, nothing was out of reach or unachievable. How little I knew then. Was it wise to be here I thought as I looked around the dark and gloomy surroundings? It was my home wasn't it? It hadn't been sold yet, and I still wasn't divorced. My heels clicked on the ash wood floor as I stepped further into the hallway. Taking a deep breath I switched on the lights their brightness making my eyes cringe. The door to the sitting room was ajar, I pushed it gently with my hand noticing how shaky I was. I laughed admonishing myself for being so stupid.

When I switched on the table lamps my heart cried out at the memories that came flooding back to me of our shared nights together, as we drank wine, being so into each other as we lay on the rug in front of the open fire frolicking around before ending up making love in front of the glowing embers. The Christmases we had spent there, the numerous kisses under the mistletoe. But now it just looked like an empty show home, the house like me feeling unloved, lonely and unwanted. I should have walked out then, through the front door and hurriedly back to my parents and to the home, which had been mine since childhood. But I couldn't. Something was pulling me in; call it nostalgia or whatever I just couldn't stop myself.

Every piece of furniture I passed, was lovingly touched by my hand, embracing the moments connected to them, refusing to acknowledge the pain of where it had all gone wrong. It was when my feet alighted on the wooden treads of the stairs that my heart began its painful trip down memory lane once more. Every picture that hung on the wall or stood on the furniture had been fervently chosen to match and blend and compliment as Dylan and I once did. I pushed open the bedroom door, my eyes immediately going to the bed, where many nights we had enjoyed our love making, always needing and taking from each other, the acts as feral and wanton as if our very lives depended on it.

I sat on the edge of the bed the coldness of the linen seeping through the damp fabric of my coat. This bed, this house had not been slept or lived in for quite a while, that was evident. Why had Dylan fought so hard to keep me out of here when he wasn't even using the house himself? The questions were becoming tiresome to me I wished now I hadn't got off the bus and stepped back into my old life. What was the point, what could I possibly gain by all of this? Nothing, that's what.

Tired and lonely and eaten up with insurmountable heartache, I lay back against the pillow almost crying out at the smell of him still emanating from it. I loved this house, I loved my life and I loved him. When had Dylan fallen out of love with me? Why, why, had he fallen out of love, with us? I had asked myself these questions so many times I lost count but unlike then, I couldn't let it go. I was sick and tired of pushing it away, pretending it didn't matter. My life was better without him I repeatedly kept telling myself, but if I was honest, it truly wasn't. As I looked around me I realised I wasn't over the marriage, or over him. When had I become such a walkover that I simply lay down and let him trample all over me like the proverbial doormat. When had this new Grace immerged? Had I been like that all along and not noticed the change? Was that why he didn't want me anymore? Where was the lust for life I once had? Where had it gone?

The click of the front door went unnoticed until I heard footsteps on the stairs. My heart began hammering imagining Dylan storming through the door demanding when he saw me what the hell I was doing here and why. But as I listened more carefully the steps were light not heavy as his were.

"Hello who's there?"

My voice was not as confident as I would have liked, so instead I stood up bracing myself for whatever confrontation was heading my way. I don't know who was more surprised Zara or me.

"Grace, my god you terrified the hell out of me"

"Likewise" I stared at her noticing her eyes scan the room checking to see if anything had been moved or taken.

"What are you doing here Zara?"

Her eyes green and bright snapped to my face suspiciously, her furtive glance at my handbag, brief but not unnoticed.

"Dylan asked me to keep a check on the house. I was just passing, I hadn't intended to come tonight but when I saw the lights on I thought..."

It didn't take much to finish off the unspoken sentence

"You thought oh Dylan must be back," my voice was mocking as I faced her with a glare as glacial as her own

"Something like that. Anyway you're not supposed to be here are you?"

"And who are you to tell me when I can and can't enter my own house?"

For a moment she looked flustered as I thrust her in the spotlight but noticing my own fidgeting hands displaying my own discomfort she recovered quickly, too quickly for my liking and like a flashlight that had been switched on suddenly I wanted to know why.

"I'm just acting on Dylan's instructions nothing more"

"Somehow I find that hard to believe. You walk into my home like you own it. You used to be my best friend and yet now you're all pro Dylan acting like you're doing me a favour by speaking to me. I thought you two couldn't stand each other? What's changed Zara?"

"Grace we haven't been best mates for over a year. But as always you're too quick in jumping to assumptions"

"Depends what I'm supposed to be assuming"

"Grace stop. None of this is relevant anymore", she voiced waving her arms around,

"It may not be relevant to you but by god it's relevant to me. I happen to love Dylan and none of that has changed throughout the months we have been apart. What else did you expect of me Zara?"

She became agitated, as she looked around her eyes avoiding facing me directly.

"This has nothing to do with me, I don't want to be involved in this, I'm just doing a favour for Dylan."

"You've already involved yourself it seems" I retorted back.

She looked away not bothering to reply, so I decided to use another tactic.

"I'm sorry if I have made you feel uncomfortable. But I have to ask, why are you checking the house? Where the hell is Dylan and when did it change between you two?"

"It's not for me to say Grace. I don't want to take sides all I know is that Dylan is away for awhile and he has asked me to make sure the house remains intact as long as it remains on sale"

I looked down at my shoes not wanting to return her gaze, not wanting to give anything away. Hundreds of questions were forcing their way through demanding answers from her, but I knew at this present moment in time it was wiser for me to keep them silent.

"What do you think Dylan will make of the conversation we've had between us tonight?"

"What do you mean I haven't said anything untoward?"

"No?" I asked enquiringly, a plan beginning to form in my mind.

"Look Grace I don't know what you mean"

Leaning back on the bed my elbows digging into the mattress for support I looked keenly back at her, making sure my voice remained light and unassuming

"I wonder how Dylan will react when he finds out you told me he was away indefinitely"

Her face paled slightly but she remained adamant.

"What do you mean?"

"Well the only reason I am living with my parents is because he made a convincing play that he couldn't bear to be under the same roof as me. You know how temperamental Dylan can be when he wants something bad enough. But, knowing now that he isn't here, well that kind of throws a different light on the situation don't you think Zara?"

"Sorry I'm not following?"

"Well I could go back to the solicitor and kick up quite a stink knowing that Dylan is not living here, and instigating you as my source. You see that was part of the arrangement of me leaving or rather being forced to leave" I added more sourly than I intended, 'Dylan was to remain here until the house sale was completed" and as I looked slowly around me to make a point I added "And well its obvious who has reneged on that agreement".

"Oh Grace. Please don't say anything I don't want to be the cause of any trouble" Her eyes bore into mine silently pleading with me as she wrung her hands nervously. This was definitely weird. Why and what had Dylan said to Zara to turn her against me?

Biting my lip to disguise my smile, I nodded looking down slowly at my feet taking a few moments of silence to show Zara that she had inadvertently given me the control.

"Well. Seeing as I don't want to get you into any trouble. I suppose I could keep quiet, if you were to do the same about seeing me here tonight"

I hoped fervently that my voice appeared as uncaring as I wanted it to sound. The seconds ticked by seeming like minutes to me before she finally answered, her voice as unsure as her expression.

"Well I think that's a good idea Grace. Best not to stir the pot eh"

"Ok that's fine by me."

I followed her out of the bedroom my eyes securely focused on the back of her head as she descended the stairs. There was something very fishy going on and I was determined to find out what it was. But now was not the time and Zara was not the right person to ask. So instead when we both reached the front door I smiled pleasantly as she followed me out securing the door behind her, which majorly riled me. This was my home, since when had she become the caretaker? I waved pleasantly at her as I walked the few streets to my parent's house. It seemed my mother was right, there was no smoke without fire and I was determined to get the bottom of what the hell was going on.

By Wednesday I had fallen into a routine of checking the house myself after work, only this time with the aid of a torch. There were a few letters lying on the doormat all addressed to my absconded husband. I could I thought leave them where they were for Zara to collect and post on as I assumed she had been doing. But by now my curiosity was getting the better of me, and I was more than willing to take part in the cat and mouse game, that had inherently come about since my initial visit a couple of days before.

I had been thinking nonstop about what Dylan's reasons could be for leaving our marital home without notice being given to the respective solicitors. So step one in my game of subterfuge was to gather information over a two-week period. If by then Dylan had still not returned, I would move back in. The thought gave me a momentary feeling of triumph before reality set in. How would my missing husband react once knowledge of my actions were revealed? Why did I care I thought as I closed the front door behind me. Not everything was about him and though it pained me endlessly to think of where he was, there was nothing at this moment I could do about it. My mother on the other hand was almost spitting feathers when I advised her of my plan at the end of my two-week vigil.

"Grace, have you gone mad? Why would you want to move back into that empty house when you can quite happily stay here with us?"

I sat at the dining room table my face resting miserably in my hands. The hard wood of the table digging into my elbows, but I refused to acknowledge my mother's gaze as she paused mid sentence expecting me to ingratiate her with a retort.

Eventually I caved in, "It's my home mum and if Dylan can't be bothered to live there, then I will."

"Have you thought this through carefully Grace?"

"Very carefully. That house is as much mine as it is his. I have every right to be there. He is the one that has lied to oust me and now I can prove it"

"And what will all this solve?"

Sighing I asked myself that same question many times. It was my home and I wanted to be there. It shouldn't stand empty. It was only a matter of time before it would either invite burglars or squatters. I reiterated this as calmly as I could and surprisingly my mother remained quiet. One Brownie point to me I thought. Sensing my silent victory my mother added,

"And what will you do when Dylan finds out and returns?"

"Nothing he won't come back because I am having the locks changed and why would he want too when he tried everything in his power to make me leave in the first place. My solicitor agrees, I have every right to move back in and that mum is what I am going to do"

"Nothing good will come of this Grace, I hope you realise that?"

"Mum come on, trust me I know what I am doing"

Now here I was sitting on the floor in my lounge in my own house a few days later, secure in the knowledge that now with the locks changed Dylan was definitely out and I was definitely in. I had not only succeeded, I was victorious. Yet for all that I still felt hollow inside. Within these four walls my marriage had begun and ended. Five years, five months and twenty-seven days. I looked around me knowing I should feel comforted by the cosiness and style of what was once our love nest, but like my heart it felt empty. I was safe within the confines of its strong brick walls but I was still the wounded chick that had her heart broken on May the fifteenth at five thirty pm.

We always met on the Friday at our local wine bar. It was close to our respective work places and started off the weekend well. Only on this particular Friday he had been late and it was me who had gotten the bottle of chilled chardonnay and two glasses. The forty-five minutes spent sipping the wine slowly had dragged, my head constantly snapping round to spy the newcomers coming through the door. I had rung his mobile every five minutes but got fed up with being fobbed off by his voice mail. So when to the minute, an hour later he strolled nonchalantly through the door, I didn't smile or kiss him, as I usually did. I eyed him suspiciously as he sat opposite me instead of next to me. He poured himself a glass of wine not bothering to refill mine, which was not the norm. I knew then something was very wrong. But hard as I tried I couldn't place my finger on the problem, so instead remaining silent I sat back and just stared at him expectantly. My nerves were on edge with the waiting I had already endured and I wasn't willing to give in easily.

"Had a good day? "He enquired politely

"Not, had a good day darling, god I've missed you." That was what he was supposed to say. What he said every Friday.

I shrugged my shoulders not wanting to engage in conversation with him. I was suddenly wary that perhaps I didn't want to listen to what he had come here to say, so I braced myself and sure enough his next words had my life reeling like an airplane spiralling out of control.

"We're over. I don't want to talk about it because there is nothing to discuss. I've been meaning to tell you for awhile, but to be honest I wasn't sure how to broach the subject."

My demeanour remained calm though my fingers clasped the stem of the glass so tightly it was surprising it didn't break. I looked at the wine glass, in my mind imagining Dylan's neck as the stem. His words were not as genuine as he wanted them to appear to me. He hadn't been waiting to broach the subject as he categorically stated because up until now, this very minute I had been head over heels in love with a man who had been head over heels in love with me. He was tall, charming and gorgeous, my own personal pinup and I had revelled in that knowledge every day since Dylan Hunt had become mine.

"Haven't you anything to say Grace? I understand this has come as a bit of a shock to you, but well, there it is."

I remained frozen as though I had been carved into an ice sculptor. This beautiful wonderful loving man that was my husband was telling me it was over. WE WERE OVER. Had I heard correctly or had I consumed too much wine and misheard what he had said?

Blinking my eyes my vision as clear as when I had entered an hour before I looked him in the eyes. He stared unflinchingly back. His jaw was set in a determined hold that I knew would not entertain any theatrics or anything remotely embarrassing. Hence, I realised, the revelation in a public place. So I remained calm just staring at him not quite knowing what to say or how to say it. As the realisation of his words sunk into my befuddled brain I began to cry inwardly, praying he had made a mistake, but his eyes when he rested them on mine were no longer the eyes of my love smitten husband. They belonged to a stranger with eyes as cold and as unknowing as if we had never met. I swallowed the remains of my glass making sure to place it as gently as I could on the table. Standing up flicking back the strands of my long dark hair over my shoulders I looked down at him, my eyes now as remote as his. It was only a moment but over the passage of time for memory's sake, it was infinity. Turning away I held my head high and walked towards the entrance. I sensed him behind me but I didn't let on. I opened the thick glass door with its heavy brass handle letting it swing back ferociously knowing he had expected me to hold it open for him. I heard rather than saw his yell of pain as the door bounded back to him knocking him sideways the thick sturdy handle smashing into him. It was only then that I smiled.

The phone rang disturbing me and I stared at it for many seconds wondering who was ringing me. Remembering we had caller ID I stood up slowly walking pensively towards the machine shrilling at me. It could only be one of two people. The only two who knew I was here. My mother or Dylan. My solicitor's secretary had duly informed me during that afternoon that my husband's lawyer had been notified of my actions and would be in touch after speaking with his client. So if this was Dylan, was I seriously considering engaging in a conversation with him when there was nothing more to say? Or, could I carry off the supreme bitch act and rub it in maliciously that his ruse not only had been discovered but also conquered. The answer machine sorted out my dilemma for me and as the silky frustrated tones of him filled the room I found my legs giving way beneath me as I sunk onto the sofa, my whole body convulsing like I was suffering an epileptic fit.

"Grace it's me pick up I know you're in there. What the hell are you playing at? What do you think this will prove moving back into the house without my knowledge or consent? He paused in his dictation my eyes seeing him now running his long fingers through the thick mass of dark hair cut short to curb the reckless curl.

"So this is it, is it? You choose to ignore me, well, what more could I expect from you and your childish pathetic behaviour." He paused again waiting to see if I was incensed enough to verbally pick up the receiver and fight back, but I wasn't and hadn't been ever since that evening at the wine bar on May the fifteenth at five thirty pm. "Fine, well ok" he continued angrily "I obviously need to use another tactic. BYE " and with that brusque farewell he was gone.

16

CHASING RAINBOWS

It took me awhile to pull myself together. It had been the first time since I had left our home that we had spoken and though now I should be lolling back against the settee with a satisfied smug grin on my face, I wasn't. Instead I was sitting upright and rigid as a mannequin. Immediately my mother's words came back at me *"And what will you do when Dylan finds out and returns?"* I don't know mum I answered quietly I honestly didn't think he would care.

The next morning I opened the door with trepidation looking in both directions for the dark blue BMW that would herald to me the arrival of the almighty and controlling Dylan Hunt. But it wasn't there and for that I was eternally grateful. I checked the front door one more time before walking down the path determined that my last day before my fortnight holiday would be calming and Dylan stress free. And so it was. Before returning home to the quiet house on Lansdale Avenue I popped briefly by to see my parents and pick up my Audi A3. My mother's eyes when she saw me were worrisome. I smiled pleasantly knowing she was hunting for any sign of deceit or distress. But no, I had overcome the initial shock of his rude interruption the night before and during the ensuing night relegated myself to the realms of sleep where Dylan had the starring role in my continuous nightly rerun movie.

"So Gracie how was your first night home" the words were spoken pleasantly enough but I detected the undercurrent in her tone.

"You know mum you don't have to worry about me anymore. I'm not a little girl and believe it or not I can stand up for myself in any given situation"

Her lips gave a grimace whilst her eyes looked into me for any signs of untruth. But there wasn't any. I had handled my first night home and though I was in two minds of whether to share all the information of the night before with her, it wasn't in me to be deceitful.

"Dylan rang last night "my words spoken casually were brief as I watched my mother pause in the pouring of the coffee to spin round and look at me intensely again for any after effects.

"And what did he have to say may I ask" emphasis on the he word, but ignoring it I smiled up at her taking the mug of steaming coffee she offered.

"Oh you know the usual, what the hell did I think I was doing blah blah blah."

"I wish you wouldn't blah blah blah me Grace. You miss out information, which you think will worry me. It does anyway so tell me exactly what he said."

"Well I didn't answer he spoke to the answering machine which he hates but, he demanded to know what the hell I was doing back at the house."

Seeing my mother's momentary glance of righteous concern I added hastily,

"He's just peeved mum that I found out and took control. No big deal."

She sat down opposite me her eyes studying my face. Satisfied that I appeared as unaffected as I sounded, she sipped her coffee before replying,

"So, what do you think he will do next?"

"Don't know, don't care. I have every right to be there as much as him, except now the scales dip in my favour as he chose to leave without informing me of his decision."

"Do you know where he has been?" her voice was acidic

I looked at her then regretting momentarily telling her. She always seemed to hit the nail right on the head even if you were sitting there with the offensive item sticking out of your skull.

"No, but then it really isn't any of my concern anymore, in six weeks we will be divorced and then we are both free to get on with our own lives," my voice cracked on the last sentence making me hang my head so my mother couldn't see the pain those words created in me. She wasn't fooled, she never was. Her hand was light on mine as she stroked my fair skin.

"I realise Grace you have to do this, to get through this, to get closure. Just don't forget where we are and that we are always here for you if you need us"

I smiled reassuringly at her wishing I felt as confident as the confidence she was obviously placing in me.

"Mum I know, and believe me I will be ok. I am my mother's daughter after all"

This seemed to placate her sufficiently enough to let the matter drop.

When I returned home arms laden with carrier bags of food I paused, inhaling the fresh clean air the house now embraced me with, as I struggled through the front door kicking it closed behind me. I plonked the bags with my keys onto the console table now sparkling instead of a dust-infested platform. As I was putting away the groceries that would last me the next fortnight I froze to the shrill of the telephone interrupting my happy slapdash thoughts. Slipping of my coat placing it on the back of the dining room chair I walked slowly towards the phone, my heart hammering loudly knowing already who was on the other end of it. The answer machine kicked in.

"Grace pick up. I know you're in there I just saw you go in."

I stood stupefied, kicking myself for not being more observant. Instead of picking up the receiver and telling him where he could shove his phone call I walked over to the bay window in the lounge freezing in horror when I saw him standing next to my pride and joy. My hands fisted automatically as I tried to calm my breathing, which had increased on sight of him.

"If you don't come out, I would hate to see anything happen to your car."

Snarling with my hands fisted I stormed into the hallway not caring for anything else but to get him away from my beloved convertible. I threw open the front door my face set in hard determined lines when he smiled triumphantly as I stepped outside.

"So Gracie you do respond. Shame though" he hesitated as he ran his hand smoothly over the bodywork of my two toned white and black audi that he had bought me for my last birthday with a big red ribbon enveloping it as his arms had enveloped me.

"Shame" he repeated slowly, "That the only chance I get to speak to my wife is via a veiled threat"

I wanted to hit him, to push him violently away, but ever since his words all those months ago which had blown my world into a million pieces, I was still unable to utter a single word to him. I knew by his expression that my face was infused with colour; it was my only visible sign that his words had got to me. He liked it I could see by the smug expression flitting across his face.

"Well there's life in my kitten yet I see"

I watched him silently, fuming inside as he continued to stare back at me knowing at this moment in time he held all the cards in his favour. Jumbled thoughts ran through my mind, each one tumbling over the other. His victorious smile sickened me so without further thought or hesitation my mouth opened into a snarl.

"Is there a point to this charade Dylan, or are you just here to majorly piss me off"

I didn't know who was the most stunned. Was that me who had just said that in that hard and relentless tone? He looked at me with renewed admiration before disguising it just as quickly.

"Well, my little sex kitten has got a little tiger in her at last."

His inferred connotation to my previous nickname did not enamour him to me. If anything it infuriated me more. Without any care for myself, or my predicament I approached him. Dylan stood his ground his eyes staring down into mine, a smirk hovering on his lips.

"I am not your sex kitten Dylan, understand," I shouted poking at his chest with my finger.

His hand suddenly clasped mine holding it still. His face was expressionless but his eyes held a depth to them that made me realise painfully I had missed for such a long time. I could feel my heart beat faster in response, but as I stood there watching him watching me, I realised what he was doing. He was reeling me in like he always had. The realisation of it had me faltering for a moment before I regained my control. Snatching my hand out of his I placed them both on my hips fending off any further chances for him to touch me. If he noticed this he didn't react. His eyes remained focused on mine I could see questions in his eyes but I refused point blank to acknowledge them or incur further conversation.

Taking one last look at him my mouth now set in a scowl I walked away my head held high.

"Gracie don't do this, we need to talk."

His words ceased my pacing as I angrily headed towards the house. Taking a deep breath I straightened up, before turning round to face him.

"I'm sorry what did you say? You want us to talk." I was incredulous at the complete and utter gall of him. "Why now Dylan. You haven't wanted to speak to me since you dropped that bombshell on me over five and a half months ago. What's so different now? What have you done? What has happened that makes you think there is anything you want to say that I want to hear?"

He grimaced at my words but I didn't care. I wanted him to hurt, like he had hurt me. I remained motionless as he advanced towards me. My mind screaming out stay firm don't give him an inch. It was so hard seeing him. His handsome features; his perfect body come towards me his hand outstretched as if to take mine.

"Grace please we need to talk, there are important things to discuss."

Defiantly I looked at him my hands still firmly placed on my hips. Before I realised what I was doing, I had stopped him in his tracks by my hand held firmly against his chest. Closing the garden gate creating the much-needed barrier between us, my body stood firm against it as reinforcement as I muttered strongly,

"Don't come any closer this isn't your home anymore Dylan"

"That's right it's not my home anymore Grace, it's ours" his purr did not go unnoticed.

Momentarily off guard my eyes searched his, my willpower still intact and fully loaded if a little wobbly.

"No Dylan"

I turned away from him my strides long as I headed for the opened door.

"Gracie please don't walk away"

"Why you walked away from me"

I stepped in the hallway immediately putting the door between us. The narrow gap I had allowed obliterated most of him from my sight.

"Go away Dylan, anything else worth discussing can be sorted out between our respective solicitors."

My mobile phone started ringing I groaned inwardly. Looking back at him I went to close the door in case it was mum ringing. He held his hand up putting it between the door and the frame.

"Don't worry, answer the call I'll be standing right here when you're finished."

"Remove your fingers then before I break them"

I closed the door hurriedly, running towards the kitchen. My eyes searched the room frantically until I spied the mislaid mobile lying by the sink. Great I'd lose my head I thought if it wasn't screwed on. I picked up the phone to see who the caller was. I froze seeing Dylan's name appear on the screen. What the hell! I turned round to see him standing close behind me.

"What's going on? How did you get in?"

He smiled lazily giving nothing away

"You didn't close the door behind you in your rush to answer my call." He replied flicking his credit card now dented in front of my face.

I stood there speechless still not fully comprehending what he had done. Noticing this he took a step forward leaning over to whisper gently into my ear,

"Did you honestly think you could keep me out of my own house?"

Again I didn't reply. I was stunned by the sheer audacity of his actions. Who the hell did he think he was? As if reading my mind he looked down at me, my senses still reeling from his breath on my earlobe and his aftershave weakening my resolve. I had bought that for him last Christmas and it hurt to know he was wearing it now.

'Stop Grace concentrate', I berated myself silently. 'He is only doing this to you to wear you down,' my mini- me inside of me admonished. 'Bitch up Girl!'

"Well Gracie as usual my quiet little lamb is as always, my obliging little wife."

'See told you so,' my internal mini-me replied.

I could feel my hands clenching again. I took a step back from him wishing with all my might that I could take a more physical stand against him. Like wipe that smug smile off with a power-wielding slap. I wanted to show him in no uncertain terms that I wasn't going to just stand back and let him walk all over me again. I floundered asking myself how the hell I was going to deal with this situation and with him. Despondently my mother's words came back to haunt me. And yet again, she was right. She knew he would come back, and she had known that in my momentary act of fiery independence I had not taken this curve ball into full consideration.

"No Dylan" I finally replied, "You just can't waltz back here just because I found you out and took back possession of what is mine"

He tutted shaking his head, his lips drawn into a fine line as his eyes caressed my face like I was a disobedient child, who had been caught stealing a cookie out of the jar without permission.

"Darling, it's not yours, it's ours"

Damn and blast him I muttered to myself silently. I had never realised until now how smarmy and cocksure he could be. I discovered I didn't like it. Had he always been like that and I had never noticed it? I frowned as I pondered this.

"Don't worry your pretty little head about it darling," he added noticing my frown lines," the house is on the market, someone will come along and fall in love with it, just as we did" he paused his eyes looking into mine with an expression I didn't recognise. It almost looked like regret or was it just wishful thinking on my part?

"Anyway now that I'm back, there are things we have to sort out."

I looked at him in horror his words not sinking in. Sighing he shook his head in mock dismay

"Like a front door key for instance"

The word key got through eventually making me stare up at him in anger as realisation dawned what he was saying.

"Dylan I don't want you here. I moved back because contrary to popular belief you weren't living here. The house couldn't be left empty, it was asking for trouble."

22

He stood still his eyes summing me up before he spoke again.

"I hadn't left Gracie I was just" he paused hunting for a plausible answer, "I was away on business for awhile"

What did he think I was, gullible? But I knew then as his words sunk in that that was exactly what I was, no I hastily corrected, 'had been.' I had never questioned him ruthlessly when at times I had been left wondering at his explanations of absence. But I had trusted him, never wanting to push my idealistic dreams of my perfect marriage to any extreme.

I needed to digest this, think it through before I made any comeback verbal or otherwise. I could feel him looking at me making me feel more inept.

"I'm ringing my solicitor," I noticed his quick grin of victory so I paused before leaving the kitchen where this whole farce had taken place.

"I'm ringing him to ask advice. I'm not happy with this, situation."

For a moment his face dropped before he quickly replaced the sardonic smile he was so fond of adopting.

"You have two choices Gracie which will save you another fee from the solicitor if you bother to listen."

I stopped walking away my back still turned to him.

"He will advise you that as the house is in both our names that entitles both of us to live here. He will also reiterate that the final decision to our, co-habitation is purely ours. So Gracie what will it be? Will you stay" his voice was heavy with derision, "or will you run back to the comforting arms of your parents, like you did over five months ago."

I swung round indignation fuelling me, "I left Dylan because you wanted me out. On and on, day after day, you were constantly jibing me to leave until I couldn't take it anymore." As my temper grew in strength so did my bravery as my steps took me hurriedly closer to where he was standing in his dark power suit with his hair so immaculate and his face so, bloody goddamn appealing.

When I stopped directly in front of him my head turning up to face his I was invincible.

"You will not push me out of this house. I have every right to be here as much as you. You on the other hand can do what the hell you like. Either way it doesn't bother me" And there it was, I had capitulated without as much as a phone call to my solicitor to verify his threat.

He stood for a long while just staring at me as though I had lost my mind. But I didn't care. He had pushed me out once and I had run back to my family with my tail firmly between my legs. But no, not this time. This time I would stand my ground. Whatever jibes he would throw at me I would throw them back. I had suffered weeks of pain and rejection, the humiliation of not knowing what I had done to have been cast aside, like I was clothing he had sickened of wearing. I knew, if I didn't stand my ground now, I would become that doormat he was so fond of using against me. As these words raced through my mind I could already feel the edges beginning to fray. Shots of self-doubt reared their ugly head, questioning whether I could do this. I ignored them, pushing them away not willing to give him any shred of visibility to my inner turmoil. When he spoke with renewed vigour I knew I had made a wrong and impulsive decision.

"Well darling, let the war of the roses begin. But, I will add I can't wait. This new side of you Gracie is very appealing and, sexy. So about the key, can you get me a copy?"

I was horrified that my actions instead of pushing him away in disgust like I was bitter and delusional had had the opposite effect on him.

"You can't be serious?" I uttered hoping my voice reflected the abhorrence I was feeling inside.

"On the contrary darling I am very serious."

Chapter 2

I didn't tell my mother that in a few days I would have a housemate. It wasn't because I was being intentionally deceitful, I just didn't want to go through all the '*I told you so's*.' I realised at some point I would have to enlighten my parents but until that time arose, ignorance on their part was bliss.

On the evening Dylan had dropped his bombshell that he was moving back in, my nights had once again become a soap opera of nightmares where he had the starring role. I hated him and not because of his over smugness. He knew what I was like and that made me uneasy. If I did not remain aware and resilient at all times it would be only a matter of time before I unwillingly handed back the reins. If someone had told me months before about this ensuing scenario, my heart would have leapt and I would have convinced myself all was not lost. But, I wasn't that same stupid fool that I was all those weeks before. Admittedly I hadn't reached the finishing line yet, but I wasn't standing at the start line looking for his guiding hand to hold.

I had to face facts. I wasn't the little sex kitten he had always lovingly described me as, but neither was I the tiger yet. I was in between. What did that make me? I'll tell you what that made me. It made me a sitting duck. I was always falling headlong into situations before I had thoroughly thought them through, and this I had come to realise was another one of those scenarios. Zara had stopped coming around, and it didn't take Einstein to deduce Dylan had been in contact. I frowned trying to think of the connection between the two of them. Until our separation she had been my friend, my only best friend. On occasions when she and Dylan had collided he had treated her with indifference and that hadn't bothered either of us. I had long since given up trying to encourage him to be nice to her, as he had always interceded saying it was me he loved he didn't have to like my friend too. So what had changed?

Musing on all of this I cleaned the worktops for the second time not noticing what I was doing. It was the first weekend of my fortnight break from work. I had made plans to do many things during this time out, but now knowing the lion in a few days was about to enter my lair it had changed everything. I had commandeered the master bedroom with its connecting en-suite for myself, which left the guest room for him. I hadn't bothered changing the sheets knowing when he spent his first night in them they would still be damp from when the house had been empty. I had also turned off the radiator in that room knowing now, that October winds already in full force would freeze his arse off. But I didn't care. It was up to him now to look after himself. I had already divided the fridge into his and mine. The cupboards were also compartmentalised his, unfortunately being the furthest away from the fridge freezer and cooker. Shame.

I wasn't going to make this easy for him. He had forced me into a situation where he had aptly forecast my solicitor had reinforced, with my reluctant although willing co-operation. It had left me without a leg to stand on without capitulating, which I wasn't prepared to do. It would be interesting I thought to myself smiling, how he would manage. When we had been together he never had to lift a finger. I had been part time then, at the office where I still worked. The remaining hours not sequested to the up and coming publishing company where I had been an assistant to an assistant, had been dedicated fully to him. It had suited us both I loved playing the housewife, being needed and appreciated for everything I did, and he had in his way, appreciated me. Dylan liked everything perfect and I had learnt quickly. Not that I needed to be tutored by him. My mother old fashioned to the core had instilled in me from an early age to be self-sufficient. There wasn't anything home related I couldn't do. Change a plug I'm your girl, home design and style, my forte, apple pie to die for, my piece de resistance. We were suited in every way. I grimaced not liking the train of thought my mind had deviated too, so wiping the taps one more time so they sparkled I put away the dishcloth in its pot underneath the sink and stood to admire my work. This was a beautiful house and I had put all my love, effort and energy into it, and it showed.

After placing the wok back in the cupboard after my oriental stir fry for supper the doorbell rang. I paused for a moment thinking who it could be. It wasn't Dylan, he had already acquired the new key from me begrudgingly, it wouldn't be Zara as she avoided me again like the plague, so who could it be. Looking around briefly making sure everything was as it should be, I walked hesitantly to the door frowning when the doorbell rang insistently again. The two-obscured glass elongated panels showed one person standing on the other side. Looking at myself in the mirror above the console table I smiled to myself wishing I felt as confident as I appeared. I opened the door my smile slipping seeing my visitor. It was my mother.

We stood there for a few moments staring at each other before I hastily stood aside to let her pass. As she did I couldn't help but give a quick glance around just to make sure the demon in the dark BMW wasn't close behind.

"Anything wrong Gracie? You seem edgy?"

Closing the door hastily behind me I followed her quickly through into the lounge,

"No nothing I was just surprised that's all"

She raised her eyebrows at me without comment before taking off her coat doing a casual sweep of her surroundings.

"You have it looking nice"

"Thanks mom. Let me take your coat I'll hang it up."

This allowed me a few seconds of privacy. As I approached the hall cupboard I was kicking myself for not being totally honest with my parents. Who was I trying to kid? If Dylan was true to his word and was moving back in a few days there was no way I could keep this from them.

"Grace shall I put the kettle on?"

"Sure thanks mum" I hastily replied groaning inwardly as I retraced my steps back into the lounge.

"I can understand why you would want to move back. It's a beautiful house, you've done yourself proud."

I looked around hastily as if in confirmation. She switched on the kettle before turning to face me as I entered the kitchen.

"Have you heard anything?"

"Heard anything?" I mumbled back feigning innocence

She sighed heavily, "From him?"

"Dylan you mean"

"Who else?"

I reached for the mugs stalling for time. Now was the moment to come clean but I hesitated. For all I knew he wasn't moving back and he had only said it to annoy me and put me on edge. Until 'it' returned there was nothing to tell.

"Well we had words. He wasn't too happy about me coming back here, but..."

"But..."my mother reiterated

"I told him he had forced me out once through his constant cajoling and this time I wasn't going to be so easily manoeuvred."

Her hands were light on mine as I put the mugs down on the worktop.

"Gracie has he been round here making a nuisance of himself?"

"Mum don't worry, you know Dylan, all mouth and trousers," I tried to make light of it but I knew she wasn't easily fooled.

27

"There's more than one way of swatting a fly." She paused, "You will be careful Grace; you would tell us if anything was up?"

Before I could reply the front door slammed. We looked at each other in confusion before a loud familiar voice filled the empty void.

"Gracie are you here? I have some stuff I want to drop off."

I cringed in horror. My mother's eyes narrowed as she faced me knowing she recognised the owner of the voice.

Dylan walked into the lounge. Instead of his usual power suit he was wearing jeans and a cream crew neck jumper. His face was red from the cold outside but his eyes flashed at me amusedly when he saw my mother and I staring at him in horror from the kitchen.

"Well, look who it is. If it's not battle-axe Fairfax"

I could feel my mother tense behind me in indignation at Dylan's ungracious greeting. He grinned at me seeing my face blanch.

"You didn't tell me you were having" he paused, his eyes glancing over my shoulder at my mother, "a visitor tonight?"

I wanted the ground to open up and swallow me as if sensing this, he stepped closer enjoying his horrified audience.

"What's the matter ladies, cat got your tongues?"

I wanted to hit him. My mother her hands positioned on her hips spoke first,

"What the hell may I ask are you doing here?"

He pretended to look shocked as he stared at me before a slow smile appeared as he answered graciously,

"Didn't your daughter tell you that since she has moved back, so have I? After all it's within my right to claim back what is mine?"

The connotation hung heavily in the air. I cringed inwardly feeling my mother's eyes bore into the back of my head.

"Grace, what is he talking about, is this true?" She asked sternly.

My eyes seared into his, my mouth firmly set as I muttered between gritted teeth,

"Not quite as he put it, but yes there is nothing I can do to prevent him coming back"

I could feel her condemnation towards me not only because I had lied to her but also been deceitful by omission. I knew as long as Dylan remained standing there enjoying the show, she would hold off on me.

"Well yet again, Dylan Hunt you're playing cat and mouse with Grace. What's the point of coming back here, my daughter is not taking you back."

He hung his head momentarily before looking sharp eyed at my mother.

"I have no intention of playing Grace as you so eloquently put it, but I have as much right to be here as my wife does."

"Oh I see she's your wife now is she? What pray tell, was my daughter to you the last five and half months of your marriage?"

"I don't have to answer to you Mrs Fairfax. Why do you always feel the need to poke your nose in where it is not wanted?"

"How dare you," my mother spluttered as I stepped forward to barricade myself between the both of them.

"Dylan stop. Why would you speak to my mother like that? Who the hell do you think you are to just stroll in here and be rude to my mum?"

He looked down at me no sign of anger evident in his eyes or his voice,

"It wasn't me who instigated this."

"I'm sorry," I uttered incredulously looking up at him, "You don't think calling my mother battle-axe Fairfax" I cringed as I said it "is being downright disrespectful?"

He sighed deeply eyeing both of us before replying,

"I class it as a term of endearment."

I could feel the antagonism rising behind me,

"Well really" my mother uttered her face red with indignation, " I have never been so insulted in my entire life, Grace get my coat, I'm leaving."

I turned round looking at her imploringly, "Mum please don't."

She paused for a moment, first staring at me then at Dylan. Her expectant stare left little to the imagination in that she expected him to apologise. Biting his bottom lip he returned her stare before casting a sideways glance to me,

"Fine if it makes everybody happy then I apologise Esther for my um... ill advised choice of words."

Hoping that was enough to pacify my mother, I waited with baited breath for her to say something. But she didn't.

"Mum please stay, I'll finish making the coffee."

She continued glaring at him before her eyes flitted to mine.

"Grace as much as I would like to stay somehow the company you choose to keep these days I find most unappealing and distasteful."

I could hear Dylan snigger behind me, as I rushed past him trying to catch up with my mother. I shot him a venomous glance trying to curtail my mother from leaving.

"Mum please don't go."

She stopped abruptly. Pulling her coat roughly off the hangar she shut the cupboard door behind her with a thud, as she looked at me with dismay and disappointment evident in her eyes.

"Please tell me Grace that you're not going to stay here with him after this," She indicated with her hand flicking towards the wall where Dylan was on the other side.

"I'm not going to let him push me out mum, like last time. Surely you can understand that? As you reminded me the other day, you raised me to be tough," my voice faltered, "So that's what I'm doing."

Knowing I had cornered her with my apt reminder she sniffed loudly as she fastened her coat.

"No good will come of this my girl, mark my words. How many times Grace do you have to fall flat on your face before you stop tripping over."

Sighing I hung my head as my mother brushed past me and out of the front door closing it none too gently behind her.

Dylan emerged from the lounge leaning lazily against the door frame, "Well some things never change"

"This is your fault why couldn't you have rung me first before walking in as bold as brass."

He grinned widely at me, "If I had I would have missed the floor show, and to be honest kitten I wouldn't have missed it for the world."

I went to push past him but stopped at the doorway partially obscured by his lounging frame,

"There are times Dylan Hunt when I hate you, and this is definitely is one of those times."

He looked down at my infuriated face his smile dissipating, "How was I to know that god almighty was here?"

"Uhhhhh" I yelled out before pushing past him. "You could have rung me to warn me you were coming over."

I stormed into the kitchen so infuriated with myself for not being brutally honest with my mother when I felt his presence behind me. I swung round.

"Yes" I shouted pointedly ignoring his bemused expression at my frustration, "What do you want now?"

"Coffee if it's still going"

I picked up the mug he was indicating too and held it above my head to hurl at him.

"I take it that's a no then," he mocked as the mug hit the wooden door he hastily closed behind him. I stared at the shard remains of my now odd numbered set of blue Denby mugs. Angrier because I had lost my temper, I knelt down picking up the large pieces with my hands and placing them carefully into the kitchen bin. As I dug in the cupboard under the sink for the dustpan and brush I heard the kitchen door open. With the implements in my hand I stood up shooting him a look of venom before I knelt down to brush away the miniscule remains of broken pottery.

"Wasn't that one of a very expensive set" he asked politely.

"And if it was" I retorted.

"Hmmm well I suppose it's easy enough for you to replace."

I emptied the contents before putting the dustpan and brush back underneath the sink. Closing the cupboard door gently I turned to face him.

"I am not replacing what you will pay for, considering it was your fault it got broken in the first place."

"Kitten all I did was come home to drop off a few items. How was I to know, Attila the Hun was here. Just because you're too scared of your parents to be honest with them, doesn't mean I have to fork out for your bad temper."

"Fine it can stay broken then, I don't care" I replied.

"Hmmm that won't do Gracie, you see when we sell, everything has to be divided strictly down the middle and if you keep breaking things as you seem prone now to doing, then... well it's hardly going to be fair, I suppose I could deduct that from your share."

I swung round to face him my cheeks infused with frustration.

"Firstly Dylan, I am not your Gracie so stop calling me that and as for smashing things, don't push me."

I braced myself for his comeback but he remained silent his eyes watching me intently,

"Gracie I'm sorry if I upset you and your mother."

I blinked unable to believe what I had just heard, "You're sorry. Did I hear you just…. apologise?" I muttered incredulously.

He nodded his face serious. Folding his arms he remained where he was just staring at me. Knowing the expression in his eyes as one of yearning rather than remorse, I swallowed hard before turning away so he couldn't see the bewilderment he was creating inside of me.

"Fine, if you've finished you should go" I retorted firmly,

"Ok I'll just put my clothes back into the wardrobes"

As he walked away I busied myself with finishing the long awaited coffee. It wasn't until I was sipping it looking out of the dining room window admiring my handiwork from the year before, did I hear him cough behind me to gain my attention.

"What" I muttered not bothering to turn around.

"You've relegated me to the spare room."

I turned to face him smiling sweetly,

"Well yes considering I am in the master suite."

He walked slowly towards me his eyes never leaving mine,

"I am not sleeping in the spare room in my own house Grace."

Putting the mug down onto the dining table I straightened my shoulders as I raised my face to his,

"Oh yes you are Dylan. You chose to leave this house for whatever reason so when I took it back I of course commandeered the best bedroom in the house. If you have a problem with that moan to the solicitor about it."

He took my hand as I went to walk away, "But I'm moaning to you about it Grace," his voice was as smooth as velvet as he leaned in "I am not staying in the spare bedroom like a guest in my own house."

His breath smelled sweet as I fought to ignore the closeness he had engineered. Taking a deep breath I looked into his blue eyes before speaking as fondly, "Well husband dear" I muttered just as sickly sweet, "your wife is not sharing with you. I happen to be fussy who shares my bed now."

I saw his mouth straighten in annoyance as his arms shot out pulling me closer to him.

"We shall see about that"

I could feel my cheeks suffuse with colour as I remained where I was, refusing to let him intimidate me.

"Let..me..go.." I hissed between clenched teeth.

My body was rigid every muscle taut as a string. My stomach on the other hand had other ideas and had begun to liquidise like molten hot lava at his touch.

His lips when they brushed against mine were warm and sensual. Biting my teeth hard I remained motionless, my mind reeling from the effect his actions were having on me after such a long absence. Taking my lack of response as an incentive he leant in closer his arms exploring my slender frame. My mind was screaming for him to let me go but I couldn't open my mouth knowing if I did he would force his tongue into mine and my resolutions to be immune to him would be momentarily lost. When he pulled away enough for my lips to open without the fear of assault I smiled at him, "Dylan stop it, it won't work."

Choosing to ignore my weak word of warning his tongue ran lightly over the outer perimeter of my mouth. Clenching my hands I looked into his eyes, their amusement plain for me to see.

"I said back off" once more but Dylan being Dylan continued ignoring my feeble protests, his breathing becoming more prominent as he continued his rediscovery of me.

Closing my mouth I bit as hard as I could on his bottom lip tasting his blood in my mouth. When I released him he yelped jumping back from me like I had scalded him.

"When will you take no for an answer? That Dylan was me defining the boundaries" Feeling more composed I picked up my mug taking it into the kitchen. Turning on the tap I rinsed it out no longer thirsty knowing from where he was standing he was watching me. Wiping my hands on the tea towel I hung it neatly back before facing him head on glad of the distance between us.

"You bitch"

"Well you know what they say Dylan, only a bastard could love a bitch like me."

Turning of the kitchen spotlights I pushed past him muttering loud enough for him to hear

"Shut the door on your way out."

Sunday morning was bright and sunny. I yawned as I languished in my bed stretching every bone and muscle and enjoying it. I felt so invigorated since the events of the night before. Never in my previous relationship with Dylan would I have been so bold and heartless. But then, I wouldn't have had to. Every move towards me, every kiss had been welcomed. I had flourished within his arms growing stronger and more daring until in my eyes, there was nothing more between us that had gone unexplored. But that was then and this was now. Don't think about him I admonished myself as I looked towards the alarm clock to see what the time was. It was nearly midday and though habit convinced me to get up and start with what remained of my day, I reminded myself it was my holiday and there wasn't a reason for getting up. I must have fallen back to sleep, for when I woke an hour later something had alarmed me. Feeling disorientated I clambered out of bed, not caring what I looked like if I came face to face with an intruder. My long dark hair was mussed, my satin camisole and boxer shorts wrinkled from my restless sleep. Not bothering with slippers I stumbled towards the bedroom door making a mental note to avoid the furniture if I could possibly help it. When I stood in the hallway I halted confused. The house was silent and for a moment I wondered whether I had been dreaming.

"Well... hello kitten."

I spun round horrified to see Dylan fresh and immaculate in sharp perfectly pressed chinos and an open camel coloured shirt. I gulped deeply at the sight of him.

"What the hell are you doing here?"

He sighed as though I was an irritating child he was desperate to shake off before his eyes slowly and provocatively inspected me from my pink painted toenails up my slim defined hairless calves to my thighs. He paused in his inspection there his eyes focusing on my skimpy satin shorts before his eyes almost regrettably continued with their journey upwards, prevaricating when his pupils dilated as he examined my pert breasts their definition clearly apparent in my figure-hugging camisole. Eventually aware I was watching him intently, his eyes regrettably ascended where they stopped when they reached my face. The smile he displayed was lopsided and very horny. Feeling my body sway towards him like I was being sucked into a vortex I shot him a disparaging glare before storming back into my bedroom slamming the door behind me as if to break his spell. All I could hear was his laughter following me, making me angrier as I tugged at my satin robe hanging on the back of the door. Eventually when it relented and fell silkily into my arms I threw it on tugging the sash tightly into a knot.

I was livid with myself that yet again he had gotten the better of me and I had been stupidly unprepared. Walking back to the bed I shoved my feet into my slippers moaning when I saw the time. It was one o clock. Grabbing my hairbrush off the bedside unit I swung round to look at myself in the mirror. My face was flushed, my eyes bright. I gritted my teeth as I ran the brush hurriedly through my thick wavy hair. How could I have been so careless? Putting the brush down I picked up the scrunchie I had left lying on the floor the night before and hurriedly tied up my hair.

When I reached the kitchen it was empty. Sighing with relief I picked up the kettle draining the water in it from the night before and refilled it. After I had switched it on I opened the cupboard to fetch myself a mug.

"If its coffee you're making I'll have one too."

Glad the cupboard door hid my face from him I replied,

"It's instant and as I know you hate that, you'll have to make your own."

My smile when I closed the unit door was fixed and bitchy. He continued to stare at me his expression bland though his eyes showed disappointment that the view he had witnessed upstairs in the hallway earlier was no longer on display.

"No worries instant will do fine."

As my face showed surprise he didn't acknowledge it.

Begrudgingly I took out another mug and almost slammed it onto the dark granite worktop. He flinched and I smiled briefly at his reaction as I hurriedly spooned coffee into the mugs. His back was turned to me as I tentatively asked whether he still took a spoonful of sugar. He nodded and whilst I sweetened mine I added salt to his. I realised I was being petulant and childish but honestly, I didn't care. I felt disadvantaged that he had caught me unaware and almost un-attired. Perhaps my mother had been right. I hadn't thought this living arrangement through. But after nearly six months of no contact at all and with the divorce imminent and the house stood empty I had never envisioned Dylan walking right back into my life the same way he had forced me to leave. Adding a dash of milk to mine and leaving his black as I remembered I picked up my mug and walked past him into the open plan lounge diner. I felt at odds with myself with him being here. It was too intimate and reminiscent of our old life together. I could hear his footsteps on the ash wooden floor as he followed me so I settled into one of the white leather expensive Italian armchairs and folded my legs beneath me. His beautiful body came into view out of the corner of my eye and hastily I covered my bare legs with the satin fabric of my robe. Whether he noticed this I didn't know as smoothly as a panther preparing for attack he sat on the leather sofa opposite, his eyes focusing on my rigid posture. I watched him with my eyes downcast as he put the coffee mug down on the nearby table without tasting it. I grimaced in disappointment as I slowly sipped mine.

"Grace."

I looked up determined not to show any sign of joy or comfort at seeing him here.

"What?"

I knew I was being petulant but I didn't care. If he was determined to move in here and try and play happy families for the remainder of my sentence with him before I was legally free, then that was up to him.

He looked pensive as he leaned back against the thick upholstery. His hands smooth with his long tapered fingers and short manicured nails folded into a clasp on his lap. His green eyes wandered to mine but I looked away, not wanting to be drawn into their deep mesmerising embrace. It had been his eyes that had first encapsulated me when he had walked into the office where I was working. He had an appointment with my boss and I a well-trained lapdog had collided into him with my arms full of promising manuscripts from unknown prospective authors. He was an agent acting on behalf of our latest acquisition and when my loaded arms had released their bounty it was him who had knelt down at the same time as me bumping heads in the process. It was then as I had looked into his eyes with my apology dying on my lips, that I was hooked. His eyes were full of concern his voice as smooth as chocolate as he enquiring whether I was all right. His hands were light on mine as they brushed my skin as he reloaded my arms. Unable to form an intelligible sentence because of his close proximity to me I had nodded and hurried away to offload my paperwork and more acutely my embarrassment. It had been later that afternoon when a beautiful bouquet of flowers was delivered to my desk. Confused, about to enquire if they were meant for me, the young guy had placed between my fingers a simple white card. It was from him enquiring politely whether I had recovered from our little mishap earlier. My heart had skipped beats and I knew my face was flushed as I ushered the delivery guy away, and that had been the start of a whirlwind love affair that had ended ten months later in my fairy tale wedding. I grimaced to myself remembering those times. There were no such things as fairy tales and as I looked at him beneath my eyelashes he was definitely no fairy tale prince.

"Grace, will you speak to me now, or are you just going to sulk?"

I was defiant when I met his gaze.

"I don't sulk Dylan, you must be thinking of someone else"

I could have sworn that he flinched but it was so momentary I could have imagined it.

"If you're angry about earlier" he broke off.

I followed his eyes to the ceiling above and the innuendo of our unexpected meeting that morning on the landing. Gnawing on my lips I met his gaze and the lazy smile I used to be so fond of.

"I thought at lunchtime it would be safe to drop off the remaining boxes. Do you normally sleep in so late?"

I wasn't stupid, knowing he wasn't referring to my unaccustomed lie- in but the reason behind it.

"What's it to do with you?"

"Ok let me put it another way. Do I assume every weekend you are prone to spending your whole mornings in bed?"

"Stop with the connotations Dylan, your becoming predictable and boring."

"Ouch. Would you like me to show you how unpredictable I can be?"

Sighing deeply I wanted to stand up and walk away from him. But knowing the action alone would reveal more of me to him than I wanted I remained seated.

"What's the point of all this?" I asked instead.

"Well, I obviously make you feel uncomfortable and as I am moving back I suppose for your, discretion, we should adopt a few house rules."

Seeing no room for argument I nodded before replying, "Fine, what do you have in mind?"

"Well I guess that's down to you as I don't have a problem with my body, or you seeing it."

I sighed before staring directly at him, "Is this how it's going to be? All innuendo and sexual connotations?"

He leaned forward his arms resting on his knees, "It could be, you tell me?"

Standing up not caring the flash of thigh he witnessed I faced him. "Oh I see what you're up to. Instead of the continual bullying you implemented before I left, this time it's going to be more basic."

Edging closer to him his folded hands on his knees almost touching my legs, I smiled wanly at him bending down knowing as I did so he would get an welcome view of my cleavage.

"There is nothing you can do or say Dylan that will remotely interest me in anyway. If you are determined to co- exist under the same roof as myself, then fine, there is nothing I can do about that at this time. But, if you think for one moment that the house is not the only thing we are sharing, then think again."

I could feel his breath on my face making my skin tingle with need. I breathed him in kicking myself for doing it. His aftershave wound spells over me making me want to lean in closer for him to touch me, feel me, kiss me. His voice broke into my reverie making me recoil from him,

"Kitten, it won't take the dwindling weeks till we are divorced for me to get between those wonderful silky thighs of yours. If I wanted to, you would be mine for the taking. But" he added smirking at my hasty withdrawal, "I like to play it slow and sensual, make it last. Don't you remember darling? I want the tiger that I believe exists in you; I always wanted you to be so much more adventurous than the obedient cat you used to be. I bet now in bed you would be a fucking mind-blowing experience. With everything I've taught you laced with the abhorrence you have for me now, would make for a damn good long sensual no holds barred fuck. Just talking about it makes me want to rip that satin of you and take you here and now rough and ready as you never had with me before ."

Feeling the colour suffuse my face I ran from the room his laughter loud in my ears as I ran up the stairs. But he was right. I ran for the shower wanting to throw away the sodden satin shorts that had betrayed me.

It was Monday evening when Dylan walked into the house confirming he had officially moved back. Since the previous day I had avoided him and fortunately he had made that easier by leaving soon after our impromptu tete a tete. His words had angered and tormented me and aroused me. But it wasn't until much later, after spending the afternoon to calm down and give myself a firm talking to, did I finally acknowledge there was an element of truth to his boasting. So what the hell was I going to do now? I didn't want to find him attractive anymore but switching of my feelings for him was not as easy as I had previously thought it would be.

In less than six weeks defined by legal law we would be disassociated with each other. Free to move on with our lives. If only it were that simple. I knew before I moved back that I still loved him and it was impossible for me to ignore it or dispel it as an untruth. My body alone was more than witness to that. I had no reason to hate him other than the dumping of our marriage callously cast aside months before at the wine bar. Aside from that I was flailing. I had nothing hurtful or recriminating to hang onto to strengthen my resolve against him. As I heard him walk through the door the next evening knowing he was here to stay for the foreseeable future I knew I was screwed. As if he had known I had doctored his coffee he had refrained from drinking it assuming instead to cajole and insult me in return. What the hell had I done thinking I could control and annihilate what I felt for him? He walked into the sitting room his face soft and inquisitive. His eyes caressing my face taking in my determined saddened expression. "Hi honey I'm home."

Chapter 3

Knowing I had taken two weeks off as holiday Dylan had done the same. It was obvious he was tormenting me, punishing me for daring to taking control of a situation that had previously been on his terms. I was under no illusions as to how clever he could be. That was why he was such a successful agent. But I wasn't an acquisition, a new proposal to push forwards to attain their full potential. I was, no had been, his wife. I had come to a conclusion the night before that if I stood any chance at all of gaining fair play out of this situation, enforced by him, then I had to resort to tactics as similar and lowly as his. Sex had always been an easy button for Dylan to press but it wasn't a ploy I was willing to undertake because against him, I knew I would lose.

Our marriage vows had meant far more to me I realised than they had to him, that was obvious. It still pained me to digest the dregs of our forgotten love, but life was for the living and I wasn't normally a person, until recently who delegated herself to living in the past. I had always moved onwards and upwards the only difference between my husband and I was, I always remained safely in second gear whilst he roared off in fifth. So I had come to a monumental decision. To be able to walk away from this intact and battle scar free, I would have to swallow my pride and principle and give as good as I got. Hell, who knows I thought despondently, my emotions needed re-evaluating and what was the worst thing that could come out of this. My romantic and fanciful notions of him would be forever shattered to be stored away under the label 'trash', its pages like our days together slowly decaying until it turned to dust.

"Why are you looking so miserable? "He asked lightly.

I was being morose, I realised that but just the sound of him noticing every movement my face made, every emotion I surfed haphazardly through, was unnerving.

"Perhaps it's something to do with your reappearance, don't you think?" I retorted back.

But as only Dylan knows how, he smiled as he knelt down in front of me his face all smug.

"Gracie don't see this as, an ending but like." He stopped thinking desperately for words. He smiled as he continued enlightened, "But as a beginning."

His words shot though me like a poison dart as I almost knocked him over in my haste to get away from him.

"There are no beginnings for us Dylan only an ending."

He looked downcast towards the floor before he stared at me as he straightened up. "See it for what you will Gracie. But there are many endings and beginnings they don't necessarily all go in the same direction."

The pain I was feeling inside I knew was good for me. What was it people always said? No pain, no gain. I looked at him then wondering if I had ever known this man that I had loved and married. Had I walked down the aisle with not only a veil but also blinkers too?

"Gracie I don't want us to fight whilst we share our last week's together. What would be the point? Can't we move on with this with as much dignity and feeling as we did on our wedding day?"

I looked at him then my eyes blurring with moisture.

"Why did you come back here? What do you hope to achieve?"

He looked thoughtful for a long moment his eyes staring over my head. Eventually he shrugged his shoulders before staring back at me,

"I don't know. We ended so dramatically that Friday night with no more between us, no contact. Living in this house before you left was unbearable. The avoidance, the silence, it was like we were scared of being in each other's company, like we would contaminate each other with our words and feelings. I missed you so much but," he hesitated, "but not enough to try and put us back together."

"Is that why you bullied me day in day out until I left?"

He nodded silently lost in thought. "Yeah that probably was why"

I felt terribly hurt and exposed his words pulling away my layers of self-protection I had spent months engineering. I hugged myself in consolation. It shouldn't hurt so much as it did, but time over the last months had not eradicated the intense feeling of heartbreak that love chose as a close friend. I looked at him not because I wanted to see the words hurting me spill from his mouth, but I needed to see if he was feeling battle worn like I was feeling right now.

He stepped closer to me as if in apology. I didn't step back from him I looked up at him with all the pain, humiliation and sorrow that he had created and planted in the garden that was my soul. He continued to stare at me, my barricade towards him coming down brick by brick. He looked penitent for making me look so stricken and openly wounded.

"I know this was all me Gracie, I am the one that's carrying all the pain and the blame. But I didn't want to hurt you anymore than I already had."

CHASING RAINBOWS

He looked down at my arms tightly folded around myself. His arms moved involuntarily as if he wanted to prise them open, but as he looked once again into my eyes he refrained putting distance between us. I was thankful for that. I felt so drained and helpless I knew I couldn't have fought him off if I wanted too. I was reeling not only from the words he had selfishly blessed me with but in how I was seeing a side of my husband that I had never seen before. Dylan the norm was perfection. From his appearance to his spoken word everything was primed and faultless. Never, had there been a crack in the impenetrable facade that was Dylan Hunt, until now. I stood motionless my eyes reluctantly following him. He seemed uncomfortable in this setting where the emotions between us were as vivid as the abstract art displayed on the white walls around us.

"I have a lot to answer for Gracie" he swung round to face me though I looked away my eyes glaring emptily through the paned glass bay fronted window of the Victorian house we both now shared.

"I can't help but feel it was a mistake you coming back here Dylan. It will resolve nothing and only incur further pain and bad feeling between us"

"Perhaps you're right but I couldn't live in this house anymore without you in it" he looked around him as though seeing it for the first time.

His posture was straight, his shoulders dejected in their repose. His hair, which I knew felt thick soft and vibrant through my fingers curled on the collar of the white shirt he wore. It surprised me that how whilst both wading through snowfalls of emotions, I had noticed how he had let his hair grow longer. It disturbed me that in as much I had noticed it and second that Dylan always immaculate in presentation had faltered in this tiny aspect of his regimen of grooming. It showed to me he wasn't as invincibly perfect as he had always portrayed himself to be. I had mistakenly placed him on a pedestal so high that even with one slight inaccuracy had him tumbling down. I looked at him again the same time as he looked at me. The distance between us was only minimal in steps. But mentally in my mind, a gorge was widening with every second that passed.

"Gracie I thought with us moving back we could somehow mend what was broken."

My heart lurched to his reference of us but my words that filtered quietly out between my lips were unassuming and defensive.

"It was only you who saw the break. In my eyes, in my world, our life was perfect."

He sighed deeply his eyes deep and fathomless.

"Everything in your world is so clear. It's black or white, no grey areas in between. Life isn't like that Grace, not in the real world and we weren't like that".

This made my head snap up.

"Do you think I wasn't aware our marriage wasn't a bed of roses Dylan? Did you think I didn't notice sometimes how far away mentally you would go from me? Do you know what I would think when those moments of greyness faced me?"

He looked at me intently,

"In those moments Dylan I would not and could not give up on us. You are the hardest person to be with, to share a life with. I waited for you to open up, to share what was dividing us, but you couldn't. Blaming it on work and anything else you could think of rather than take the responsibility. Even now you stand there saying to me how everything that has happened of late was of your own making. But you don't mean it. There is no repentance, no remorse in you. Perhaps as people go I am transparent in how I see life but how can that be so bad when compared to you?"

"Grace it takes two to make a marriage and two to break it. I may be responsible for the majority of it but you don't get away scot free."

"Is this what it comes down too Dylan? You did this, I did that. Did we not mean more to each other? "I flailed my hands outwardly emphasising my words.

He let himself drop onto the armchair his whole body a reflection of the conflict he was evidently fighting inwardly.

"Gracie don't you see? For over five years we shared a life that was so faultless in its design it never allowed any room for change. Each day was habitual; I could almost quote each scene in this house. It got boring and monotonous Gracie. I have a stressful and demanding career but you know what it gives me? It gives me the incentive I need to survive and to be someone. Within these walls as beautiful as they are had just become a glorified prison. Neither of us felt the same desire and excitement towards each other like we had in the beginning," he paused running his hands frustratingly through his hair,

"Christ Gracie I realise complacency breeds contempt but we were both so much more than that. We had dreams"

I stared back at him his every word cutting into me like a knife. I looked around the home so lovingly put together. I had placed every part of my heart and soul into this home. It wasn't just a pretty house to me it was our

42

sanctuary where we could both shut out the rest of the world. Leaving just the two of us. When had it become a prison to him?

"My dreams, my hopes and ambitions Dylan they never diverted from you they were always there. They were never as prominent as yours. Not everything in life is about you. How you feel, what you want is not the be all and end all... I have needs too but one thing I realise listening to you now is that I had put them all aside for you. That's what love does. One of you has to compromise more than the other. That's all I ever did where you were concerned was give and give to you Dylan and I always felt desire towards you regardless of how you felt towards me. What Dylan, did you ever give back to me?"

He looked around him his eyes avoiding mine. I followed his gaze understanding his thinking,

"You mean you gave me this beautiful prison as you describe it. You see that's where the difference between us lies. I saw this as a home for us where nobody but us mattered. A home that would eventually be a home for the children we would make together. But you didn't even want that did you?" I paused as he cringed and looked away from me. Ignoring him feeling angry for his indifference to my words I continued, "It was ours for the taking, where all our love and dreams could come true. If only you had seen it for what it was. I loved you Dylan and that never changed, unlike you." I remained standing my body tense as my eyes looked down at him, the full shock of what I had just said reeling through me. I had used the past tense in my feelings towards him when until now I had still thought of it as the present.

I walked into the kitchen suddenly feeling the space we shared too claustrophobic. I hoped Dylan would take the hint and leave me alone. I took a glass out of the cupboard filling it with cold water from the fridge. I felt weighted down with everything that had transpired between us, but I also felt incredibly unburdened at the same time. All those questions I had demanded in the beginning of our separation had now all been addressed if not yet fully resolved. I looked at him staring quietly out of the window. I at one time had loved this man more than life itself. But now as I watched him I felt pity towards him. He wanted so much he would never be able to attain it all. But how long would it suffice. What he had, what he wanted before that bored him too. I had come to realise very quickly throughout the conversation that Dylan would never be truly happy. Nothing ever was enough for him and if it was, it wasn't permanent. He grew bored and restless very quickly and it made me feel sick to the core that I hadn't seen this down side of him before. Though I didn't want too against my better judgement I did momentarily as I watched him, I felt sorry for his shortcomings.

He had never intended when he had started the conversation this evening, that I would be the one walking away enlightened. As much as I was the victor it left me feeling hurt and used. He would be outraged if he knew his speech instead of pulling me closer to him, had had the opposite effect. He had been bored with his marriage, and with me. When had he lost his disinterest in us, when he knew the divorce was on-going by his instigation, when eventually the ties holding us together would be severed he had taken this last opportunity to regain what he had thrown so carelessly and selfishly away. Only now the tables had turned. My blinkers had been removed and as if I had been given second sight I could see how his world, that I had been living in, had been nothing but a temporary illusion making me feel sick inside at how willing I had almost selflessly thrown away, all my hopes and dreams.

The atmosphere was still strained between us when he entered the kitchen where I was still musing over my glass of water. I watched him silently as he made himself a hot drink. It wasn't until he was sipping it did I realise he hadn't requested as usual for me to make it for him. Things were changing between us and whether the change was heading in a good direction at the moment it made little difference to me. I was hurting inside at the realization of where our fairy tale had ended. If it ever had been the childhood fantasy I had always envisioned having. The granite edge of the worktop was digging into the base of my spine making me suddenly stand up straight. My unexpected movement made him look at me. His face normally masked in confidence and absolute surety was not present as his eyes stared back at me. I could see unanswered questions in his eyes but I wasn't ready to address them. My mind was still reeling from the disclosure that had taken place less an hour before. Throwing away the remainder of the water I placed the glass gently upside down to drain. Wiping my hands absently on the tea towel hanging close by the sink I ran my hands nervously down the front of my jeans. When he spoke to me I felt myself jump. My mind was so consumed with all the information we had shared earlier I hadn't expected anything more from him.

"Grace"

My hands stilled as I fought to quiet my heart, which was racing. I looked at him feeling very much out of my depth. I wasn't used to this side of Dylan who normally swept issues of the heart under the carpet. It was evident by his expression that he wanted to carry on the discussion and as I looked at him doubtfully I could see he felt as uncomfortable as I did.

"Dylan I really don't want to talk anymore about this tonight."

"Why? Don't you think it's about time we thrashed this out?"

I sighed deeply my head too jam packed to be able to take anymore in.

"What's the point? What's done is done. I understand you're sorry for the breakup of the marriage, and I understand you feel doubtful about it. Well don't Dylan, it's too late in the day for your change of heart to make any difference."

He took my cold hands between his. He said nothing as he just stared down at them; His thumb caressed my skin making my senses run top speed into each other again. I shut my eyes not wanting him to see the pain his caresses were creating in me.

"Please don't," I cried pulling my hands away from him.

"Grace, please listen to me. This has to be sorted out."

I hadn't realised I had started crying till I looked at him his face blurry and concerned.

"I don't have to listen to you anymore Dylan. The time for talking was five and a half months ago when you dumped me remember? In less than six weeks we will no longer be married and then you can do what the hell you want."

"Is that what you want?"

Confused I looked away not getting what part of the conversation he was referring too.

"I don't understand"

"Grace, look at me"

Reluctantly I turned back my eyes focusing on the wall behind him.

"Grace, look at me damn you not the sodding wall behind me"

He so rarely lost his cool that it had me obediently obeying.

"Do you really believe it's too late? I don't want the next six weeks to be the countdown to our demise. I want it to be our rebirth. We know all the pitfalls now we can avoid them" his last few words stuck in my head, he just didn't get it, didn't get what he was doing to me. Even now after all the words it was us not him that had brought our relationship to its untimely end.

"You keep referring to us. Don't you understand Dylan there is no us anymore."

I stormed past him my eyes blurry with tears. I ran up the stairs slamming my bedroom door behind me. The bed still unmade from earlier, looked as out of place in the surroundings as I did. Everything in this home was co-ordinated and correct. Every colour, every painting, every piece of fabric blended seamlessly into utter perfection. This house I realised didn't reflect me in any way it was all Dylan. Why had I never noticed that before? I had been so blissfully happy in this house, so settled, so much a part of its tapestry. Yet now, as I looked around I realised compared to all this beauty, I was the ugly duckling.

    I lay back on the bed my eyes staring aimlessly up at the ceiling. When had I changed? I froze as I heard his footsteps ascend the stairs. His feet paused by my bedroom door. I sat up quickly my eyes riveted to the door handle to see if he was turning it.

    "Grace?"

    "Dylan, just leave me alone"

    "I don't want our first night home together to end this way"

    Our first night home, had he heard nothing that I had said? What the hell was he talking about? What was going on with him that continually propelled him in my direction? What wasn't he getting?

    "This isn't our first night home Dylan. Nothing about this is united. So just go away and leave me the hell alone."

    I had never spoken to him in that way before. The silence on the other side of the door was deafening to me as I waited for his response. But none was forthcoming as I heard his footsteps fade away.

    It was a dull grey day the next morning the rain pelting down so hard it was bouncing off the pavement like pellets. I was glad I was on holiday, I hated the rain. I had showered and dressed this morning determined not to embarrass myself as I had done the morning previously. My hair was still damp and I couldn't be bothered to dry it so I tied it back into a high ponytail. My face I left free of makeup on purpose. My jeans old and faded I matched with a hot pink t-shirt. Everything about me screamed out ill matched old and carefree. I hadn't slept much the night before but I had made a decision. Whether I was on the rebound or not I was determined to show Dylan that I no longer was the person he left broken months earlier. A part of me still yearned for him, still wanted to be with him and it pained me to feel I was not completely free of him yet. But the verbal open-heart surgery the night before had cut away a lot of the tubes that had connected me to him. Why it had happened I didn't know, but what I did know was I liked the slowly emerging new Grace.

    Of course the moment I left the sanctuary of my bedroom my resonance was not as strong but I was determined not to be taken for granted by him anymore. Dylan was lounging on the sofa flicking through the channels not looking at any of them. He was as usual as pristine as ever. His jeans unlike mine were new and sharp, his shirt freshly pressed and colour co-ordinated. The aroma of fresh coffee assailed my nostrils I looked back at him in surprise but whether he noticed me doing it he didn't acknowledge. Getting a mug out of the cupboard I poured the coffee into it. As I was adding a dash of cream and one sugar cube I could smell his aftershave.

"Morning Dylan did you sleep well? "My tone purposely polite

I was determined to get past the events of the night before. What had been said had caused me long hours of heartache before eventually sleep had claimed me. When I looked at him I could see it had been the same for him. His face was expressionless his eyes tired.

"I didn't know whether you wanted breakfast"

"Err what?" I stammered wondering whether I was in the right home and this man was the man I had married.

He smiled at me before opening the fridge, "Omelettes okay?"

"Dylan I don't think..."

"You have to eat right?"

"Err yes," I muttered

He paused with the box of eggs in his hands as he stared at me

"Go sit down Grace I'll call you when it's ready"

Not saying a word I obediently complied my feet as confused as my brain as I edged past him. When had Dylan learnt to cook I asked myself. Still brain glazed I sat on the sofa picking up the remote and switching off the telly. I looked sideways at him still not believing what my eyes were telling me but there as bold as brass was Dylan masterfully cooking breakfast.

"Egg white omelette ok" he asked casually from the direction I was looking at

"Yes" I mumbled now more confused than ever. I wished I hadn't been so impulsive in switching off the telly. I had nothing to divert my attention from him so instead I picked up the nearest magazine to hand and flitted through it my eyes only scanning the pages. When he handed me the tray I almost gasped from surprise. A perfect omelette with a few sliced strawberries for accompaniment stared back at me. The cutlery lay upon a white linen napkin. The small glass of orange juice was fresh and the rose in the small crystal vase beside it was a nice touch. He saw the look of shock clearly apparent on my face his only response was a wry smile as he waited patiently for me to take the tray from him.

"Err thanks. Dylan, when did you learn to cook?"

He shrugged his shoulders nonchantly as he headed back towards the kitchen I assumed to retrieve his own food. When he returned he sat on the armchair smiling at me, as I tasted the omelette nodding in approval.

"There are a lot of things since our...parting Grace that I've been doing anew"

It wasn't until I had finished the delectable food did I realise we had eaten in the lounge instead of at the dining table which had always been strictly adhered to in the past. Rules were rules in Dylan's book never to be deviated from or broken.

Noticing my stupefied expression he walked over to me taking my tray from me his eyes narrowing as he looked at me,

"What are you wearing Grace?"

"Why don't you like it" I replied sweetly not caring whether he did or not.

He stopped on the threshold of the kitchen turning around to look at me. His eyebrows rose whilst his eyes slowly took a tour over my attire,

"It's very different to how you used to dress, but...there is a sexiness to it"

I turned my head from him towards the window my mouth falling open in surprise. Ok what the hell had happened? This is my home, that, I recognized but who the hell was that man in the kitchen?

"I was wondering whether you had any plans today?" his voice was polite and enquiring.

I was beginning to feel I had walked into the twilight zone, but I could play along I thought see how long this charade would last. It wasn't ideal after the conversation the night before but it was definitely more preferable than what I had expected from him.

"Nothing much why?"

He joined me back in the lounge smiling down at me, "I thought we could go out together, and do something, whatever you like"

Again I looked stupefied at him. This was beginning to freak me out. I had fully expected Dylan to be his normal obnoxious self. I had prepared myself for it and instead I had been given a version of him very much preferable. What was he doing? Trying another ploy to make me change my mind?

"If this is another tactic of yours Dylan, to sway my decision, stop because it won't work"

He sat down his eyes gentle on my face, "I guess I can see how you would see it that way. But last night Grace I had to force the issue, to see how intent you were on the divorce"

So I had been correct.

"But after you went to bed last night, I realised you've changed. I've changed. I deeply regret hurting you but I am not sorry for what I did"

Seeing my eyes narrow at him expecting another repercussion of the night before, I pulled my legs tightly under me. He was too close to me and suddenly I didn't want to hear what he had to say.

My eyes must have taken on their woeful wounded expression for immediately he shook his head before reiterating quietly,

"Grace, what I mean is if we hadn't have split, all of this wouldn't be happening, both of us would have been content to just go on in the lives we were used too. But, now things are different between us I can't force you into what I want you to do, so instead I am going to show you how I have changed"

"Why" I whispered

He looked down at his feet for a moment before his eyes caressed mine

"Because I love you and I want us to remain together"

Chapter 4

Two days later my mind still unclear I walked to my parent's home my feet slow and dragging. I had been avoiding this not wanting the fall out I was sure my mother was waiting to dish out to me. It didn't help that for the last couple of days though fighting hard against it Dylan had swept me away making me almost believe his intentions were sincere. I wasn't convinced. Perhaps it had been that first night after his return when we had the heart to heart or whether the following days after it had just confused me more, but though my resilience was still intact it was seriously weakened. The man I had been seeing since my move back to the marital home was only a brief reminder of the man I had dated and married over five years before. He looked the same but that is where the comparison ended. Courteous and attentive nothing was ever too much for him and as much as I was freaked out by it I had also greatly enjoyed it. But, as my mother always said a leopard does not change his spots and just for once I wished she were wrong.

As I turned into Rosemary Avenue my feet stopped knowing my parent's home was only a few steps away now. Dylan had offered to come with me being as he was the one and only reason the falling out had taken place. But I refused strongly shaking my head at him at the suggestion. I could imagine my mother's face as she opened the door to see him standing beside me. Her face would have turned red and I would have been frantic she was having a sudden heart attack.

"Grace you shouldn't have to do this alone. I am the one who instigated this in the first place. Your mother has a right to hate me, I hurt you but I'm sure I can put this right"

"Seriously" I had yelled at him my hands firmly on my hips, as my mother was prone to do when annoyed

"You don't think the mere appearance of you will create world war three. Dylan, I don't know what is going on with you at the moment, and though I am appreciative of all the courtesy and attention you have been showering on me it's not real," I pointed my finger directly at him, "And it's not you."

The old Dylan would have been outraged at the audacity of my behaviour and my lack of respect but this version just smiled ruefully nodding his head in agreement.

"Ok you're right. I'm sorry."

There he said it again making me take a step back loving it one minute, freaking out the next because who was this man and what had he done with my husband.

I stopped abruptly at the dark wood stained gate latched securely and looked up at the house. The house was very similar to ours I thought shuddering when I realised the plural I had subconsciously used. He was getting to me I knew that but I was fighting it every step of the way. Where my house was of yellow engineering brick with tall white painted bay windows to the front my parent's home was darker. The red brick with its ivy clinging to it covered most of the front of the house. The front garden was large with its gravelled driveway and neatly weeded borders. My father had a passion for roses and this was evident as I looked at them now pruned back for the winter. Since his retirement six years before, he had adopted many new hobbies, most of them alone. As much as my parents were devoted to each other my father always avoided the highly excited temperamental side of my mother. Where he was docile, my mother was fiery, where he was a great listener; my mother was a great adviser and so on. I looked towards the garage tucked back neatly amongst the trees wondering if he was home. Chicken I thought to myself as reluctantly I opened the gate and walked down the path.

I pressed the bell not daring to look through the clear paned gleaming panels of the front door. I turned away taking in deep breaths for courage as I heard it open. My mother stood there clad in her apron, which meant she was cooking. I looked at her doubtfully my mouth grimacing trying to achieve a smile. Hers was straight though her eyes were not as reproachful as I had expected.

"Grace"

Not a good sign, if it were, she would have called me 'Gracie', which as much as I hated would now have been gratefully welcomed. She stood aside allowing me to enter which I reluctantly did so. I took off my coat hearing the thud of the front door behind me. My mother's hands brushed my arms as she took the coat from me and hung it on the coat rack standing obediently to attention in one corner of the hallway. Nothing or nobody disobeyed my mother and lived to tell the tale, well not anyone that is except Dylan. She looked me up and down her eyebrows raised at my too casual clothing, which I had recently adopted. I followed her into the kitchen dismayed not to see Dad sitting at the table enjoying his elevenses. I thought I had timed it justright but obviously not.

"Would you like some tea Grace," her austere voice requested as I nodded silently sinking onto the old Victorian chair my mother was so fond of. The table and chairs had been discovered at an auction my parents had gone too. It had been their one and only experience but with the parting of a few hundred pounds they had come away with the table and chairs that I was now sitting at. I looked down at the wood its deep mahogany colour gleaming back at me mockingly.

"I won't be a moment I just have to find your father in the garden and call him in for his elevenses"

"No" I piped up too quickly, "I'll do it for you mum its cold outside"

Before she could reply I had grabbed my coat from the hallway and was rushing out of the back door thankful for the fresh air and welcoming atmosphere.

The garden was wide and rambling. This house had one of the largest gardens in the avenue being a strong and only contender for my father when they had bought it thirty-five years before. Whereas my mother had been happy tending after her flock which consisted of my brother Andrew and I, my father when not too tired returning home from work would wander the winding paths deep in thought. He had lovingly planned his garden which was now an abundance of fruit trees and flowers and most importantly his vegetable garden and roses. As I wondered slowly down one of the winding paths I smiled to myself remembering the games I used to play here as a child. Each path would have a different fairy tale at the end of it. My father had built me a doll's house that resembled more of a castle than a house. I had loved it and played with it almost every day during my childhood. Now relegated to the depths of the attic I had defended its sentimental value when my mother had wanted to cast it upon the bonfire one November fifth. I had loved it so much and I knew if ever I had a daughter she would also love it too. So the castle had stayed and my father secretly had repainted and repaired it for me. Thinking of him now I spied him partially hidden by the bushes at the end of the garden obscuring the garden refuge he would burn later when he had time. My father wasn't a tall man nor was he sturdily built. But what he lacked in stature he more than made up for in love and humour. His face was round and unlined belying his sixty-eight years. His brown eyes twinkled like stars and his smile encompassed most of his lower face when he grinned which was often. Hearing my footsteps as they crunched on un-swept leaves he hadn't gotten round to sweeping yet he looked up at me. A huge smile broke over his face when he saw me. Putting the garden fork to one side he roughly brushed his hands clean on his garden trousers before embracing me tightly.

"Snicket, what a lovely surprise"

I wallowed in his hug never wanting him to let me go. This was my dad. The one person I loved more than any other. Whereas my mother during my growing up had been the one to moan, scold, love, punish and repair, dad was the one who made everything better and whole again. He was never mean spirited, never intrusive unless invited; he was to me my very own prince charming. My hug- a -lot and sweetie- giver when I was sad, this was my wonderful and forever loving dad.

"Dad it's so great to see you, I'm sorry I haven't been round"

He nodded his lips grim as his eyes looked towards the house to where my mother was preparing a snack for his tea break.

"Well I understand Gracie, you and your mother have fallen out"

I looked down at my feet as I used to when I was a child and knew I was in the wrong.

"I couldn't tell her Dad that once Dylan found out I had moved back he was moving back too. I was hoping he was just irritating me, I didn't think he meant it"

Pulling the pipe out of his mouth that he had been smoking he looked at me intently,

"Are you sure what you're doing is what you want Gracie?"

I nodded, "For the moment anyway."

"Are you happy baby girl?"

"Kind of"

He looked at me beneath the brim of the flat cap he was wearing. He harrumphed to himself at my non-committal answers before replying gently,

"Well that's all that matters then"

Hearing my mother's voice call out for us both to hurry up he looked at me below his brows

"Come on then snicket let's go in before your mother blows another fuse"

His arm was tight around my shoulders, as I laughed glad to be home.

The kitchen was warm and inviting when we both entered my father pausing at the door to remove his wellies. His slippers stood side by side waiting for him to slip his feet into. As I hung up my coat and sat obediently at the table where my mother had placed a setting for me I looked at my father quietly for comfort.

"Esther"

My mother stopped pouring the tea into our cups when he spoke. Her eyes read his and without any indication of the message shared between them she placed the teapot gently down on its mat before looking at me,

"Grace help yourself to a sandwich, you're looking so thin these days"

I obediently did as requested looking at my father as we both shared a secret smile between us. My mother wasn't one that offered apologies quickly or often but knowing the comment to my figure was unwarranted we both understood it was her way of welcoming me back and forgiving me.

"How's work these days snicket?" my father asked enquiringly as he helped himself to a cheese and pickle sandwich.

"Well ok my hours have increased recently, not to what they were" I hastened quickly, "But enough for me to cope with"

"Has old man Lewis given up the reins yet to his son or is he still making the poor young fool pander to his every quivering command"

I laughed out loud at his description of my boss. Gerald Lewis as old as my father and still unable to walk away into retirement. He was as harrowing to Julian his son and heir as he had ever been when I had started my last eight and still on-going years at the firm.

"He is trying dad but Julian is more interested in other things shall we say, than the publishing of books"

"Well that young whipper snapper should take a few leaves out of your book Gracie, mind the pun," he grinned wickedly at me, "If he wants to command that empire"

"He's okay dad, when Lewis senior isn't there he manages just fine, but his father, well you know what he's like."

My dad nodded in assent turning to my mother,

"You're very quiet dear"

My mother munching sedately on her sandwich only nodded as her eyes met both of ours staring at her.

"Well it's nice hearing the old chit chat back."

Knowing her innocent reference was solely meant for me for leaving home a week before; I swallowed my food before answering.

"Mum you don't have to worry. I'm okay everything is fine. We had a phone call the other day about a couple wanting to come and look at the house. I'm hoping they'll like it enough to put an offer on it"

Both of my parents stared at me with puzzled eyes.

"What did I say?" I enquired

CHASING RAINBOWS

My mother was quick to intercede, "We, Grace?"

I coloured as I realised what they meant.

"Mum it doesn't mean anything. It's just with Dylan being there..."

I faltered not wanting to continue in case I slipped up any further.

"Have you forgotten the way he spoke to me last time I was at your house Gracie?"

I shook my head in answer avoiding both of them as I hung my head hurriedly wanting to finish my food.

"It's not that important now Esther, don't read too much into it" I knew my father had come to my rescue but I also knew my mother wouldn't be sidestepped.

Feeling her full attention on me I breathed deeply before raising my head. I had nothing to be ashamed off. I hadn't done anything wrong.

"Mum it's our house and we are selling it. I know how Dylan was to you and I'm sorry for that it was my fault. I should have told you of his intentions, but to be honest I thought he was just winding me up, I never thought for one moment he was serious about moving back"

"And how is that working out for you!" Her tone was civil but cold

"Well it's had its up and downs shall we say" I really didn't want to delve deeper into my co-habitation with Dylan but to be honest I should have known better. My mother wasn't a person to let things slide or go by unnoticed.

"Is he behaving himself?"

I looked at my father but his expression was as interested in my reply as my mother's.

"Now it's fine, in fact more than fine. When he moved back after you two met..." I paused before continuing, "Well we had a rather heated discussion." Seeing the immediate worry in my parent's eyes I raised my hand to alleviate their concern, "No it was nothing like that, he just wanted to talk and as we hadn't since our separation well it cleared the air"

My father seeming satisfied with my answer nodded his head in agreement before getting up.

"I'm going back to the garden. Lovely to see you Grace, take care wont you?"

I nodded wishing I could follow him.

"I will Dad no probs" I replied far too brightly.

My mother started clearing the table, her actions swift and precise. Me, I sat there like the teenager I once was, twiddling my thumbs wondering how to overcome the awkwardness that had appeared in the room since my dad had left.

"Mum you have to stop worrying about me. I am not a child anymore I know what I am doing."

She stopped running the water in the sink to wash up. Turning round to face me she looked at me for a few seconds before answering,

"Do you know what you're doing Gracie? Or are you just trying to pacify your father and myself?"

"I know what I am doing" my tone was firm as I stood up

"He wants you back, you know that don't you?"

I was glad she had turned back to the sink because as her words sunk in my mouth gaped open in surprise.

"A man doesn't go to all the effort Dylan Hunt has unless he wants something in return"

I couldn't refute what she had said because that was exactly what Dylan had said. My mother noticing my silence continued without looking round

"Come and help me Gracie, you can dry"

Reluctantly I picked up the tea towel trying to assume a bland expression as I joined her.

"Mum" I stammered before taking a deep breath, "It's not like that. My reasons for going back to the house were as I said. Dylan has, reiterated what you have said but I don't believe the sincerity behind it."

My mother paused in the washing of the cup she was holding to look at me intently, "You know Gracie people don't change regardless of how emphatically they may try to persuade you otherwise."

I sighed deeply as I took the cup from her and dried it slowly.

"I know" I replied wistfully.

The walk home two hours later was tiring. My feet were lethargic knowing their destination. I had chosen to take the long way home to give me time to think. My mother was right. People didn't change. Dylan as much as I wanted to believe was capable of that I knew was too set in his ways to be able to change. When we had married, my husband ten years older than my twenty-two years was already established in his career. He was well known and admired for his prowess and no nonsense business dealings, which was why he had risen quickly and comfortably. That was why I had been surprised that out of all the women he could have chosen he had chosen me. Compared to most of the hearsay floating round the office concerning him I had never seen myself as a woman to attract such magnetism and power. Because power was what exuded, out of every pore of Mr Dylan William Hunt. I looked up suddenly noticing my surroundings realising my steps had taken me to the park close to my parent's home. I looked at my watch it was a little after two in the afternoon. Why not take a stroll I asked myself as I walked slowly along the path through the big iron gates of the entrance. For nearly the end of October the weather was cold making me snuggle deeper into my long thick coat. My boots fleece lined were old but very comfortable so instead of retracing my steps back to the house where I knew Dylan would be waiting for me I walked further into the park. All the trees now looked as sorrowful as I felt, their deep green leaves long gone, their barren branches reaching nakedly out to the sky as though seeking comfort. They looked as lonely as I realised I was. Noticing an empty bench straight ahead of me I walked briskly towards it. My ears were freezing so as I sat down I pulled my knitted hat further over my ears. Why did life have to be so complicated? No correction, why did Dylan have to be so bloody-minded.

The elderly woman heading towards me her hand firmly holding the leash of the Old English sheepdog leading her looked happy and contented. I wondered why she had chosen such a large dog considering how small she was. Reaching me she sighed deeply giving me a smile as she settled next to me trying to curb the dog from continuing his hurried pace.

"Buster sit"

I chewed my lip to hide my amusement as eventually the dog obeyed but not before clamouring all over me.

"I'm sorry dear are you alright?" She asked her voice full of regret and concern

I looked at her sideways nodding one eye still focused on the dog that now placated after licking my cheek repeatedly had at last slumped haphazardly down on the ground between our feet his eyes closed. My cheek was sticky and I had no tissues in my open pocket I inwardly groaned cursing the beast laying reposed in slumber at my feet.

As if in answer to my unspoken need she looked at me offering me a clean paper tissue.

"I'm sorry about Buster he can be quite excitable at times, I don't know how Jerry manages"

Taking the tissue from her I wiped my cheek shuddering at the thought of the dog's saliva drying rapidly on my skin.

"My grandson Jeremy loves this dog. Though how he manages with him I'll never know, he can be so boisterous and disobedient most of the time"

I smiled back at her, "He definitely seems a handful" I replied politely.

She looked at me, and then back at the dog, who by this time was in a deep comatose state judging by his snoring.

"He is but we love him regardless."

I looked away not knowing what else to say.

"I've never seen you in the park before, are you new to the area? I walk Buster here most days when it's not raining of course. Can you imagine walking this monster in the rain trying desperately to keep my balance" she laughed not noticing I had remained quiet.

"I'm sorry," she continued " ignore me I'm always chattering on."

"No it's ok" I replied, "I work so I don't often have the chance to visit the park"

The old lady nodded, "It's hard nowadays for you youngsters. I look at my grandson Jeremy always working" she shook her head, " it doesn't seem fair to receive so little for all the hours he puts in"

I smiled seeing her eyes look at my left hand now bare from the bands I had worn with such pride and had treasured so dearly.

"Haven't you got a nice young man to come home too?"

I followed her gaze shaking my head immediately, "I did have once, but well soon that will be all over"

She shook her head again, "It's a shame that these days nobody tries harder to keep things together. I suppose now what with divorce being so acceptable it's almost odd to see long standing marriages survive"

I nodded thinking of my parents and feeling envious of what they had. I had imagined lifelong wedded bliss as I had walked proudly on my father's arm down the aisle to meet Dylan. But what did I know. Obviously not a lot.

"Sometimes it's not always possible to hold on, especially when one of you walks away."

She shook her head in agreement, "That's true but then you must always look on the bright side, you know what they say. As one door closes another opens"

My companion reminded me so much of my mother that I grinned

"Yes my mum says the same thing."

"Well I suppose I should get this ruffian home before it starts getting dark"

Standing up with her, I turned to look at her, "Are you sure you'll be ok"

CHASING RAINBOWS

She laid a hand gently on my arm, "It takes more than this mischievous pup to get the better of me"

I looked back at the dog wondering how she could describe the big hairy reprobate as a pup. We headed in the same direction towards the entrance. Although I hadn't had the solitude I needed to think through my troubles I had been glad of the company.

"Which way are you going?" I asked not knowing why

The elderly lady looked at me a slow smile appearing on her lips

"Well normally I go left out of the entrance its a little longer for buster, but today I am heading right. It's shorter and well he has clean wore me out"

My decision was immediate and before I realised what I was saying I had offered to accompany her including taking control of the leash.

"Are you sure dear he can be quite naughty, especially when it's getting near to his food time as it is now?"

I smiled reassuringly at her, "No I'm sure, I'll be glad of the challenge and the company."

Why I had offered I didn't really know but the thought of going straight home to where I knew Dylan would be waiting, wanting to know how my day with my parents had gone was not something I was either looking forward too or willing to share. Buster as prophesised pulled at the leash nearly dragging me twice into the road when we tried to cross.

"Are you sure you're ok..." the old lady floundered looking up at me, "This is silly I don't even know your name."

"Grace" I replied yanking Buster back as forcefully as I could without result.

"Grace what a beautiful name. My name is Florrie" she grimaced "Short for Florence."

The walk was short with Buster being fairly obedient after our tug of war. We hadn't spoken much or well I hadn't, as Florrie had continuously chatted on as prophesised earlier. By the time I willingly handed back the lead to her I had been fully versed about her life including that of her grandson Jeremy. She took my hand giving me a warm smile as she opened the garden gate.

"It was a pleasure meeting you Grace. I normally take Buster out to the park most afternoons; it would be nice to see you again."

Smiling I muttered vaguely I would try as I waved goodbye and made my way reluctantly home.

The house was quiet when I returned. Hanging up my coat burying my hat deep into one of the pockets I heaved a sigh of relief that Dylan wasn't there. I had had an enjoyable day I realised and what was more important other than the conversation with my parents concerning my estranged husband I hadn't thought of him more than a few times. I had certainly come a long way in the several days since I had returned to this weird set up of a life I was entertaining now. I hadn't felt like the whole world was caving in on me like I had been feeling since our initial separation. As I walked into the kitchen feeling the desperate need for a strong coffee I noticed the coffee pot simmering on the machine. I picked up the glass jug inhaling the aroma, which wasn't acrid as I expected. It hadn't long since been made and then I wondered where Dylan was. Opening the cupboard I helped myself to a mug and poured coffee into it. Adding my one lump of brown sugar I opened the fridge to get out the cream. Lying on the top shelf was a bottle of champagne that hadn't been there earlier. Staring at it I wondered what he was up to now. Pouring the cream into the coffee watching it swirl I thought more about what my mother had said earlier. As loathed, as she was to admit it she had noticed in me a change, which hadn't been there when I had moved out. Her eyes were weary, as she looked at me her hands resting gently on my forearms.

"Are you sure you're ok Grace?"

I nodded forcing a smile not wanting to dispel the moment. "I'm fine mum."

She pulled me tenderly into her arms hugging me close. I missed this, I missed them and I was immediately contrite for ignoring them since the evening of Dylan's initial arrival when my mother had been present.

"Have you thought more about what you are going to do when eventually the house is sold and the divorce is behind you?"

"Not really" I muttered.

"Well Gracie don't you think you should start dating again? How long has it been since you buried yourself away here?"

Shrugging my shoulders I continued drying up the remainder of the crockery.

"Mum it's been a long time since I was free. I wouldn't know what to do or how to go about it"

"What about Zara. Couldn't you two go out together like you used too?"

Placing the damp tea towel back onto the handle of the oven door I sat back down at the table not wanting to meet my mother's gaze.

"We don't talk to each other now"

"Why not Gracie you two were the best of friends what happened?"

"Remember when I went round the house the first time. Well Zara turned up. Apparently Dylan had asked her to keep an eye on the house whilst he was away"

My mother's lips set into a firm line, "Really. Well you don't have to read a book to know what's going on between those lines do you."

My heart shuddered to a halt. "What do you mean?" I asked not really wanting to hear her version of the answer.

Her eyes were gentle as they rested on my face. Stretching out her arm her hand clasped mine tightly,

"What do you think it means?"

"If you're thinking there is something going on between her and Dylan mum I doubt it. She's not his type"

"Neither were you"

I bit my lip anxiously.

"Grace, it doesn't necessarily mean that, but don't you think it's strange. I mean it's not as if Dylan gave her the time of day when he was around you both or am I completely barking up the wrong tree?"

"No you're right in fact if I remember correctly he was always rather rude to her"

The satisfied look that flitted across my mother's face had my stomach churning. I knew from that first evening when Zara had found me poking around the house that something was up. She was cool and offhanded with me but regarding the circumstances of our meeting that night I hadn't given much thought to it being anything other than what it appeared. Had Dylan and Zara been in cahoots behind my back or was it something more sinister than I originally assumed?

"Mum I don't believe it"

"Don't darling, or wont?"

I sat on the armchair in the dusk of the lounge sipping at my coffee wondering if my mother had assumed correctly. Looking around me I wondered whether any clues were visible. Knowing Dylan and how sly he could be I finished my coffee quickly. Leaving the empty mug on the side table close by. I walked tentatively out into the hallway calling his name. The house remained silent. Walking slowly up the stairs I breathed in deeply trying to figure out my next move. There was nothing in my bedroom because when I had returned all the drawers and wardrobes were empty, so if there were anything to be found it would be in his room.

As I reached the top of the stairs I had to ask myself what depths I was willing to sink too to find answers. I had never in all our years together ever contemplated rummaging through Dylan's private things even when his distant and sometimes obnoxious behaviour would have warranted it. I paused by his door my heart hammering heavily at what I was considering doing. I knocked tentatively a big part of me hoping he was sleeping. I knocked three times before I had gained enough courage to open his bedroom door.

The room was empty, his bed made. Although this room was not as luxurious as mine with its own en-suite it was appealing but as my eyes quickly scanned it I saw nothing out of place only ruthless tidiness. I looked over my shoulder expecting Dylan to be standing behind me asking me in cool tones what the hell I was doing in his room. But there was nobody else there except myself. My body felt pumped the adrenalin coursing through it as I stepped gingerly into his sanctuary. What the hell would I be looking for I wondered not used to doing what I was about to do. I remembered then he carried a diary and I looked quickly around hoping it would be helpful and would be lying on a surface easy for me to find. But the only surface filled with any of this things was his bedside table and that consisted only of an alarm clock and his book and specs which I noticed was a habit he still continued to do at night when he had trouble sleeping. It came to me then I knew this man as close as any person he allowed into his world. Dylan was not a man that embraced many into his private life; it wasn't because he was reclusive but very selective who shared his domain. Should I be doing this I began to question myself my feet still unable to step further into the room. He had given me no cause to consider my actions now, and with the divorce pending did I honestly have the right to be so intrusive when the outcome of the consequences if any, was fallout anyway because it was over between us. My mother's words came back to me encouraging me to probe. With baited breath I walked hurriedly over to his bedside and opened his bedside drawer. The diary was there. I looked at it for a moment wondering now whether not only should I do it, but also if I were to find anything did I really want to be hurt even more than I already had. My dilemma was decided for me when I heard the front door open and Dylan's voice calling my name. Panicking I shut the drawer and ran out of his room closing it quickly behind me before taking the nearest exit which was my bedroom. Shutting my door as quietly as I was able I laid my hand on my rapidly beating heart trying to gain some composure before he came upstairs to find me. I knew I had only minutes for Dylan was very astute and I was lousy at lying. Looking hurriedly around me I could see no place for me to hide, for that is what I wanted to do until I was calm again and in control. As I heard his footsteps on the treads of the stairs I shot into the en-suite bathroom in enough time to close it before I heard his gentle knock on my bedroom door.

"Gracie are you in there?" his voice was light and amusing.

I remained silent, which was a bad move on my part as I heard him enter the bedroom. I stood against the bathroom door the key quietly turned waiting hesitantly for him to leave. But he didn't.

I looked frantically around me why I didn't know, but I wasn't used to spying and being discovered almost immediately.

"What are you doing in there?" his voice was suddenly so close to me that I shook even though I knew I had a wooden barricade between us.

"I was just about to take a shower," I mumbled shaking my head at myself, my mouth grimacing at my answer. What! Couldn't I have thought of anything better to say than that?

"I don't hear the shower running"

I clenched my teeth sighing quietly to myself.

"Why are you in my room?" I enquired hoping my voice was as cool as I had meant it to be.

"I was looking for you" he replied silkily

"Well now you have found me so you can go?"

"Oh I don't know" his voice was playful, "I might just wait here"

No longer feeling guilty for my intending misdemeanour I bit down on my lip kicking myself for creating this situation.

"Go Dylan, get out of my room. You are not allowed in here, remember?"

He was silent for what seemed a long moment before his answer filtered through the door to me

"Your stipulation kitten not mine"

I groaned inwardly. Hitting my forehead repeatedly against the palm of my hand I paced the small en-suite determined not to give an inch. I knew pig stubborn as he was he would remain waiting in my bedroom until I showed my face. Looking down at my clothes I shook my head as I quickly shed them picking up a bath towel and wrapping it tightly around my now naked body. As farces went this was ridiculous but if it meant getting rid of him then that's what I had to do. I checked my face in the mirror quickly tying my hair into a high knot as I always did when taking a quick shower. My reflection showed a young woman her face suffused with colour her eyes bright. Clear signs of guilt I thought as I leant down turning on the cold tap and quickly flushing my skin with water. It was better I thought as I looked at myself once more. I now looked more annoyed than guilty. Unlocking the bathroom door checking once more my towel was tight around me I opened it. He was lying on our bed. His eyes were closed with his left forearm resting gently against his eyes. When he heard my entry he immediately opened them and sat up. I stood still as we both looked at each other and I think it was then that I realised, as catastrophes went I had just made a major catastrophic boo- boo.

His eyes lazily and intentionally roved slowly over my body. I had since our break up lost a little weight and though I had never been overweight I was now extremely slim. I could see in his expression that Dylan was approving of the weight loss. I gritted my teeth but remained silent as I watched him watching me.

"You've become very svelte Grace" he nodded his head approvingly, "I like it"

"Really and you can tell that through a thick long bath towel?"

The gauntlet I had unwittingly thrown down, made him stand up and walk slowly closer to me

"I have memories which were," he faltered off for a moment before his eyes settled steely on mine, "stunning then. I can only imagine now how much your body looks better now" his eyes were mentally removing the towel I was holding onto tightly now. As he stepped closer to me I stepped back groaning inside when my body hit the wall behind me. He smiled at me sensing my inner distress and entrapment. He leaned in his arms trapping my body on both sides.

"Well, this could be a rather compromising position don't you think?"

I breathed in deeply before I answered hoping my voice wasn't as tremulous as my body was feeling at his close proximity. As much as I was angry with him for my present predicament my body thought otherwise. My heart was beating so wildly in my chest I swear he could hear it. My stomach was churning doing aerobatic somersaults inside, my legs and arms as weak as jelly. I knew I was blushing because I could feel the heat. I moaned inwardly again as his eyes picked up on it. He raised one hand to caress my cheek lovingly with his forefinger. I remained transfixed unable to speak knowing if I did my voice would give me away. He stepped closer now pinning me tightly against the wall. His other hand tugged at my band holding up my hair pulling it free so my dark tresses tumbled haphazardly over my shoulders. The action had his eyes smouldering as he stared deeply into my eyes. I knew he was going to kiss me and as much as I wanted to turn my face away from him in denial I couldn't move. He smiled knowing the effect his actions were having on me. I hated myself for being so transparent. My head was screaming at me to shout at him and push him away, but my body and my heart melted like molten toffee as his lips hovered over mine. I closed my mouth tightly my only act of defence. It amused him. His tongue ran slowly over my dry lips poking gently to open them. I gulped wanting so much at this moment to have the guts to knee him in the groin but the space between us was so limited any sudden movement on my part would only act in his favour with my towel falling away. So I remained still. His hands began to wander. The softness of his palms caressed my shoulders before slowly trailing over my rigid arms. His lips pressed lightly on mine still probing for entry but I remained firm. Not showing any signs of annoyance he just smiled at me his eyes pulling me further in to his hypnotic trance. Softly and provocatively his tongue skimmed my cheeks in small circular motions before descending slowly down to my throat. I could feel his mouth pause on the vein on the side of my neck telling him my heart was pumping erratically. He didn't stop. I had a weakness and he had remembered it. Sucking gently on my earlobe I could feel all my strength drain away from me as I could feel my body lean into him responding. His hands when they clasped each side of my face were firm and gentle as sensing my mouth opening in surprise his lips abandoned my ear to possessively take control. His tongue was hot as he thrust it deep into my mouth. I moaned forgetting my defences as my arms encircled his waist clinging onto him for support. He was a master at this and he knew it as his arms lifting mine to around his neck then encircled my waist pulling me into him so tightly the knot of the towel dug into my chest. My legs felt numb as his hands slid lower to caress my bottocks. He squeezed them gently I could feel his lips smirk against mine as the rigidity left my body and oozed into him. The towel had loosened with our combined gyrating making the fluffy fabric between us the only weakening barrier. His hands lifted the towel his fingers caressing the skin of my bottom pausing at the crack as slowly his forefinger eased itself between my cheeks moving slowly up and down leaving me with no uncertainty as to what was on his mind. Feeling him lift me my feet dangling like puppets I didn't protest, as he carried me to the bed. His kisses hot and demanding paused on my neck as I felt the edge of the divan bed hard against my calves.

"Grace?" his voice was fevered filled with emotion as he looked into my eyes and I knew as I nodded assuring him it was ok that I wanted this as much as he did. I also knew that when this was over I would hate myself for what I was about to do. But the recriminations could wait I needed this, wanted this; I had missed this, missed him for so long. I wanted to feel alive again instead of the zombie I had been for the last few months. He lifted me further onto the bed tugging at the towel until it gave way reluctantly falling to the floor taking my virtue with it. As I lay there looking at him kneeling over me I helped him out of his shirt almost tearing at the buttons to release them. I didn't want to withdraw to have a change of heart as if sensing this he stood up quickly tearing off his jeans and boxers before covering my body again with his. He leaned on his elbows framing each side of my face looking intently at me. His blue gaze examined every part of my hazel eyes intent on him assuring me that what we were about to do was right. His fingers raked gently through my hair his thumbs pausing at the side of my temples to caress them. His mouth slowly descended onto mine our tongues meeting, searching each other's mouths desperately. I couldn't get enough of him and I groaned as his lips pressed harder on mine, the feeling was mutual. His teeth gently nipped on my lips the tip of his tongue probing gently then forcibly into my mouth making me moan as I raked my fingers through his hair. He moaned too in response his tongue withdrawing quickly his lips covering my face in gentle light kisses.

"I love you kitten and tonight I am going to prove it again and again until you believe me."

I moaned in reply my hands pulling his head down to mine his tongue again taking possession of my mouth, in and out thrusting then caressing me. My tongue wound around his urging him to take control.

I could feel his manhood hard and firm against my pelvis as I moved seductively beneath him making him growl taking deeper possession of my mouth. I couldn't breathe his weight heavy on me but I didn't care. I closed my eyes luxuriating in the warmth coursing through my body, I wanted him to take me now I couldn't wait another moment but Dylan ignored my frantic hands as I held his buttocks trying to force him into me. He lifted his face his forefinger caressing my swollen lips; I moaned again at him my eyes imploring him to take me. He shifted his weight grabbing me he rolled onto his back lifting me so I was on top of him. I looked down at him my breathing hard, my legs embracing either side of him. His hair was ruffled from my fingers his skin damp and glowing. He held me firm against him his hands on either side of my hips. I looked down at him ignoring the tug of conscience at the corners of my mind. His hands releasing me held my face forcing me to look at him his smile was languorous as his fingertips trailed slowly down my neck caressing my breasts rubbing my nipples until they were as hard as bullets. I let out a long moan my teeth biting my lower lip as I moved my hips against him in a circular fashion throwing my head back my mouth open my eyes closed as his hands caressed my stomach. His hardness beneath me lay motionless but I could feel the heat coming from it, the stabbing thrusts as his cock edged closer. I moved my hips lower hoping the motion would get him inside me, he looked at me another feral growl escaping him as grabbing my hips he thrust himself inside me again and again. I cried out in pleasure moving with him wanting him to take deeper ownership of me. My arms hung limply by my sides, my skin wet from perspiration. As the momentum increased I felt myself being turned as my back landed on the bed his body still connected to mine. He raised my legs folding them tightly around his waist as I clung onto him my face buried deep into his shoulder. His hair was as damp as mine, his mouth was hot his tongue plunging as deep as his sex. I could feel my orgasm building as his thrusts became faster and harder. Crying out in ecstasy I came he paused slowing down preventing his ejaculation from escaping. His name died on my lips as he kissed me again, slowly he moved downwards until his head was between my thighs. His eyes captured mine as his tongue licked the juices oozing out of me. I moaned in response my hands holding his head firmly. He smiled slowly at me before his face lowered again as his mouth sucked harshly on my clit making my body spasm and my body lift backwards of the bed. I couldn't breathe the ecstasy coursing through my body was like a drug leaving fire in its wake. The more I squirmed the more he sucked. When I felt like my heart would stop he slowly entered me one finger at a time. The more my body betrayed me the more fingers entered the tiny space until feeling like I was being fucked to death he pulled his fingers out and entered me thrusting so hard I cried out in delicious pain as my arms and legs pulled him in closer. Kissing me harshly on the mouth he yelled out

"Grace you are mine never forget it"

I heard him but did not respond.

Heaving himself up he lifted my legs onto his shoulders as he leaned into me demanding, his thrusting penis punishing me for my silence

"Grace you are mine and I will fuck your brains out until all you think of is me. "

He lunged harder into me with every spoken syllable demanding my verbal compliance

"Do… you…hear…me…baby?"

"Yes" I screamed as my second orgasm erupted, his thrusting increasing as he yelled out my name as he came holding me tightly to him as his seed filled my womb, and his body my soul.

His body jittering from the last throes of his orgasm did not release me. Unable to move I lay there my eyes closed my breathing coming thick and fast. Dylan his body slumped over mine shifted slightly as his lips tenderly kissed the tip of my ear. I looked at him his face buried in my hair. Turning away I bit back the nagging doubts knowing as much as I had wanted this, wanted him I would come to deeply regret what I had just done.

Chapter 5

The next morning I woke up alone in my bed. For a moment I was confused knowing the night before I had done something I knew in the cold light of day I would deeply regret, and then I remembered. I turned over hugging the duvet closer to me in comfort. My body ached and I was sore, very sore. We had made love three more times during the night and I hated myself now for every single one of those acts. The bed was ruffled with our frantic writhing the smell of our lovemaking jeering at me, reminding me. Why had I done it. I admonished myself because, "you had wanted to my heart reminded me." Angry for being so weak and foolish I sat up hurriedly wincing at the soreness of my lower region. There was no use mentally beating myself up for what I had done I thought, as I threw back the covers and gingerly got out of bed. I picked up the towel where it had been discarded so carelessly the day before and wrapped it around me. My hair was tangled and as I looked into the mirror in the bathroom my lips were very swollen.

I was glad Dylan hadn't been beside me when I woke for the last thing I needed at the moment was any reminder especially when knowing his sexual appetite he would have re-instigated another session and I as helpless as the night before would have complied. I turned on the bath taps wanting nothing more than to soak my aching limbs and sore areas in hot soapy water. If only my mind could be rinsed as clean as my body I thought miserably, as staring at my image once more in the mirror I reached for my toothbrush. It was then I stopped. My mind reeling in sudden shock and horror, I had been more than careless with my deceiving body the night before I had risked sexual intercourse many times without any consideration for protection.

"No" I shouted out how could I have been so stupid?

I had always been on the pill during our marriage Dylan not wanting to start a family. A few months before we had separated I had stopped taking them because there was no point. We had often discussed starting a family since the house had been completed, but Dylan had not been supportive saying the time wasn't right for his career. So I had quietly decided to change his mind over the next coming months and if I had fallen pregnant during that time it would force him to capitulate and welcome the next natural stage of our life together.

NATASHA JACQUES

Running towards the bedroom I pulled open my bedside drawer frantically looking through the contents. I sat down on the bed the pills I was frantically searching for in my hand. I quickly scanned the expiration before searching through my mind for today's date. Sighing with relief that they were still viable I pressed out one of the tablets taking it into the bathroom and swallowing it quickly with a handful of water. When Dylan had discovered what I had done he had gone berserk shouting entrapment at me and that he wasn't ready to become a father. Knowing I wasn't yet pregnant and immediately regretting my impulsive decision I had gone to the doctor's and got the morning after pill to make sure no pregnancy mishap occurred until I was safely back on the pill. He had forced me through bouts of arguing long before our separation that he wouldn't and couldn't entertain being a parent. It was then he had truthfully stated he never wanted to be one. I had been heartbroken and for a time I had wondered whether I could accept the decision that he had made so coldly without my acquiescence or knowledge. When he had proposed he had not been abhorrent to our discussions of starting a family in a few years and I wondered then as now what had happened to change him so emphatically in another direction. I turned off the taps dropping the towel and sunk slowly into the depths of hot foamy suds. I remembered being heartbroken at his unwavering resentment knowing that even though what I wanted most of all was a family he had gone back on his word not willing to give an inch. I had tried everything to make him change his mind and when that hadn't worked I had accepted the two choices he had left me and learn to live with them. I could either leave him and one day hopefully fall in love with someone else and have a family, or I could stay and remain in his life. I had after lonely days of crying and soul searching, chosen the latter. I loved Dylan with all my heart and as long as I had him, he would show me every day how right I was in my difficult choice to stay with him. Initially I had been correct and when conjugal rights had almost immediately ensued it continued to tear me apart every time we made love that all I had was all I would ever have with him. Now I was grateful for his self centred greed, but it made me feel even worse to think I had submitted so easily to him the night before. I had let myself down in more ways than one. How much more of a doormat could I make myself become? It was so clear to me now, why hadn't I noticed this before? Throughout our life together I realised everything had been about him. The house, the furniture, the project from start to finish had been achieved through me but to his stipulations. Even my most treasured hopes of

70

becoming a mother he had taken coldly and heartlessly away from me. I shook my head in dismay unable to believe that throughout those five and half years of marriage I had not only considered myself fortunate to be married to such a man I had been blissfully happy or so I thought.

I sunk further into the foamy water feeling for a moment that if I were to duck my head under the water the thoughts depressing as they were, would be washed away. But it wasn't a baptism and I would not be cleansed of all my sins. So instead I just lay there. When the bathroom door opened I turned my head towards the wall rather than face Dylan.

"Good morning darling"

Choosing not to reply I lowered half my face under the water so I wouldn't be expected to answer. Dylan sitting on the edge of the bath smiling mistook my action for embarrassment

"Ah feeling a little shy this morning after our lustful night"

I closed my eyes wishing he would go away, but he didn't. Instead I felt his hand on my leg his fingers swirling gently in the water. Opening my eyes I stared at him my expression clear that I was not amused at his antics. He continued with his actions his eyes focusing on the watery illusion of my body occasionally visible as his hand pushed away the bubbles.

"Dylan stop" my tone was harsh.

His hand froze on my thigh his eyes meeting mine. The smile faded quickly from his lips as he looked at me intently trying to figure out why I was in a mood, because by his interpretation if I disagreed and put my foot down, I was not having my fair say like in any other normal relationship, I was just being bloody stubborn and disagreeable. He took his hand out of the water slowly wiping it on the towel I had dropped on the floor by the bath.

"What's the matter with you?"

My head screamed out 'you, you bastard that's what's the matter with me.' Instead I shrugged my shoulders not willing to discuss our previous night's carnality whilst I lay naked in the tub.

"Tired" I stammered wishing he would go away and leave me alone.

"I can understand that I don't feel too bright myself."

"Then would you mind leaving the bathroom so I can take my soak in peace?"

"Why don't I join you, the bath's big enough remember," the glint in his eye left nothing to the imagination as I grimaced at him.

"No I'm, too sore."

He smiled as he leant down his hand diving into the water before I could stop him. I could feel his fingers touch my lower area as his fingers slowly made their way into me.

"For God's sake Dylan fuck off will you, I said no" I screamed out the words kicking his hand away with my leg sending waves of soapy water spilling over the edge of the bath drenching his jeans.

"Grace what the hell is the matter with you?" His face fuming as he stood up. His shirt was also soaked and if I hadn't felt so foul tempered I would have burst out laughing at the sodden sight of him.

"You just never listen do you? When I say back off it doesn't mean bug the shit out of me."

He walked towards the door not bothering to look back. Breathing out a sigh that he had eventually listened to me, the door closed quietly behind him. Before it clicked shut he stuck his head through the small gap wiping the look of relief of my face

"I don't know what the fuck's wrong with you this morning but hurry up I want to talk to you."

Drying my body gently with the towel he had casually discarded to its original place of rest I looked in the mirror wishing I could feel as soothed as my body now felt. An hour later tentatively opening the door I poked my head round making sure the bedroom was empty. As my eyes took in the bed recollections of the previous night flooded my mind once more making my face colour and my body repulse in shame. Picking up the brush from the bedside table I sat down running the brush through my wet strands. It had been over an hour since his departure from my bathroom and as much as I wanted to just stay where I was and pretend he wasn't there I knew if I didn't hurry up he would stroll in demanding why I wasn't downstairs. Not wanting a repeat performance of the night before or this morning I hurriedly put on my underwear. Tying my hair back in a low ponytail I put on a long skirt and jumper. I stripped the bedclothes and remade the bed picking up the wet towel I dropped all of it into the laundry basket before slowly vacating the room.

When I entered the lounge he was sitting on the armchair in fresh clothes with a definite scowl on his face. Normally worried knowing his temper tantrums could last for days, I didn't as in the past rush to him kissing him telling him seductively how sorry I was; instead I walked past him to make myself a cup of coffee. Emptying the jug I rinsed it out leaving it on the drainer. Opening the fridge I picked up the cream pouring it into my mug as I dropped in my regulated sugar cube.

"So don't you think you owe me an explanation?" His voice was sharp. He lounged against the door frame watching me as I stirred my coffee, dropping the spoon in the sink instead of the dishwasher, which I knew would irritate him further and took a sip. I turned my back on him not wanting to face him.

"I owe you nothing" I retorted stubbornly wishing he would walk away.

The silence that followed made me uneasy, more so because I still had my back to him.

"So that's how it's going to be is it?" his tone held a sense of finality to it, which I recognised, did not mean the end of the conversation as I had hoped.

"Dylan" I voiced out loudly, "What happened last night, I really wish now it hadn't "I said sombrely.

I turned to face him as I spoke the words watching his expression change from pissed off to angry.

"Really" his tone was dry and mocking as I continued to drink my coffee for something to do.

"Well unfortunately Grace I don't share your wish. Whatever is wrong between us sex isn't it. In fact if anything celibacy has improved your sexual appetite."

I cringed at his words hating him for tossing my momentary weakness for him last night back at me.

"What makes you think I've been celibate during our separation?"

He smiled languidly as he approached me. Leaning in his lips resting on my ear he whispered triumphantly, "Because my darling wife if you hadn't been celibate you wouldn't be so sore."

I turned away from him ignoring his laugh then a thought struck me

"Does that mean you haven't been?"

He looked confused for a moment before catching the jist of my question,

"If you're inferring whether I also have been abstinent then I'm afraid Grace its none of your business."

"That sounds like an omission of guilt Dylan."

"Separation my darling means exactly that. For awhile we both led our own lives, to do with as we choose without consideration or accusation from the other, meaning you."

I expected the return of the raw pain I had suffered since we had split up. But none was forthcoming only anger at his reply.

73

"Well then as the situation still applies then I also can do whatever I like with who ever I want"

His hand grabbed my arm pulling me to him. His face was expressionless his tone laced with underlying jealousy,

"Don't push me Grace. It's one thing to be separated out of each other's lives completely, it's another to flaunt it whilst cohabiting under the same roof"

I shrugged off his arm my eyes meeting his; "I never said I would flaunt it in front of you now did I?"

Taking the mug out of my hands and dropping it into the sink he grabbed both my arms forcing me to face him.

"Grace after last night do you think I would have screwed you just for the hell of it. Hell if I want sex it's easy enough to get. I made love to you last night because I wanted too, because I love you, and because I want to put this separation behind us and start anew."

I gulped my eyes riveted to his. I didn't bother replying because I knew I couldn't say the same back. Whatever had happened to me since his moving back in it hadn't wanted me to want him back like I previously thought I did? Without realising how I was feeling, which direction I was heading in, I had accomplished partial disconnection from him without even being aware of it. The sex last night should have proved to me that I loved him and wanted to make a fresh start. But the feelings that had heralded my awakening that morning had left me ashamed and repulsed by my behaviour.

"Let me go Dylan, unless you have something more you wish to share with me, aside from that? "I looked pointedly at his groin, "Then let me pass."

He waited unmoving his grip on me tight as his eyes looked intently into mine, trying to read what I was feeling.

"Grace what the hell is going on with you?"

I fidgeted until he let me go putting space between us.

"I don't want what you want anymore"

His mouth tensed. I could see his jaw clenching as he tried to control the sudden anger he felt at my disclosure.

"You can't just switch off your feelings for me like that Grace, he clicked his fingers to reiterate what he was saying. I know, I can remember how we were, how you were. That just doesn't disappear in a flash. Last night you were as desperate for me as I was for you."

"It's not a flash Dylan. It's been five and a half months if not more, since you dumped me remember? Do you think you can just pick up from where you left off? I am not a robot; I no longer bow to your every command as I used to do. When you threw me away Dylan you did something to me. As if denying me a family wasn't enough you threw me aside what eight weeks later? I didn't realise until after last night what effect that had on me in relation to my feelings towards you. Yes my body still wants you but my head and heart does not."

"So what was last night then, a goodbye fuck?"

I cringed at his words unused to his blasphemy. "I don't know what last night was. Perhaps it was just the timing, hell I don't know, I only know I hated the way I felt this morning when I remembered."

"You could be pregnant Grace. Isn't that what you have always wanted from me? A baby, hell Grace if it means that much to you then fine let's do it."

I shook my head looking away from him, "I took the morning after pill, so no Dylan, there won't be a baby"

He pushed past me to turn at the door stopping me vacating the room.

"Why, I thought that's what you wanted from me?"

I looked at him square in the face, "I did. Remember months before we finished. You found out I had stopped taking the pill. Can you remember how you reacted? How you accused me of trapping you. How could I trap you Dylan when we were already married? It's the most natural thing in the world to want to procreate. It's what people in love do Dylan. Create families"

"Grace we have that now. We don't have to settle for one, hell let's have two kids one of each."

Frustratingly I looked at him pitying him, "Dylan relationships makes babies not the other way around. You're not ready, I don't even know if you ever will be, you're too self centred."

"So that's it we're finished just like that?"

"Dylan you threw us away remember not me,and now, now it's too late."

Hugging me close his lips caressing my hair he whispered urgently, "Gracie, don't do this. I made a big mistake I can change. I will do anything for you to keep you"

"I'm not a possession. I'm not yours to keep."

"Are you punishing me for the way I ended us? Hell Grace I didn't know what I was doing back then. I was confused. I've missed you. Why do you think I came back when I discovered you moved back here?"

I shoved him away not believing a word he was saying, "Dylan if you missed me that much you knew where I was. You could have rung me, texted me. I would have met you. But, you didn't. What you are doing now is too little too late. I've grown apart from you and though my body still remembers you, it's just sex right."

I left the room not wanting to give him another opportunity to try and change my mind. There were no doubts that our sexual liaison the night before had weakened the chains binding me to him but I still wasn't free from him.

Chapter 6

I was restless. It had been a day since our argument and Dylan had opted to ignore me, which suited me fine. I shook my head not believing how childish he seemed to be when it had been an accusation he had often thrown at me. Firstly, fresh after the row he had thrown himself into the armchair his arms rigid across his chest. Me though I was not sorry for being the perfect bitch I was also proud of reaching that status. I had gotten a light snack together for myself. Passing him on the way to the sofa I had offered him, off handedly a helping, which he refused with a rough shake of his head. So I had settled stretching fully out and slowly and gloriously filled my belly to overflowing whilst watching one of my favourite romcoms. Dylan hated these kinds of films, stating they were soppy to the point of nauseating, which is why I put it on expecting him to retaliate demanding we change channels, or even better vacate the room. But he didn't. So forgetting he was there I thoroughly enjoyed my romance as Tom Hanks got his woman Meg Ryan both of them being my all-time favourites.

Sitting up I stretched my back, stretching my arms as I yawned as politely as I could. Dylan no longer in the armchair I presumed had gone out or upstairs. Picking up my plate I sauntered into the kitchen placing it as quietly as I could into the sink.

"Enjoy your film," he asked pleasantly making me jump as I turned to face him.

"God Dylan" I cried holding my hand to my chest, "You scared the hell out of me."

He gave me a rueful smile before approaching me slowly,

"Sorry didn't mean too"

"So you're speaking to me again then" I enquired nonchalantly as I headed towards the fridge to get myself a cold drink.

"I was angry Grace; you really have changed since we were together. I 'm not sure as to whether I find it an attribute you should be proud of."

I sniffed at him my eyes scanning the fridge.

"Each to their own" I mumbled in response,

Turning my head to look at him I asked, "I meant to ask Dylan, why do we have champagne in the fridge?"

He didn't reply so momentarily forgetting my thirst I closed the fridge door to look at him.

"Oh I forgot" he replied airily as if he only had just heard me, "We've sold the house"

Falling back against the worktop mumbling an ouch as the granite dug into my lower back I could only stare at him staring at me.

"Why didn't you tell me sooner?"

"Because of our earlier conversation "

I looked at him in confusion wondering whether I should probe him further. Deciding against it I muttered a vague 'oh'.

"Is that all you have to say?" his voice was silky smooth.

"What else is there?"

Sensing he was dissatisfied with my answer I turned away from him intending to walk away. His words stopped me dead in my tracks.

"The reason we finished months ago is because I had an affair."

Thankful I had been holding onto the door frame, I froze, my confidence spiralling out of control at his words. The lump that formed in my throat felt like it was going to suffocate me. I could feel tears burning my eyes as with a deep breath I walked shakily into the dining room, not bothering to switch on the light to see where I was going. Don't react I screamed inwardly, that's just what he wants you to do. I had wondered over the months apart from him, whether there had been someone else. Now he had confirmed it and I was gutted. I managed to reach the sofa where I sunk onto it trying to keep a calm facade. Picking up the remote I switched off the telly, all the good vibes from the film I had just watched having vanished. I didn't want to look at him knowing he was standing watching me intently.

"Is it someone I know?" I stammered a small part of me praying he was lying.

"Yes" was his curt belated reply.

"Is it Zara?" I asked remembering my mother's assumption.

He didn't reply so I turned as he entered the room.

"Yes"

"Explains a lot," I mumbled suddenly deciding my feet were a good focus point of attention.

"What do you mean?"

"Our friendship isn't what it was and when I came back here to take a look around she came in checking the house when she saw the lights on."

"Oh" he replied, "She didn't tell me that."

"So if you and Zara are an item why are you here?" I forced myself to say,

"Because we are not an item anymore."

"Oh" I repeated stupidly, "Why?" still dazed from his revelation.

He shrugged his shoulders, "Wasn't working out."

It took me awhile to digest the dialogue that had conspired between us. I felt out of it like I was on Tramadol unable to comprehend what I was hearing or feeling.

"So you came back because you needed a place to stay?"

"Partly"

"You should have said" I uttered, "I wouldn't have come back."

"I know, which is why I didn't tell you."

Shaking my head in confusion I looked at him, "Am I being dense here, or is there a point to all of this?"

He stood up and walked over to me sitting down beside me where I had unknowingly collapsed onto the sofa. His body closer than I would have liked facing me.

"It didn't work because of you. When I found out you had returned here via my solicitor it had quite a profound effect on me. I realised I had made a monumental mistake and she wasn't the woman I wanted to be with."

"So you dumped her?"

"I wouldn't put it quite like that, but yes we did end almost immediately."

I nodded as if I was in total agreement with his decision, "You rather seem to enjoy doing that," I snapped at him. He ignored my verbal comeback choosing instead to look at me closely before replying.

"I realise Grace this has come as quite a shock to you, but after everything that has happened I realised to get you back I had to be brutally honest with you. I know in the past I haven't been forthcoming on occasions but it wont be like that anymore."

My God I thought to myself the bastard wanted closure on his affair and easy acceptance and forgiveness from me. Knowing Zara was once my longest and dearest friend the chances of me finding out were averagely higher than normal. But now through clearing his own conscience he had completely obliterated every possible ounce of trust or feeling I had ever had in him or her.

So calmly and serenely I looked at him, "Dylan seriously? Do you think after this admittance of guilt it changes anything between us? Do I appear so needy to you that you would think I could just forgive you and pretend it had never happened?"

He took my cold hand between his rubbing my skin gently to warm it up.

"Grace, I know how you admire honesty regardless of the consequences. The old me would never have admitted it let alone own up to having a relationship with someone else. But, I am trying to prove to you that I have changed and that I love you so much I would never leave you or repeat another indiscretion."

Was this guy for real I asked myself? I looked at him not believing a word that tumbled willingly out of his deceitful lying cheating mouth. Did he really think I was so weak that I would just nod, say it was ok and pretend to play at being happily married? I thought of my friend Zara then, not feeling an ounce of pity for her. She had gotten her just desserts and I had been the one that had paid dearly for it.

"How could you have made love to me after being with her?"

"It was my way of showing you Gracie how much I still love you."

I stood up not wanting to share another moment of air space with him.

"I'm going to my room."

He stood up walking quickly towards me, I swung around pointing my finger at him, "And don't you dare follow me Dylan."

Shutting the door loudly behind me as if to make a further point I wearily climbed the stairs unable to digest what Dylan had willingly, no almost proudly offloaded on me.

I sat on the bed or rather collapsed on it, the words flooding my mind creating a battle of bewilderment and betrayal inside of me. Not bothering to switch on the bedside lamp, I remained where I was until dusk had settled into darkness. I could hear muted movements from below telling me Dylan had not gone out which I hoped he had. I had trapped myself in this room unable to eat not that I was hungry or to make a drink, which I discovered I wanted and had forgotten earlier. Sighing I stood up walking over to the window pushing aside the heavy cream brocaded curtain. The street was quiet with only the occasional car driving by. The street lights lit up muted areas making the trees bordering the green opposite appear daunting in grotesque and intimidating swaying shadows. I chewed my bottom lip still no further in my inner battle than I had been when I had entered the bedroom hours before. I was taking his admission of guilt very calmly I thought, though my stomach churned every time I thought of it making me feel unwell and queasy.

Dropping the curtain I headed back towards the bed making sure my footsteps were light so as not to alert the cheating rat below. I could feel the beginnings of a headache coming on which only fuelled my feelings towards him. There was one question constantly nagging away at me, which I needed to know the answer too. Had the 'affair' between him and Zara ignited as a result of our separation or was it the reason we had split? Either way it wouldn't change the outcome but it would go a long way to explaining why my perfect marriage had dissolved on that Friday night at the wine bar. I tried to recall their intense dislike for one another. If there were any different interactions between them when she had come round which I hadn't noticed, but hard as I tried I couldn't retrieve any. But then I thought sourly I hadn't known to look for it. I could feel myself sink further into the depths of self-pity making my headache more effective. Damn him I thought angrily. Why should I be the one sitting in my room moping when I hadn't done anything wrong? I had two choices. Option one was to continue as I was now or option two curse them both to hell and move on with my life. It was his loss not mine. Feeling more assertive, I stood up angrily storming into the bathroom making sure my footsteps were heard below. Taking a quick glance in the mirror I rummaged hastily through the medicine cabinet releasing a couple of painkillers from the packet I was holding. Shoving them into my mouth I turned on the tap running my hand under the cold water. Scooping up a handful I swallowed. Wiping my mouth on the hand towel I ran my fingers quickly through my hair before leaving the bathroom in the manner I had entered.

Slamming the bedroom door behind me to alert him I was still angry I made my way downstairs. When I blew into the lounge like a tornado ready for round two I stopped dead in my tracks. The bastard was asleep on the sofa like he hadn't a care in the world. Gritting my teeth I wanted to kick him awake. He had offloaded on me the worst thing a married woman could ever hear from her husband, and whilst I had been agonising upstairs, here he was sleeping guilt free. I headed for the kitchen in desperate need of coffee. Picking up the kettle I threw the dregs of the water into the sink before refilling it. Placing it back on its stand I flicked it on my eyes diverting to the lounge where he still lay dormant. Opening the cupboard I got out a fresh mug placing it quietly on the worktop. Waiting for the kettle to boil I tapped my foot on the slate tile beneath my feet evil thoughts of what I could do to him right now running through my mind. Pouring the boiling water onto the coffee I had spooned in along with my solitary sugar cube I breathed in deeply trying to curb the nasty scenarios that were urging me to act. Opening the fridge door I picked up the milk pausing as my eyes alighted on the bottle of champagne lying on the top shelf taunting me. Undoing the lid of the milk I poured some into my hot coffee. Stirring the mug briskly I picked it up and sipped gingerly as I put the milk away.

Re-entering the dining room I looked around me at the home we had created between us. I would miss this house and all the things in it, but they were material items that could be easily replaced unlike my heart. I sat down on the armchair my hands embracing the heat from the mug I held. Crossing my legs at the knee I stared out of the window not caring that the blinds were up allowing passers-by to look into the room as they passed. The light from the table lamp stood close to where he lay, shimmering its golden glow over the floor and the rug in front of me. He had fallen asleep with the telly on, the volume low and as my eyes watched the characters on screen my brain was not registering what I was looking at. I had neglected earlier when he had dropped his bombshell on me to probe him further on the buyers that had fallen in love with our house. Where had I been when they had called? Looking at him tempted to rudely awaken him I refrained from the strong urge realising I had to gather my thoughts first. Our divorce was imminent; the sale would take longer depending on the financial situation of the buyers. Who would stay behind until the house was finalised, him or me? Now that the property was no longer an issue I had no reason to stay, but as I looked around me it would take time to divide and pack the belongings that had once been our life together. That said I wondered how much I could take. I would be moving back to my parent's home for the time being and as spacious as the house was it wouldn't be able to digest what I would be bringing with me. I could always rent space I thought despondently till I had decided what I was going to do. The savings account Dylan and I had between us had a few thousand in it more from him than from me. He also would be in the same situation as me but he had been living somewhere else until he had discovered my re-entry into this house. I wondered where he had been living and if it had been with Zara. But knowing her place I couldn't see him in it. It was small and dingy as bedsits went and Dylan if nothing else had a high standard of living. I shrugged my shoulders not caring where he went after we finalised the house. He was no longer my concern and though for a moment I felt a pang of pain I squashed it just as quick.

Feeling my folded legs go dead beneath me I shifted slightly allowing them the freedom. I could feel the pins and needles in my toes and I stretched them slowly out in front of me. Dylan mumbled in his sleep turning over so he was facing me. I paused with baited breath in case he awoke to see me staring benevolently at him, but he didn't. His mouth dropped open his fine display of white teeth shining in the light from the lamp. His hair was ruffled where he had run his hands through it in his sleep. Once that would have been endearing to me, but now it only left me cold. To think my best friend from as far back as our school days, had lain in those arms, kissed those lips, run her fingers through his hair screwed his brains out had me almost jumping out of my seat. But I stayed where I was, knowing every thought running negatively through my mind would only make me stronger.

A buzzing sounded made me turn my attention to the room wondering frantically where it was coming from. Spying his mobile lying on the corner table by the lamp I got up hastily hoping to retrieve it and silence it before he woke up. He stirred as I held it in my hand, my heart hammered loudly thinking of his response if he was to wake now and see me holding it, like I was some paranoid jilted wife rifling through for secrets he had withheld from me. Not stirring from the interruption I looked down at his phone about to end it when my eyes froze when I saw who was calling. Looking quickly down at Dylan to verify he was still sleeping I ran as quick and lightly as I could towards the kitchen. Opening the door to the utility room at the end of the kitchen I darted inside and closed the door gently behind me. My decision was quick my voice pointedly tired when I answered.

"Hello?"

I could hear breathing at the other end of the line and knew Zara was shocked when I had answered his phone. I waited patiently jogging from one foot to the other in anticipation until finally she replied vaguely,

"Is Dylan there?"

I smiled conspiratorially to myself before feigning a purred reply

"No he's sleeping "

Again silence although I could tell by the change in her breathing that she was not happy with my reply.

Her voice was firmer when she asked, "Can you wake him I need to speak to him"

"Look Zara I don't know what this is about, but you disturbed us we were both sleeping after our..." I paused on purpose hoping she would catch my drift. She did. I thought I heard her inhale quickly but I couldn't be sure so I remained quiet as I examined my nails refusing to feel sorry for hurting her. It wasn't retribution that was making me act so bitchy towards her because I didn't feel sorry for what I had said. She deserved everything I threw at her and I had been truthful if only a day late.

"Are you still there? "I asked making my tone sound innocent like I didn't know

Before I could wait for her reply I heard footsteps from the lounge. I pressed the end button before I began to panic as to where I could hide the phone. Knowing I was trapped I looked hastily at the washing machine full of dirty bed laundry. It wasn't an ideal place to hide my deception but for the moment it would have to do. So without further hesitation I opened the door shoving Dylan's mobile deep within the dirty items. I had just shut it when Dylan appeared in the doorway.

"What are you doing? Did I hear you speaking to someone?"

Before I could answer I watched his eyes quickly survey the small confines of the room, which was ridiculous considering how small the space was.

"Oh just talking to myself, I was just about to do some washing" I lied turning away from him as I filled the compartment drawer with soap powder and conditioner. He nodded accepting my answer as I pushed past him

"Haven't you forgotten something?" he enquired

Pausing my heart beating erratically in case he had found out my secret after all I looked at him with an expression of annoyance to hide my guilt.

"And what would that be" I retorted.

"To switch it on" He leant down and pressed the button. The light came on humming quietly before the sound of water was heard gushing into the machine. Walking away I chewed my lip realising frantically what had just occurred. He called my name demanding why I had snapped at him. Turning round I looked at him hoping the disbelief I was feeling was not openly displayed on my face. His phone whilst we were standing there looking at each other was going through the first cycle of the hour wash. It would be ruined I thought despondently and with it every single work and personal number he had. He would go mad my mind was repeating continuously as I stood there unable to tell him to stop the machine immediately as his mobile was inside. I could imagine the inquisition that would immediately follow and I was neither willing nor gracious enough to stand there whilst he shouted at me at the stupidity of my actions and why I had done it. He was the one that had switched the machine on and if he hadn't dallied around in the first place with my best friend the scenario now unfolding wouldn't have happened.

I had wanted vengeance on him earlier but not in this way. So I just shook my shoulders, smiled wanly and told him in as pleasant a voice as I could manage that owing to his confession earlier I was still reeling and had no wish to discuss it with him at this time. Dylan looked saddened by my words but as I continued to stare at him it was like my heart had turned to stone. So with a shrug of my shoulders I walked away cursing myself for coming downstairs. I sat back in the armchair and picked up my mug grimacing that my drink had already gone cold. He also had walked into the lounge and as I saw him out of the corner of my eye sit on the sofa I remained facing the window curbing the need to shout out what I had done. I thought of Zara and why she had rung him when apparently it was all over. Curiosity was building up inside of me to question him about it, but then if I did I knew he would ask me why I wanted to know and what had made me think of it now. So I refrained ignoring my conscience trying to think of something else.

"Have you seen my mobile?"

Looking down at my half empty mug I shook my head. I could see out of my peripheral vision that he checked the side table and then under the cushions of the sofa.

"I need another drink," I murmured using any excuse just to get away in case I blurted it out. Switching on the kettle I looked sideways at the open utility room door. The washing machine stared back at me the soapsuds covering the glass bubble of the door. I looked closely in case Dylan's black mobile would go spinning by or knock against the inside alerting him. But nothing happened. Closing the utility room door I swirled round as his voice made me jump.

"Are you okay you seem jittery?"

"How do you expect me to act Dylan" I retorted back more viciously than I intended. I was not cut out for this and with his constant attentiveness it was just making it worse. He held his hands up backing off leaving me alone again in the kitchen. I looked at my watch quickly sussing out how long till the wash cycle ended. There was no fear of Dylan emptying the machine but not only did I have to find the offending item I had to dispose of it. The house phone began to ring and before he could begin to move to answer it I grabbed the receiver off the wall phone close to me in the kitchen.

"Dylan?"

It was Zara again. Seeing him look at me curiously from the lounge I turned my back on him as I spoke spitefully down the phone.

"What part of leave us alone don't you understand. Stop ringing or I will report you for harassment" Not giving her any chance to reply I slammed down the receiver jumping when Dylan touched my shoulder.

"Grace what's going on?"

I swivelled round making my head spin as I hurriedly replied, "Nothing just some jerk who won't leave us alone."

His eyes looked concerned as he looked at the phone and then at me.

"Why didn't you tell me? How many times has he rung?"

"A couple today, it doesn't matter he'll back off when he gets tired of getting nowhere."

"Give me the phone I'll see if I can trace the number."

"No" I shouted out smiling immediately at him, "I mean Dylan I really don't think I can take much more today," my voice quivered on purpose hoping that would be sufficient in stalling him. It did. He looked at me with compassion in his eyes before he stepped closer taking me in his arms.

"I'm sorry; all of this is my fault."

How right you are I thought to myself stiffening at his embrace. My body was rigid as he held me. I felt a strong urge to beat him away with my fists but what would be the point. It would anger him and probably make him suspicious as to why I was behaving so irrationally. So I suffered his embrace, the feel of his skin on mine and the aromatic enticement of his aftershave.

"I'm fine now Dylan" I muttered too quickly as I slithered out of his arms. The kettle had boiled and I was glad of the distraction. Spooning in my coffee with shaking fingers I moved my back so my actions wouldn't be visible to him. Pouring the water I placed the kettle down not wanting to face him to reach the fridge for the milk.

"Here let me" he pushed me gently aside as he undid the cap of the milk and poured some in my coffee. I nodded thanks as I slowly sipped the hot refreshment wishing he would just bog off and leave me alone to think. But, of course Dylan never does what you want him to do and instead of reading my body language correctly and leaving me be; he hovered not saying anything but I could feel his eyes on me watching almost trying to anticipate my next move. It was restrictive and suffocating and I suddenly felt a strong urge to go to bed. I felt tired with the excitement of the last hour if you could call it that but knowing the machine would finish in less than fifty minutes and the risk too great of Dylan maybe emptying the machine proving he could be pro active I unwillingly stood my ground hoping eventually my rejection of him would filter through and he would leave. My eyes alighted on the wall phone hoping Zara unlike Dylan had understood my message loud and clear and backed off. Considering she had rung twice within a short space of time I almost felt like a ticking time bomb wishing I could disconnect the bloody thing. Of course! I only had to pull out the wire from the wall in the lounge and I could relax knowing there would be no more phone calls until I chose to reconnect it. Remembering Dylan was still behind me I turned round to face him smiling falsely at him as I manoeuvred past him. He stood his ground though I could still feel his eyes pinned on me. I had to get him out of the lounge if only temporarily but how to achieve that simple task I hadn't yet quite worked out. It came to me as I sat down in the armchair my hand rubbing my temple.

"Dylan could you do me a big favour?"

He was by my side almost immediately his expression contrite

"Of course. What's the matter?"

"I have a major headache starting. Would you get my tablets out of the bathroom medicine cabinet for me?"

My voice was pleading as I looked at him with sad eyes. He stared at me for a long moment. His blue gaze penetrating

"Isn't there any downstairs?"

"No" I replied, "I haven't had time to go to the chemist and restock."

"Ok kitten I won't be a minute."

As I watched his retreating back my mouth almost snarled at him. I didn't need to take any more tablets considering less than half an hour before I had swallowed a couple. But I would deal with that scenario shortly. Hearing his steps on the stairs I shot up. Leaning gently behind the telly I stretched my arm grabbing the wire and pulling. It wouldn't give so I tugged harder as I heard Dylan close my bedroom door on his way down. Come on I shouted inwardly tugging at it harder. Just as I was about to give in it gave way. I dropped it hastily and only made it back to the chair in time before he entered the room.

"Would you like some water with them?" he asked concernedly

"Please" I mumbled. I gave him a quick smile as I chucked the two tablets he gave me into my mouth.

He was back within seconds as he handed me a glass of water. Spitting them out the moment his back was turned I lifted the seat cushion slipping them underneath. I had just settled back when he returned looking questioningly at me.

"Is something the matter with the chair"?

"Why" I replied confused looking up at him

"I was watching you from the kitchen"

Damn him I thought. Considering the swine he was in the marriage department he certainly didn't miss a trick.

"Know I was just making myself comfortable."

Sipping the water from the glass he gently handed me I swallowed deeply wishing he wouldn't remain so close. Handing him back the glass I rested my head against the cushion of the armchair closing my eyes. He backed off returning the glass to the kitchen, as I knew he would. It was then that I realised that although I had disconnected the main phone from the wall I had neglected to unplug the other two phones. Looking over my shoulder I watched him as he put the glass in the dishwasher, my heart thumping loudly in case Zara determined to speak to Dylan would ring a third time. I shot out of the lounge and up the stairs. I could hear him somewhere behind me shout out what was the matter but I replied I had forgotten something and opened the bedroom door. Shaking my head realising I was hopeless at subterfuge it would be so much easier to come clean with Dylan in relation to Zara. I unplugged the phone wondering why I hadn't, but I knew why I had chosen to remain quiet. Our friendship had been important to me and to think that she had jumped into my place and into my bed nullified any guilt I normally would have felt towards her. But I did realise in that instant I did want to talk to her before I confronted Dylan.

As I stepped out of my room there he was standing at the top of the stairs with concern etched all over his face. For a moment I almost felt myself sway towards him before I remembered that no matter how innocent his face appeared beneath the coating of his skin lay a treacherous two timing bastard.

"Are you ok?"

"Yeah I'm fine," I mumbled as I pushed past him and down the stairs ignoring the hand he held out.

He didn't follow me into the kitchen, which gave me a quiet sigh of relief. But to be sure I glanced back just to make sure before I unplugged that phone as well. I didn't feel proud of myself for what I was doing because I knew it was only a temporary stall. I would have to see Zara soon because I knew I wouldn't get the information I wanted out of Dylan. Why I wanted to know was immaterial but I had to know. I looked at the clock on the wall noting it was shortly after ten in the evening. The day had sped by in a blur.

"I am off to bed" my voice was clear and concise as he stood in front of me as I went to pass him on my way to the hall.

"But you've only just come down and we haven't spoken yet."

I chewed my lip trying to think of a plausible excuse but I couldn't find any so I looked up at him with eyebrows raised and replied.

"Like what?"

"You haven't asked me about the buyers for the house?"

It was true I hadn't, it had completely escaped me when Zara had rung.

"When did they come round?"

"The afternoon you went to see your parents"

"Did they offer the full asking price?"

He nodded his eyes never leaving my face.

"They wanted to know whether we would be interested in selling any of the furniture."

"Oh" was all I muttered. I had accepted the selling of the marital home, but the furnishings and knick-knacks were very personal to me. I had spent a lot of time hunting for each piece and now some stranger wanted to buy what remained of our life together.

"I'll think about it and tell you tomorrow", I paused in the lounge doorway turning my head to look at him, "I suppose you'll need most of the stuff for when you buy another place?"

He shrugged his shoulders in answer before turning away to sit down on the sofa. Picking up the remote he switched on the telly. Realising he had dismissed me without an answer to my question, I watched him for a moment or two as gently I closed the door behind me and climbed the stairs.

Feeling refreshed from the shower I lay in bed the pillows propped up behind my head listening to the muted sounds from the television below. I was tired but I couldn't relax, something was niggling at me about his behaviour earlier when I had questioned him about the furniture. It was unlike Dylan to act so nonplussed when he had made such a stringent point about halving the assets when I had thrown the mug at him in temper. Something wasn't right but I was nothing if not determined to find out why suddenly something so important to him a few days before now seemed so inconsequential. I looked at the widescreen on the wall, its black face staring back at me. I wasn't in the mood for entertainment and neither was I in the mood for the romance thriller lying open on my lap. I thought again of Zara and why it was so necessary earlier for her to speak to Dylan. I chewed on my lip trying to quell the nasty feelings running riot through my mind. As my mother had often remarked, it took two to tango and though I was tempted to lay all the blame at Zara's door because of my husband's revelations, it wasn't fair to make him the innocent one when I realised with an aching heart it was probably him who had instigated it in the first place. Looking down at my mobile laying charging on my bedside table I toyed with the idea of ringing her, but to be honest the way I was feeling at the moment she was the last person I wanted to speak to. So instead I decided to message her and arrange a meeting. I picked up the phone pressing the message button. Inputting her initial her name sprung onto the screen at the top under Z. Once that had been accomplished I wondered what I was going to say. I had a varied choice of expletives but none eligible to achieve my goal. So instead I texted, 'Zara, are you doing anything tomorrow? I think we should meet.' Without giving myself a chance to change my mind I sent it. I waited for five minutes my eyes glued to the screen for a reply. When none was forthcoming I reluctantly placed the mobile back on the bedside cabinet. No sooner had I done so than my phone vibrated informing me it had a message. I grabbed it ignoring my heart palpitations. 'Ok but I can't in the morning I have an appointment, I'm free in the afternoon" I pulled in my lower lip as I read it surprised the message was so cordial so without further thought I replied back. 'No problem. Four o clock ok? I take it you still live in the bedsit?'

'No I've moved I live in an apartment near the river now I'll text you the address tomorrow. See you at four'

I stared at her words for a long time wondering how she could afford on her wages to be able to live in an area, if memory served I knew to be exorbitantly priced for the apartments recently built there. Just then I heard the television below go quiet which meant Dylan was probably going to bed so I hurriedly switched off my bedside light making him think as he passed my door that I was already asleep. His footsteps were light as they walked past my room not stopping at the door like he had before to see if I was awake.

I stirred moaning in my sleep. My stomach felt like it was on fire. I tried to open my eyes but my lids felt so heavy from the lack of sleep the night before I just moaned as I spread-eagled my body over the mattress my hands tucked firmly under my pillow. My dream was so consuming I could almost feel the fingers gently caressing my stomach and lower down. The more they investigated the more I responded my mouth opening slightly my tongue wetting my dry lips. I had these dreams often since our separation so I welcomed the intrusion as the fingers delved slowly inside me making my body squirm. My body was very proactive to the attention I smiled muttering more as a tongue moistened my clit and sucked softly. I began to pant as the yearning starting building. I tossed and turned my arms flailing until they hit skin. It was moist and sweaty like my own and I pulled it into me. When I was impaled with one thrust I yelled out my eyes opening to find Dylan on top of me. His eyes stared at me, his tongue plunged my mouth stopping me shouting out.

"You want this as much I do admit it to me Grace" He lunged back into me relentlessly in and out whilst his eyes held mine

The crescendo inside me was building rapidly all I wanted to do was ride this roller coaster and I did.

"Yes don't stop," I cried out as I kissed him hungrily back.

He covered my body in one swift movement his hands on either side of me supporting him as he repeatedly rammed into me. I stared up at him hating him and wanting him at the same time. The love making that he did so well had me begging for more. I was angry and I was hurt and the more he gave me the more I took. Unlike our night before his revelation today had made me hate him and hate them both. I felt revengeful and angry. This was my time now I realised to show him what he'd lost. I had never been the tiger he had always wanted me to be in the bedroom but tonight my revenge would be sweet

"Flip me over" I cried out

When he was beneath me I rode him like a bucking cowgirl harder and deeper taking what I wanted from him. My hands pinned his to the bed, biting him when he tried to move them. He looked at me in amazement as I continued my assault on him.

"Grace what the hell," he growled in surprise "don't stop."

My breasts were full as my nipples caressed his chest as I leant into him nipping at his mouth enjoying the shock still displayed there. I didn't care anymore, tonight I was released from the chains of the obedient Grace I had once been, and tonight I was going to control him. All the hurt and pain of betrayal inflicted by him and Zara came flooding out of me. It was payback time.

"Grace stop I'm going to come" he cried out.

I lifted myself off him my breathing laboured as he reached for me. I slapped his hand away,

"Stay where you are" I purred. Reaching down into the bottom drawer of the bedside cabinet that had been his I took out the handcuffs he had failingly tried to make me wear. Now they would come in very useful.

Looking down at him his eyes narrowed when he saw what I was holding.

I kissed him long and hard "I want to be your tiger tonight" I lied

He smiled willingly holding his arms up for me to encapsulate them with the handcuffs to the wooden headboard.

"Grace what are you doing to me," he crooned his eyes taking me all in

"This" I whispered, as the gag was next. He fought me when he realised my intention but it was too late. His eyes were bulging with anger as he fought to break free but I just smiled as I leaned in closer

"Now now darling isn't this what you've always wanted?" He shook his head muted sounds escaping from him

"Oh wait a minute I've got this wrong haven't I. Isn't this what you always wanted to do to me. Unfortunately this time you don't get to control this."

Sitting on top of him plunging him into me again I began to move. He struggled trying to release himself. I leant closer to him holding his head still with my hands. Kissing his face I smiled at him before I whispered

"Now you know what it feels like, to feel helpless when the one that you love takes away everything. I could have been all of this and more to you if only you had let me breathe."

Breaking one arm free Dylan pulled down his gag. Grabbing my head his mouth hungrily met mine his tongue pushing deeper with need almost making me gag.

My body tightened knowing my orgasm was only seconds away. Seeing my body tense Dylan broke free his other arm and turned us over before I realised his intention he had withdrawn and entered me from behind. I yelled out in pleasure gyrating higher to meet his thrusts. His hands positioned on my hips pushed me relentlessly in and out whilst I clung to the bed for balance. When the orgasms came we both screamed out in unison. His body tightened around me totally possessing me and by god I loved it. "Oh fuck," I muttered, "why did you have to be such an unfaithful bastard and ruin it".

He collapsed with me his breathing as erratic as mine. He took my face between his hands and answered, "Because this fucking idiot didn't realise what he had."

Having forgotten to close my curtains the night before the sunlight streamed in waking me up early. My bed was empty and knowing I wouldn't be able to go back to sleep I reluctantly got out of bed as I fumbled for my slippers. My pyjamas I put on after my shower were long and covered everything of me from my neck downwards so I felt relatively safe going downstairs. As I closed the bedroom door behind me I could hear Dylan snoring quietly from his room, which meant I had time to myself.

Rubbing my eyes I went quietly down the stairs yawning widely as I shuffled into the kitchen. Switching on the kettle I closed the cupboard door putting my mug gently on the worktop. It wasn't until I heard the water boiling did I remember the washing machine. Regardless of my previous intentions the night before I had totally forgotten. Opening the door I breathed a sigh of relief ignoring the light flashing at me telling me it had finished. Pressing the button the door sprang open. Grabbing a laundry basket nearby I pulled out the washing separating each item until the phone fell out landing loudly on the tiled floor. Picking it up quickly I stared at it. Pressing a button I almost groaned out in agony, as the screen remained blank. Damn I had well and truly broken it. I could try and take it apart and put it somewhere to dry out but there was nowhere I could put it where Dylan wouldn't find it if he was looking for it. Tapping the phone against my lower lip I quickly pondered a way out and smiled when I found it. I was going to my mum's this morning. I could dry it out there. Feeling pleased with myself I walked into the lounge and into the hallway opening the hall cupboard. My coat was the nearest to me, putting my hand in the pocket I pulled out my hat and put the offending phone in its place before covering it with the hat. I knew Dylan wouldn't be long in rising and it was imperative I was out of the house before he came down. After last night I didn't want a confrontation. I had no regrets if anything I felt liberated. Hurriedly I retraced my steps to the kitchen drinking my coffee in a hurry.

The air was cold even though the sun felt warm on my face. As my fingers enclosed around Dylan's phone I couldn't help but smirk knowing now as I turned the corner into my parent's road he would be up and annoyed that I had left already. He hated being shut out because before I had never acted in that way. But life was changing rapidly for me and so were my actions along with it.

My father answered almost immediately hearing my knock. Smiling his beaming grin at me he hugged me close as I stepped inside.

"Hello snicket, this is a surprise or does your mother know you're coming?

Shaking my head at him knowing my mother had related to him my intention to visit the last time I was there, dad being dad with other things on his mind had completely either not heard at all or was busy dreaming about next day's gardening expedition at the local garden centre.

"She remembers unlike you" I smiled at him returning his hug.

"If you hurry there's still some tea in the pot. I'm off out into the garden, loads to do and precious little time to do it"

I watched his retreating back feeling such a surge of love for him flow through me. Hanging up my coat I took out the phone pausing for a moment as I stared at it wondering how to broach the subject with my mother. Honesty was always the best policy she was fond of saying and sighing I knew she was right, but it would still lead to explanations I wasn't sure I wanted to go into. My expression of dread must still have been evident on my face when I entered the kitchen for my mother's voice was immediately inquisitive.

"Hello Grace, what's the matter?"

Bang and there it was instantaneous mother radar.

In a few seconds before I joined her at the table I had to make a decision. Do I lie and avoid the I *told you so,* or do I just think the hell with it and suffer the onslaught? I knew from the expression on my mother's face it was definitely going to be like summer followed by winter heading my way.

"I've done something I don't think I'm very proud of."

Her brows furrowed at my words as she sat back and folded her arms.

"Pour yourself some tea Gracie and then tell me everything."

I noticed my hand shaking as I poured in the milk and my proverbial one sugar. Stirring slowly trying to lengthen out the moment before revelation, I stared at her smiling briefly before sipping my tea.

"Well?"

Clearing my throat I took another mouthful before taking the phone, which I had placed on my lap when I sat down and placed it on the table between us. My mother's eyes diverted immediately to it before looking up at me with questioning eyes.

"It's a phone Grace."

"Its Dylan's not mine," I immediately blurted out kicking myself for being so cowardly.

"Why have you got his phone?" I noticed her voice had hardened realising as harmless as the item was because of its connection to Dylan it was like him unwelcome.

"Well" I stammered licking my lips, "It was totally unintentional but I didn't have any other choice but to bring it here to dry out."

Picking up the teapot my mother shook it gently before pouring herself another cup. Her eyes looked into mine.

"What have you done Grace?"

Knowing every word I was uttering hurriedly to her was jumbled and disorganised in its event, she remained quiet until eventually in my haphazard way I had reiterated what had happened the evening before. She remained quiet for a time as she sipped at her tea her eyes now focused on the mobile.

"Hmmm" was all she said as she looked up at me with a devilish smile on her face.

"It couldn't happen to a nicer person."

I knew I was sitting there staring back at her like she had lost her mind, but her behaviour had been the last thing I'd been expecting.

"Well I suppose you should dry it out then "she continued not bothering to move.

My fingers were clumsy as I took the back off and took the battery out. My mother getting up laid a heavy thick towel on the lid of one of the aga burners and swiftly laid the disembowelled phone on it.

"Is that all you have to say?" I enquired still dumbfounded at her.

She raised her eyebrows at me as she began to clear the table.

"What else do you expect me to say Grace?"

"I told you so," I spluttered as I hurriedly drank the dregs of my tea before she took it away from me.

"Would it make you feel any better if I said it?"

"No" my voice was low.

She sat down extending her hand to me and grasping it tightly, "When you were here last time Grace it was quite evident what was going on, but, I'm glad you found out, its closure for you after wondering all those months why he did what he did. Though..." she paused waving her finger at me as she removed her hand from mine, "That Zara is a stupid girl if she thinks he won't do to her what he did to you."

At the mention of her name it reminded me of my plan to see her later. I wondered whether I should share this information with my mother, but as she stared at me with a pitying smile I decided it would be beneficial for me to keep it to myself. I could imagine my mum staring at me in horror exclaiming loudly why had I contacted her, when all it would achieve would be further pain and betrayal from both sides when it didn't matter anymore. But on one point she was correct, I did need closure and Zara having been a friend to me since childhood I wanted to sever the loose end that still bound us. Realising my mother would never understand the way my mind ticked in this situation, I spent the next couple of hours idly willing away the time trying to ignore the building tension inside of me.

Chapter 7

I had left my parents house earlier than I needed too explaining there were a few chores and shopping I desperately needed to do before returning home. Whether my mother saw through my lie she never said. Hugging me close she stroked my face her expression understanding as she watched me walk away which was something she wasn't prone to doing. My dad too enthusiastic about his immediate garden plans to really listen to me looked almost guilt stricken when he realised I was still lolling against the shed waiting for an answer.

"Snicket you still here, I'm sorry I'm so busy today" his voice trailed off as he looked lovingly at the recently dug vegetable patch he had created alongside the other. Knowing as much as he loved me he was desperate to get on. I smiled pretending it didn't matter as I hugged him briefly leaving him staring perplexed at me as I walked back towards the house. I looked at my watch moaning inwardly that I was too early for the appointment with Zara. I had received her address via text just as she had promised the night before and although I was having doubts that I had done the right thing in contacting her it was too late to back off. It wasn't until I reached the entrance to the park did I realise what route I had taken. I still had a few hours to kill and as there were no chores or shopping to do I shrugged my shoulders hoping as I entered the park that I would see Florrie and god forbid that tempestuous dog that had taken such a liking to me.

The park wasn't busy with only a few strollers and joggers running along the path. I looked at every bench that I passed disappointed that they were all empty. There was no sign of the elderly woman that I had met a few days before and for a moment my heart sank. I hadn't realised until now how much I had enjoyed her company, which was utterly bizarre considering she was a stranger and of a totally different generation. I stopped to look at the winter plants recently planted by the council and realised for the first time how close to Christmas we were. It was already early November and in a few more weeks I would be divorced from Dylan. My thoughts left me pensive, totally consuming making me oblivious to everything else around me. I heard the riotous barking but paid it no heed as slowly walking over the grass to the other side of the park to where the fountain stood. As a child my father had convinced me it was magical and still to this day I lost count as to how many wishes accompanied by a penny I had made.

It brought a brief smile to my lips as I wedged my hands deeper into my pockets my head bent, as my booted feet walked over the wet muddy grass recently dampened by the rain. The barking got louder making me look up just before a large muddy shaggy sheepdog leapt at me sending me flying onto the ground landing with a heavy thud onto my back. I lay there winded and confused as the huge hairy monster licked my face like I was an ice cream that he couldn't get enough off.

"What the hell" I cried coming to my senses trying unsuccessfully to push the dog of me. This only encouraged him further and knowing I was beat I shut my eyes and pressed my lips together as suddenly his weight was lifted off me. I lay there for a moment waiting for an encore but it never came.

"Are you ok, I am so sorry?"

The voice was male and his tone gentle. Slowly I opened my eyes. They were met with a pair of intense blue eyes framed by long dark lashes. He was tall and slim and took my breath away. His face was slim and angular and captivating with his short blonde hair ruffling in the breeze. I gulped feeling such a fool for my predicament. I slowly turned my head committed to breaking my acute embarrassment. There, sitting as good as gold with a smug grin on his face was Buster. I shot him a venomous look, which made him hang his head sideways wondering why I was being so unfriendly.

"Here let me help you," the voice offered as a hand strong and lean offered me salvation.

"Thank you," I replied awkwardly as he gently pulled me to my feet. My hat in the tussle had fallen off and now lay muddied on the grass. My hair hung around my shoulders and though I didn't have a mirror to hand I knew I looked a sight.

"Again I must apologise I don't know what came over Buster, he's not normally so... so over friendly with strangers" he replied handing me back my muddied hat.

"I beg to differ" I replied caustically, "I had the misfortune to meet Buster the other day and if I remember correctly he got the better of me that time too"

"Oh" he replied looking at me more closely, "You must be Grace? You know my grandmother Florrie."

"Yes I do but how do you know..." my voice trailed off

"She mentioned meeting a nice young lady the other day. I take it you must be the nice young lady she was referring to?"

I said nothing as I looked down at my coat grumbling loudly at the large muddy patches displayed all over it. He followed my gaze as an awkward silence fell between us.

"Is there any way I can help you considering it was my dog who...um molested you"

I could sense in his voice a hint of amusement as I looked at him annoyingly,

"Well I can't exactly go to my appointment looking like this can I?" I knew I was being ungrateful but I didn't care. Not only were my clothes muddied but I could also feel the beginnings of a bruise making its intentions known on my posterior. I looked down at Buster who looking up at me looked away towards the ground. His lead now firmly embedded in the stranger's hand I looked at him defying him with my eyes to wipe off the innocence that was so apparent on his face.

"I'm Jeremy please to meet you" he held out his hand, which I looked at in disgust.

"This doesn't exactly solve my predicament does it?"

"No that's true" he retorted his hand still firmly outstretched.

I looked at him again my expression evident. Did he really want me to shake his hand when I looked like a cross between a mud pie and a scarecrow? Realising he wasn't going to move until I returned the greeting I took his hand briefly withdrawing my hand quickly at the mild charged electric shock that passed between us. He looked as surprised as I did, which made me realise he must have felt it too.

"Um I could give you a lift home Grace."

"No" I replied immediately not because of the ride he offered but because I knew from rejected phone calls received continuously throughout the morning on my mobile that Dylan was waiting impatiently to see me. Realising he had misunderstood me I hastily replied,

"No I don't want to go home."

He looked at me closely as I lowered my eyes growling inwardly at Buster sitting close to me as obedient as a cruft entry to the infamous dog show.

"Well, considering it was my dog that got you in this predicament you could come back to mine and get cleaned up. And before you say it you have nothing to be afraid off I am as harmless as..."

"Your dog" I interceded cheekily with a false smile on my lips.

"Um yeah" he replied looking at me with big blue eyes and an enticing lopsided grin.

I had two options. Either go back to my parents or take Jeremy up on his offer. I looked at him his eyes as honest as his expression. I thought of Florrie then and how much she had ranted on about her wonderful grandson. Making my mind up I nodded reluctantly before answering,

"Well you come highly recommended by your grandmother so...it seems churlish of me to decline."

His smile widened, his eyes twinkled and just for a split second I was reminded of my father.

"Ok well follow me my car is just over there"

My eyes looked in the direction he was pointing. A black Volvo estate stood by the kerb at the edge of the park. The railings I was looking through were bereft of shrubbery that normally would be thick and lustrous in the summer. We fell into step, Buster as meek and mild as though he had been tranquilised ambled obediently alongside us. Jeremy caught me staring intently at his dog and when I met his eyes he asked.

"What's the matter?"

"Nothing" I retorted "I just have never seen Buster so well behaved and compliant before."

He grinned at me, "Well we are going to dog training classes and slowly we are breaking through his defences. Though I must say I have never seen him so overjoyed at seeing someone like he was when he saw you."

"Is that supposed to be a compliment," I asked drolly.

"Absolutely, your obviously the apple of his eye."

"Hmmm" I begrudgingly murmured as we walked out of the park.

When we reached his car I looked quickly inside at how clean and tidy it was considering it was an old car. He caught my glance as he opened the boot door and let Buster inside.

"It's open Grace get in."

"I'll mess your car up, the back of my coat looks like a mud pit"

Opening up the back door again, he took out a large plastic carrier bag. Reaching me he looked down at me as he opened it,

"Here take off your coat and put it in here"

I did as he requested without hesitation which until recently was very unusual for me. As he took the coat off me he folded it up placing it neatly inside the bag. Laying it on the back seat he smiled at me as I watched him.

"Are you ok Grace?" I nodded mutely wondering why I was acting like a prized potato. He must think I was some kind of sociopath. One minute I was like a raging bull the next as compliant and soppy as Buster was acting now on the back seat. I stood back as he opened my car door and waited patiently for me to get inside. I did so looking down at my hands as he closed my door gently. When he sat next to me he gave me a warm smile as he started the car, all his attention focused on the oncoming traffic.

I took little notice of where we were heading until suddenly I noticed my parents road whizz by. Noticing me look back Jeremy smiled at me as I looked at him.

"Everything ok Grace?"

"Yes" I mumbled returning his smile.

Buster sensing he was close to home started barking as Jeremy took the next left turn.

"Is this where you live?" I enquired as I looked at the houses we were passing all very similar to my parents' house.

"Yes just a little further down. I recently bought the house to renovate but even though I have hardly made a dent in it I have grown quite attached to it."

"My parent's home is only a street away so I'm quite familiar with this area."

He smiled encouragingly at me, "Have your parents lived here long then?"

"Yes about thirty five years."

He stopped the car to look at me, "thirty five years, wow."

"My father would never move he has spent too many years cultivating his garden, I think it would break his heart if he ever had to let it go."

He nodded understanding the sentiment in my voice, "You must have had a wonderful childhood Grace growing up in such a lovely and safe area"

I nodded smiling warmly at him.

He parked the car pausing to stare at me as I looked at the house. The front drive was spacious but not as wide or as neat as my parent's front garden. The house which was a double bay fronted similar to my family home was large with a veranda running along the front. The windows were high and big although through years of neglect the paint had worn away to show rotten wood beneath. He winced as he caught my gaze as I smiled at him.

"I know what you're thinking and you would be right. I have so much work to do to this place it will take me forever"

"Is it just you that lives here?" I enquired.

"Yes, but I am turning the attached garage and adjoining outbuilding into an annex for Florrie."

"That's a nice thing to do" I replied.

"Come on let me get you inside before your coat starts drying out"

Realising the reason I was here I looked down at my muddy jeans, which had already begun to dry. I looked back at Buster my eyes serious under my brow. He hung his head looking away from me bounding out of the car as Jeremy let him out. I went to open my door but Jeremy had already opened it and offered me his hand. I smiled hesitantly at him wondering if I touched him again would I receive another electric shock. His hand was cool and firm as it held mine. Closing the car door behind me I followed him to the front door pausing to caress the wooden columns of the veranda, which acted also as a porch covering.

"What a shame that nobody has ever loved this house enough to look after it"

He stopped and smiled at me his eyes caressing my face making me blush. I hung my head immediately only realising as I looked down that our hands were still interlinked. Removing mine quickly I looked away as he turned and opened the door. The hallway when I stepped inside was long with beautiful covings painted a hideous jade green colour. He followed my gaze grimacing at it

"I know sacrilege right."

Walking behind me he led me through the kitchen to a utility room recently renovated. The units were old lightened oak with a large Belfast sink and brass taps. The window, which had recently been replaced, looked fresh and white as my eyes looked through it to the jungle beyond.

"Whoa you have your work cut out there," I muttered.

He nodded, "I know, trouble is I'm not much good with gardens I was thinking when the house is finished getting in a landscape gardener to finish it off"

"My dad could be of help to you there, he planned and planted our garden and it's beautiful."

A silence fell between us when I realised what I had said. I blushed again looking away wondering what on earth I was thinking off being so familiar with a guy I didn't even know.

"That would be great if your father has the time"

Knowing he was trying to make me relax I smiled awkwardly at him before he turned on the taps until the sink was a quarter full. Reaching into a top cupboard above the washing machine and tumble dryer he handed me a thick blue towel and cloth.

"There's soap too, call me when you've finished."

Leaning on the sink I hung my head calling myself all the stupid names I could think off. What had come over me? I was acting like a silly teenager all gaga over a great looking guy.

Turning towards the sink I immersed the cloth soaping it well before attacking the mud stains on my jeans. When I had finished there were still vague signs of my mud attack but it was sufficient until I got back home after my meeting with Zara. Looking at my watch I still had over an hour and a half to kill till our appointment and though as I emptied the sink and cleaned it out the dreaded thoughts, which had been nagging me on and off throughout the morning were not as irritating as before. When I opened the door he was waiting for me with a hot mug of delicious smelling coffee. Smiling shyly I took it off him looking round for somewhere to sit in the large semi gutted kitchen. Sensing what I was thinking he pulled a stool from beneath the large oak table and beckoned for me to sit down. I did, watching him sit close to me as we both sipped our drinks.

"I forgot to ask earlier where is Florrie? I went to the park knowing she usually walks the reprobate in the afternoons."

His face looked serious as he looked away.

"Florrie is in hospital. She fell over a couple of days ago and hurt herself."

"Oh no is she all right?" my concern was genuine for I really liked the elderly woman.

"Well since her confined recuperation in hospital she's getting better but she's not healing as fast as they would like."

I nodded silently sipping again at my coffee not noticing the lack of my one solitary sugar cube.

"Does she live on her own?"

He looked at me then his eyes serious, "Yes she does which is why I am desperate to get the annex finished. As active as she is, she is too old to be living by herself."

His words warmed me. The love, grandmother and grandson shared, was warm, sincere and heartfelt, and for a moment it left me envious that I no longer had a partner that thought of me that way.

"Would you like to see what I've done so far?"

"Well if you have time I don't want to intrude."

I put my mug down on the table as he had and looking warningly at Buster lying in a heap asleep in the corner on his bed.

Next to the utility room was another door, which I hadn't noticed when I had come in. He opened it pausing as he took my hand,

"It's pretty dodgy; I wouldn't want you falling over."

I nodded trying to ignore the somersaults my stomach was doing as I held his hand tightly. The room we walked into was partially finished and it was evident that it would be a large lounge diner. There were French doors looking out onto an area, which overgrown at present would make a nice sitting area for Florrie. The ceiling was high with an ornate ceiling rose of which hung a suspended crystal chandelier wrapped in plastic for protection. The walls were partly painted a warm summer yellow, the floor a light oak. On one wall stood an iron fireplace, which had been recently blackened, above it hung a large mirror also wrapped for safety.

"Florrie will love this room," I murmured confidently because I loved it too.

"There's still a lot of tools and stuff lying around so be careful Grace, I wouldn't want you getting hurt."

He urged me over to a door close to the fireplace. He looked back at me smiling as he opened it.

"I just finished this"

The room was a bedroom. Again the walls were of a paler shade of yellow with a pale grey carpet. The window faced onto the side of the house where wisteria grew creeping along the brick wall.

"It's so lovely" I whispered.

He nodded pleased that I liked it; another door he led me into had been turned into a bathroom with Florrie in mind. There was a wet room with bars screwed to the wall for her to hold onto. Everything had been designed with her safety in mind.

"Do you think she will like it?" he asked me gently.

"How can she not, its beautiful."

"I wanted her close on the ground floor so I could keep an eye on her. Its hard for her managing the stairs she can be a bit of a tyrant at times."

"You mean with walking Buster every weekday afternoon"

"Exactly. I worry about her, but do you think she will listen," he shook his head in answer to his own question.

We retraced our steps back to the kitchen when suddenly I remembered my coat.

As if reading my mind he beckoned me to follow him into the hall where hanging from a make do coat peg knocked into the wall was my coat. It had been cleaned for there was no trace of Buster's misadventures.

"I cleaned it whilst you were washing."

"Thank you," I murmured thinking how Dylan would never have done anything like that. He would have shrugged it off and demanded it be sent to the cleaners. I looked over my shoulder towards the back of the house and all the work he had completed for his grandmother. His voice when he had spoken about her was so tender and touching it left me cold for no matter how hard I tried, I couldn't convince myself or recall Dylan ever being so thoughtful towards another person, without there being something in it for him.

"I have to go,"

"I know," he murmured quietly.

He held my coat so I could slip into it and before he removed his hands for one moment he was holding me and it felt so familiar.

"Well" I uttered awkwardly as I walked towards the front door with Jeremy and Buster in tow.

"Thank you Jeremy for being so kind it was a pleasure meeting you."

As the front door opened Buster pushed his way forwards placing his wet nose into my opened hand.

Bending down no longer fearful of his acrobatic behaviour I ruffled his hair smiling as he licked my hand in playful response.

"Grace."

I turned as I stood in the doorway my eyes enquiring and bright.

"I'm going to see Florrie tonight at the hospital, would you like to come?"

My heart leapt doing a thousand somersaults before I could verbally reply.

"Yes" I mumbled, "I would like to see her again."

"When and where shall I pick you up?"

I thought for a brief moment my happiness once soaring now sinking faster than the Titanic. I wanted so much to go with him and it was then I remembered I couldn't. In just over an hour I was meeting Zara and although I was sorely tempted to take a rain check I knew I couldn't. I had initiated the first move towards her and though it was imperative for me to find out what had been going on in the last five and a half months I knew I wouldn't be able to move on completely until I had left everything behind me. So as I looked up at Jeremy I realised my face must have shown him the battle I was fighting within. His face was no longer smiling but looked disappointed as though I had been trying to think of a way to excuse myself from going with him.

"It's fine, I mean I understand you hardly know me and well you hardly know my grandmother."

My hand shot out taking his arm as he began to back away,

"No it's not that. I really want to go with you and see her...but I just remembered a previous engagement that I now wished I had never made but I still have to go to."

I knew I was rambling and I knew it sounded like the excuse he was thinking I was making because I had changed my mind.

He stood for a moment and I knew he felt uncomfortable for he stuck his hands into his jean pockets as he hurriedly thought through what I had said. He looked at me still looking at him, my face pensive as he came to his decision.

"Okay then we could do it another day, Florrie won't be home for awhile so I suppose there's no rush."

Although I didn't know him I knew the latter part of the sentence he had just muttered was to try and make me feel better and that endeared him greatly to me.

"Seriously Jeremy I made an appointment to see a friend and its going to be a difficult meeting and it would be so easy for me to cry off and avoid the whole thing altogether," but... I chewed my lip looking away from his intense stare, "I need to do this."

He stepped closer saying nothing, as he looked down at me his stare gentle and unassuming.

"Grace it doesn't matter I understand. You don't have to explain anything to me."

"But I do" I interceded quickly cutting him off.

"Why?" his voice was gentle his breath warm on my face.

"I don't know" my voice was low and husky, I felt very awkward blurting out what I just had, but suddenly as I had said it I realised it was essential to me that he knew I wasn't stringing him along.

"Would you like a lift to where you are going?"

I looked up at him feeling the need to suddenly hug him just because he had offered unselfishly to take me where I needed to go. It would mean I didn't have to return home to fetch my car, knowing Dylan would try to stop me demanding an explanation and when he knew my destination his intent would be to stop me going. So I nodded my head in thanks, my blood coursing through my veins as he gently took my hand and beckoning to Buster to follow as we left the house. Once the dog was safely ensconced in the back I looked at him shyly as he got in looking over at me briefly before starting the car.

"Where is it you're going Grace?"

"Do you know the new development by the river?" I murmured.

His eyebrows raised in reply as he nodded his head and drove away from the kerb.

"Lovely plot I've been watching as the apartments went up. Nice but too modern, too boxy for my taste."

"I know what you mean I much prefer the older style home much more space and character."

He looked at me nodding in agreement,

"You ok?"

"Yes...and no. What I am about to face is every married woman's nightmare."

He looked at me quizzically before returning his eyes back to the road,

"Hmmm sounds interesting. Want to talk about it?"

I looked at him debating whether to share. Here was a complete stranger, someone I vaguely knew yet the impulse to tell him everything was so strong, that after a brief moment I nodded in agreement.

"I was happily married for over five years when my husband told me out of the blue one day that our marriage was over. That was nearly six months ago. One evening whilst on the bus going home, I lived with my parents then, I looked out of the window realising I was outside my old home," I shrugged my shoulders, "Before I knew what I was doing I was outside the front door. I had left some months previously owing to my husband forcing me out." I paused "The agreement was until the property was sold he was to live there. But it was empty and had been for quite awhile. So to cut a long story short I moved back in, he found out and also decided to do the same. He only recently admitted that the reason we split up is because he was unfaithful and didn't want me anymore."

Jeremy was quiet for a long moment as I stared at him from beneath my eyelashes. Though his eyes were intent on the road ahead I could see he was digesting what I had told him. Suddenly he turned his head looking directly at me.

"Grace, I'm so sorry. What a bastard if you don't mind me saying so"

"I don't and he is" I replied his lips matching mine in a brief smile.

"So where are you going this afternoon? Is that related?"

I shrugged my shoulders, not really wanting to talk about it anymore. "Yes" I said briefly.

"Hmmm, may I ask, in what way?"

I turned my face to stare out of the car window not noticing the houses passing by.

"Zara was my best friend and the woman my husband broke our marriage vows over"

"Will you be ok Grace or would you like me to wait for you?"

I stared at him, "You would do that?"

He pulled the car to the side of the road pulling on the handbrake as he stared at me,

"Of course"

I shook my head exclaiming, "But I don't know how long I will be up there for and"... I paused before continuing, "I don't know what state I will be in when I come down."

He laid his hand gently over mine before adding quietly, "I know, that's why I'll wait."

"Are you always so gallant?"

His voice held the hint of a smile as I shyly looked up at him, "Only once..." he let the words hang in the air before he continued, "This being the once" he added more quietly "Are you sure you'll be okay and that you want to do this?"

I nodded looking down at my hands realising to stay where I was at this very moment was far more appealing than what I was about to do, but I had come this far I wasn't going to back out now.

"I have to do this. I have to know." I looked at him then, my face as solemn as my voice, "I have ghosts that need to be laid to rest. For nearly six months I have struggled to put myself back together, I am not quite there yet." my voice faltered as I recalled the last few weeks of my co-habitation with Dylan. Although I had made some major faux pars recently, it was only now I realised that my marriage to Dylan was well and truly over and through it all I had survived and put my self back together, even though there were still a few missing pieces to make me fully intact and healed.

My mother was always fond of saying when your relationship breaks down for whatever reason only a fool would repeat the trip down a dead end road. I frowned then wondering how the hell she would know that after such a long and happy married life to my father, her only one true love?

I stared at the high wall enveloping the new housing estate. I opened the car door putting my feet on the ground when he stopped me with his hand on my shoulder. I looked back at him as he leaned over and gently hugged me, "That's for good luck" he said quietly his eyes intense on mine. I was all choked up as I nodded my head silently looking away as I got out of the car. I took a few steps forward stopping and turning once more to look back at him thankful he was there with me.

I could feel his eyes following me as I walked away from the car. The urge to just run back to him, to forget about the whole thing was so tempting, but if I wanted closure this was the last step to make it happen. The front gates were high, solid and impenetrable as I faltered for a moment wondering how to get in. The solution was easy when I noticed to my left a long metal plate fixed to the wall with an entry button to each apartment. Pressing firmly I waited saying my name when Zara's voice came through the speaker. The gates opened silently I looked back once more at Jeremy before I walked slowly up the drive. My feet crunched on the gravel as I walked slowly towards Riverside View Apartments. To my left were gardens new in their creation with trees and bushes freshly planted in designated areas with benches and tables for the inhabitants to enjoy picnics and BBQ's in the summer. It was nice and pleasant and I could see the appeal the developer was trying to create, imagining when the trees and shrubs were fully-grown how breath taking it would become. I heard what sounded like a bubbling brook and as I looked more closely around me I spied an endless lawn sloping down to what must be a small manmade outlet from the river. Nice I thought to myself but as my head swung round to look at the four storey building looming up in front of me I wasn't prepared for the intimidating facade with its reclaimed old red brick and glass balconies which I hadn't noticed as I walked reluctantly up the short driveway. The building was obviously an architectural design in its own right, with arched windows and large planes of glass to what I presumed graced every apartment. I paused for a moment wondering again how Zara was able to afford to live at such a prestigious address. I hadn't bothered taking much notice as the building had got underway but as I walked closer towards the large glass entry doors I remembered vaguely reading in the local rag the uproar of neighbouring residents when the plans had first been introduced. The argument over this development had been on going as the local residents complained and campaigned ruthlessly not to lose their frontal riverside view. Obviously they had not been successful. The steps to the entrance were large and of dark stone with ornamental trees bordering the doors like soldiers on sentry duty. Before I reached them I stopped and turned around. I needed a moment just to focus my thoughts but as my eyes glanced around me I looked at the row of cars parked opposite to the gardens noticing every one was new and expensive. Again I pondered on Zara's luck and how she found herself living here. She had either won the lottery or inherited a lot of money either way I didn't care but I was curious.

Taking a deep breath of courage I looked back at the door noticing my reflection in the glass. I wasn't suitably attired to be calling at such a privileged address but what did I care. My eyes looked sorrowfully back at me as I watched my chest rise and fall alarmingly. Take deep breaths I thought it's only Zara but as I raised my head to look up at the building it only made me feel more inadequate and dizzy, so instead I pressed another buzzer for entry. She lived on the fourth floor or as described in the building plaque the penthouse suite. I suppose that should have alerted me. I chewed my lip apprehensively as I pressed the intercom for the apartment and within seconds her voice greeted me as the buzzer sounded and I opened the door. The first thought that struck me as I entered the hallway was how sterile it looked. It was and looked expensive with its white grey veined marble floor and snowy white walls. The prints were sporadic but adorned the space with style. The centre of the floor held a large glass circular table with a glass circular vase filled with a variety of flowers, all classy and colourful and apt for their surroundings. To the right of the table were what I presumed to be metal post boxes inserted into the wall. Streamlined and labelled but to me a smaller reminder of the corpse's cabinets you found in any mortuary. God I was being morose I thought as I walked towards the lift and pressed the button. The interior was mirrored so for a few moments of upward travel I had my image staring back at me. My whole posture was one of dread and as the doors opened notifying me in a tinny voice I had reached the fourth floor, I straightened my back and forced a smile on my face.

When I stepped out, the first door that greeted me was open with Zara filling the doorway in a cool white ensemble very unlike what she used to wear. Her hair blonde hung long and thick past her shoulders their curls obedient and glossy. Her eyes what I normally described as cold green were warm and inviting as she stood aside to let me pass and if I had been my normal self I would have been aware of this and forearmed myself. The floors were also white marble; the walls white with recessed lighting and genuine abstract paintings hanging strategically in places of light to gain their full effect and beauty. I looked back at her feeling more uncomfortable. She stood watching me a false smile on her lips like lady of the manor and me the ever-grateful cleaner clad in jeans and t-shirt. I ran a hand nervously over my hair not wanting to think how scruffy I must look compared to her. The roles had definitely reversed I thought to myself as I followed her. Being married to Dylan I was always immaculate and well turned out. Hair appointments twice a week to keep my hair as manicured and glossy as the designer clothes and shoes I wore upon my slim frame. Zara had always been the one who dressed down as long as they fit and coordinated, fashion wasn't an issue.

Her smile was gracious but it wasn't Zara's normal way. Her actions were controlled and preened as I had once been. It made me feel very confused as to what had happened to her to incur this dramatic change in her. The room she led me into was large, white, open plan and soulless. The kitchen stood to the far right with its units and integrated appliances, again all white and streamlined. It was high style and expensive but it only made me frown more. The lounge diner was minimal in style with a long glass table adorned with white upright leather chairs. A large crystal vase stood upon it filled with white lilies perfectly arranged. I began to feel I was in the twilight zone as I looked around me in awe knowing she was silently watching me. The white leather sofa's arranged around the built in chrome fireplace were reminiscent of mine and that should have a given me a clue, but I was too awe struck to take notice how familiar and yet unfamiliar my surroundings were. I walked over to the large glass paned wall looking out over the front of the building. I stood there quietly my eyes looking frantically for Jeremy's car below. It was partly obscured by the high wall surrounding the perimeter of the site, but as I raised my face to stare at the magnificent view of the fields and houses surrounding this complex, I spied a lone figure with a bounding dog playing ball in the field opposite. The scene gave me a feeling of warmth in what was otherwise a cold and sterile environment. The balcony in front of me was bare except for a small glass table and two chairs.

"Do you like it?" she asked breaking me from my reverie

I swung round a smile immediately appearing on my face.

"It's very chic, but I wouldn't have said it was you Zara."

Her smile faded for a brief moment as she turned away towards the kitchen.

"Would you like some wine?"

Again this knocked me off kilter. All Zara had ever had in her cupboards were the usual tea, instant coffee and occasional cheap carton of orange juice and out of date milk.

"Err yes that would be fine" I replied.

I had to sit down my legs were unsteady and for a moment I felt that this was all an illusion and soon like a lamb I would be led off for the slaughter. The glass she handed me was crystal, again unlike her normal tastes but I chose to remain silent opting instead to put the ball in her court. She sat down on the other sofa facing me with a glass of cool sparkling water in her hand. I refrained from frowning as my eyes alighted on hers waiting to hear the reason for the sudden and definitely unexpected life change.

"Grace" her voice faltered as she looked down at her glass before staring back at me.

"What" I managed to mutter feeling a sudden sense of dread.

"I'm glad you contacted me...we need to talk."

I knew my curiosity was getting the better of me as I placed my wine glass down upon the glass coaster strategically placed near where I was sitting.

"Ok"

Taking a small sip of water she followed suit before staring back at me with a mixture of pain and regret in her eyes.

"Are you with Dylan?"

Her question stunned me but I didn't show it as I stared back at her before answering.

"Why do you want to know?" I hastily replied confused before realising the impression she must have received when I took her last phone call.

"If you are referring to our last conversation I was just annoyed and bewildered as to why you wanted to speak to my husband when you rang the other night."

Ouch I cringed inwardly knowing I was being bitchy but not caring either way. I could feel her sense of relief as she digested what I said. My stomach began churning unable to piece together what was unravelling. A few moments passed before she looked at me again. Her eyes were gentle as she clasped her hands together. She was uncomfortable and embarrassed and it made me wonder why.

"This isn't going to be easy Grace, with what I am about to tell you"

I felt my back stiffen as I sat upright dying to take a large gulp of my wine but knowing if I picked it up I would most probably drop it from nerves. So I refrained, licking my lips instead, as my eyes fixed on hers.

"I don't understand what you mean?" I heard my voice reply calmly.

"Dylan and I have been seeing each other."

A bolt of electricity shot through me my senses reeling from her words, my stomach churning convulsively. I took a few deep breaths trying desperately to digest what she had just said.

"You mean you and him had an affair, I know that he told me."

Even though Dylan had thrown that at me it hadn't rung true, I had taken it as just another decoy thrown at me to hurt me. But, to hear my friend admit the same knowing now it wasn't just hurtful innuendo from Dylan had my head running off in multiple directions. My heart was hammering in my chest as I tried unsuccessfully to steady my shaking hands.

"It was more than an affair and he knows it. Why would he say that to you?" Her voice was vehement like she was the injured party and for a moment that threw me.

I could barely utter the words but seeing as she had started this I found myself wanting to know what the lying cheating bastard had really done behind my back.

"More than an affair?" I broke off trying to comprehend what she was saying and knowing anything more would hurt as much as when he had initially dumped me.

"I've been wanting to tell you for some time Grace, but...Dylan wouldn't hear of it."

"Long time?" I repeated stupidly.

She nodded her head at my words as she looked down at her lap before continuing.

"Do you remember that last party you threw at your house?"

My mind went blank as I fought hard to recall. What was she going on about? The last party I had thrown at the house had been just over a year ago. It had been a celebration as Dylan had acquired a new promising writer destined to make him rich. I nodded blankly as she continued.

"Remember you walked in on us in the garden and Dylan said we had been arguing?"

Again I nodded blankly.

"Well we hadn't been arguing. We had been kissing," she admitted hurriedly before continuing, "But it was also the beginning. Dylan pushed me back when he heard you coming calling his name. I suppose I must have looked angry and confused at his actions, but it obviously worked because you believed him."

I looked at her dumbly as I remembered the moment she was speaking of. I had wanted more wine for the guests and couldn't find him. The

113

garden was cool and I hadn't known why I'd gone out there to find him, but I wasn't surprised to see him there. I was taken aback to find Dylan with my best friend and his worst enemy, but I had shrugged it off hoping at last the snide indifferences between them were over.

"I'm so sorry Grace you have to believe that. I never meant it for it to go any further, but..." she broke off looking away.

"But?" I repeated my eyes demanding her to finish.

She looked at me with a defiant look in her eyes, "But you know how persistent and persuasive he can be?"

I nodded recalling how he had been the same way with me after we had met. She got up and sat beside me taking one of my cold hands between hers.

"Please I am so sorry Grace. I never meant to hurt you but I became so enamoured with him, I just couldn't let go he was like a drug that I couldn't stop taking."

I wanted to prise my hand away from her, but instead I just sat dumbly nodding like an idiot as she continued more strongly now.

"So I need to know if he has moved back in with you?"

It was a few seconds before I registered what she was saying,

"Why?" was all I asked.

"Because things have changed between us and I want him back...no I need him back"

"You can have him" I replied my voice dead.

"Then please tell him to come back to me."

I stood up needing the space between us. Was I receiving this information correctly? For a moment I was confused and off kilter the next angry and outraged. I turned on her not caring how callous my voice sounded.

"I don't know how you dare say that to me. Zara you who had the audacity to screw my husband whilst we were still married? You were my best friend, how could you do to this to me, to our friendship after all these years. You were like the sister I never had. My parents welcomed you into our family. I trusted you and this is how you repay me?" I walked towards the large paned window wanting desperately to leave. Dylan was dead meat I knew that. He had led me to believe that he and Zara had had a fling since we had separated and the reality of it all was he was deeply embroiled in an affair that had been the cause of our separation, I turned on her.

"Were you living together when I moved back to the house?"

She nodded silently, "We had an argument shortly after he discovered what you had done. We had been at odds with each other for a while. I was hoping he was coming to terms with what had happened between us, but instead he just came home one day announced we were finished and packed his stuff and went. I've been hunting for him everywhere, never thinking for one moment he had returned back to your marital home."

"Why were you at odds?" I asked dejectedly.

"It would be easier to show you," she replied quietly as she stood up. I looked at her for a brief moment before I found myself following her. We walked down a long narrow white hallway before she stopped at a door at the far end. We looked at each other; her expression was soft as she turned the door handle. I followed her gaze, hers becoming dreamy and gooey eyed. In front of me was a bedroom, no correction a nursery fully kitted out.

"You see Grace I'm pregnant with Dylan's baby"

I leant against the wall for support my mouth dropped open as I stared at her face and then more closely at her mid section. The clothes she was wearing hid very successfully the significant bulge I now noticed.

"That's why he finished with you" she continued, "Because if he didn't I threatened to tell you everything."

Chapter 8

I was quiet when I returned to Jeremy's car. Buster exhausted from his run lay in the back of the car snoring. Jeremy smiled at me as I opened the door and got in.

"Hi how are you feeling?" his voice was gentle as he lay a hand on my arm. I looked at him with a deadpan expression on my face not replying. I was mentally drained and broken and as glad as I was that I wasn't alone he wasn't the person whose arms I could fall apart in.

"What happened Grace? You look shattered?"

I couldn't answer as I sat there looking out of the car window trying desperately to control my emotions, which were threatening to erupt at any moment. My eyes were blurred with unshed tears as I heard the car start. The silence was deafening inside and I knew I was being extremely rude but I couldn't bring myself to utter a single word.

I had thought nearly six months before, when I was unceremoniously cast aside that my life as it was had ended, but it was nothing to how I was feeling now. The anger and gut wrenching pain coursing through my veins with yet another revelation of betrayal, was so strong I could feel my hands clench and unclench into tight fists. I could see out of the corner of my eye Jeremy's worried expression as he drove slowly along the road, his eyes casually straying to me but as I continued my silent blinding appraisal of the passing scenery all I could do was wallow.

"Grace?"

When I eventually registered his repetition of my name I looked at him unable to see him clearly through my tears. The car stopped by the side of the road as he pulled up the handbrake and leaned over taking me gently into his arms.

"You're going to be okay."

I wanted to shout at him that he didn't know what the hell he was talking about but I couldn't. It wasn't his fault that yet again Dylan had broken my fucking heart. I thought of Zara in cahoots with him stabbing me in the back at every stolen opportunity, whilst he merrily and without remorse broke my heart into a million little pieces. How could two people who claimed to love me so much rip out my very soul without any regrets.

"Take me home."

I lay my head back against the headrest. I didn't know and I didn't care. He remained quiet for a moment looking at his watch then giving me a warm smile before he started the car.

"I have a little time before going to see Florrie, I'll take you back to mine if you like so you can have a strong cup of tea and chill for awhile."

"No it's ok honestly. I don't want to put you out anymore than I have already. Can you take me to my parent's house?"

He nodded though the look of disappointment on his face did not escape me. I muttered vaguely where my parents lived before I returned to my vigil of looking aimlessly out of the window. When the car drew to a stop I remained where I was wishing I had gone back with him to his house. My mother would be all over me like a rash demanding what had happened and why I was in such a state. It wasn't something I wanted to rehash but right now knowing he was in a hurry I took a deep breath ignoring the pain and loneliness ripping me apart inside.

"Grace" I stopped to turn and look at him as I got out of the car.

He walked over to my side and took my hand smiling down at me.

"Do you want me to come in with you?" I looked at him then feeling a small surge of mixed signals. To have him with me would stun my mother and keep her at bay from harassing me until I was ready to tell her what had happened. But gradually as common sense returned I also realised how uncomfortable it would be for us both, knowing my mother as I did. So it was with regret I shook my head at him. I hardly knew this man, this stranger that I had only met a few hours before. But in that time I had grown to like him very quickly, as though I had known him all my life. That acknowledgement should have had me reeling back in horror after what had just happened but it hadn't. In his presence I felt safe.

"Snicket?"

I turned my head quickly at my father's concerned voice. He was standing not far from the garage the inevitable spade in his hand. His eyes were wary and questioning as he saw the exchange between Jeremy and myself. He also saw the tears glistening on my cheeks, as he dropped the spade he had been carrying and hurried over to the gate where we were standing.

"Dad" I cried out suddenly holding tightly the hand by my side. He looked down at me in question as I straightened my back to face my father wiping the tears hurriedly from my face with my free hand.

"Grace what on earth is the matter?" The question was asked innocently enough but I knew what my dad really meant. His expression

117

firm and territorial was quickly summing up Jeremy immediately portraying him as the cause of my sadness. About to speak again I interrupted him.

"Dad this is Jeremy. He brought me home."

I could see my father's confusion as he looked between the both of us like he was watching an avid tennis match.

"Hello sir, pleased to meet you" Jeremy's free hand was outstretched throwing my father momentarily off guard.

"Um, yes pleased to meet you," my dad replied unsure as he reluctantly shook his hand. His eyes strayed back to mine his questioning glare clear,

"Dad..." I wanted to offer a brief explanation but when it came to it I didn't know what to say. I looked at Jeremy with blank eyes as he met mine.

"Grace has had a distressing meeting this afternoon; she didn't want to go home so I brought her here."

I looked at him with gratitude in my eyes as he smiled back squeezing my hand gently in response.

"Well...um thank you" was all my father managed to say before the front door opened to reveal my mother staring enquiringly out.

"Grace, John what's happened?"

I groaned loudly looking up at Jeremy with apologies in my eyes. He looked back at me confused before looking up to stare at my mother.

"Nothing Esther, go put the kettle on Grace has brought a friend round to tea."

"No" I interceded releasing Jeremy's hand quickly as I stepped forward,

"Dad he has to go and see his grandmother who's in the hospital, he hasn't the time for this."

"Oh I'm sorry to hear that" my father could always be relied on to be cordially understanding.

"I have time if you want?" Jeremy replied softly taking my hand again and squeezing it. My father noticed this brief interaction looking up at me quickly his brows furrowing with questions.

"Well okay please come in" he muttered his tone uncertain

"What about Buster" I cried out grasping at straws to delay what I knew was coming.

I could see his expression change, as Jeremy turned round to look at the dog still snoring loudly in the back of the car.

"Buster?" my father repeated looking at me like I had gone mad.

"Buster is an old English sheepdog dad. He's sleeping in the back."

CHASING RAINBOWS

Pushing the top of his cap back my dad scratched his head trying to look over our shoulders.

"If I could have a bowl of water he should be fine for a few minutes "Jeremy interceded.

"No we can't have that. Bring him in he can run around in the garden"

"No dad" I interrupted, "You don't know Buster."

Jeremy looked down at me biting his lip,

"Grace is right, he can be very boisterous."

"Well, bring him in then I'd like to see him pit himself against your mother" my dad smirked as he turned around. I looked at Jeremy shrugging my shoulders whispering 'sorry.'

"Dad I need sort to my face out before seeing mum."

He looked at me nodding his head in silent assent,

"Off you go then Grace I'm sure we can manage."

When the three of us followed my dad inside the house I diverted whilst the others went into the kitchen. Shutting my old bedroom door behind me I let the tears escape as I unceremoniously collapsed onto the bed. Clutching the duvet around me I cried like never before. The pain inside of me continued to eat away at me as memories of Dylan and Zara together whilst we were still happily married continued to thrash away at me, their baby already well in the making, whilst Dylan cold-heartedly denied mine. I curled up in a foetal position hugging my womb for the baby that would never be.

Hiccupping I buried my face deeper just wanting to die. I had never grieved for my baby because I hadn't been allowed too and like a fool I had obeyed like the obedient little wife I was. The pain had never been replaced by what I had lost and still mourned after. Now that missing part of me interlaced with the revelations of today, had utterly floored me leaving me devastated, abused and defenceless.

The arms that embraced me and pulled me close all the while whispering into my hair that everything would be all right belonged to my mother. As she rocked me gently all the while crooning like she had when I was a child woken terrified after a nightmare.

"Is Jeremy still here?" I asked between sobs suddenly remembering him.

"No he left almost immediately after you didn't come into the kitchen. But, don't worry," my mother added hastily as I reacted, "He said he would see you in a few days if he didn't hear from you first."

I nodded as I buried my head deeper into my mother's arms.

119

"Do you want a drink love, you must be thirsty after so much crying?"

"Please" I snivelled as my mother releasing one arm reached to my bedside table and placed a hot mug of cocoa into my shaking hands.

"Take care Gracie, that will hurt if you spill."

The coldness I felt when she released me to puff up my pillows, take the mug and ease me against them made me want to tell Mum everything. I had never told another living soul about the baby and as I looked at my mother now sitting on the side of my bed looking concernedly at me, I felt what I was about to tell her would be the worst act of betrayal and would break my mother's heart.

I smiled briefly as she handed me back the mug. As I gingerly sipped my cooling cocoa my mother as usual put my bed back to rights. Taking off my shoes she pulled the duvet neatly over me smiling at me as she sat down beside me. I had decided that nothing could make me feel worse than I already did, and I knew as I returned her stare that if I didn't tell her now I never would. I hadn't been comfortable keeping the news to myself, for my mother was, in fact, my best friend even though half the time she drove me insane with her all prying intuitiveness she had nothing but my best interests at heart. I chewed pensively on my bottom lip as I fought my inner demons. I felt abused, betrayed and ashamed. Dylan and Zara between them had totally demolished everything I had held dear. My parents had raised me to be a good honest person. Believing when I grew up I would be treated with the same respect and honesty as I bestowed upon others. So what had gone so terribly wrong? The Dylan now was not the man I had married or was he? Had I been so naïve that despite parental advice I believed they were wrong and I was right? Because I was so head over heels, had I been blinkered resulting in him treating me so harshly and disrespectfully, but if so where did that leave Zara?

I could see my mother growing impatient with my silence so putting down the mug I sat up straighter.

"Mum, I know you are waiting for an explanation about today, I'm sorry I just didn't know what to do or where to turn."

She nodded watching me intently, "That young man mentioned that you had been so see Zara?"

I nodded lowering my head as I felt the tears collect in my eyes again.

"Honey, is this related to Dylan"?

I nodded before the tears erupted. My shoulders shook as I buried my face in my hands reliving the pain stirring up inside me again.

She moved closer stroking my hair.

"You know Grace, all things in life happen for a reason. What breaks your heart now will make you stronger and wiser. Do I take it that what Zara had to say has done this to you?"

I nodded again trying desperately to stop the tears but they just kept on coming relentlessly.

"Were Dylan and Zara an item?"

"Oh Mum", I blurted out throwing myself into her, "They had been having an affair for over a year before he dumped me, can you believe that" I spluttered out leaning back to look at her.

Her lips thinned as she shook her head in disappointment, "Grace I am so sorry, but why, I don't understand, those two are like chalk and cheese. It will never work but...knowing what they have done to you they both deserve each other."

"It gets worse mum" I managed to say before a fit of tears silenced me
"You mean they are still together?"

I nodded looking at her.

"But if that's the case what is he doing back in the house with you?"

"She's pregnant with his baby mum, not that he owned up to me about that, he has been trying to convince me to come back to him, all the while dumping Zara and their baby."

"Why the two-timing lying heathen. Ohhh Grace what did you ever see in him."

"Mum, stop that's not all." I paused arguing inwardly whether telling her all of it now would be wise. Before I could talk myself out of it I hurried on,

"Please forgive me."

"Grace" my mother halted mid sentence looking intently at me, "Tell me you weren't stupid enough to believe him, tell me you didn't let him seduce you?"

I looked down nodding gently.

"Grace no, tell me you didn't, oh my God tell me at least you were careful. Grace you could be pregnant with his child."

"Mum stop" I screamed out my fists hitting the duvet repeatedly, "I WAS pregnant with his child. When I told him, he was so convincing telling me it was too early, that he couldn't handle it. Still I couldn't cave until eventually he gave me an ultimatum it was him or the baby. He forced me to make the appointment to get rid of the baby, but it didn't matter anyway. I miscarried a couple of days before the appointment. I loved him so much, and like the stupid gullible person I was, I believed that in the future he would eventually relent when he saw how important it was to me." I'm sorry mum that I didn't tell you."

I paused then wondering whether I could finish. I couldn't look at my mother knowing what I would see in her eyes so I continued with my head down,

" I didn't want to raise a child on my own; it's not how I wanted to raise a family. Little did I know he had acted that way because Zara was already pregnant."

My mother moaned putting her hands up to her mouth. Doing the sign of the Holy cross, she kept shaking her head as she stared horrified at me.

"Mum please talk to me, tell me you understand?"

Instead she stared at me like I was a stranger to her. Scrabbling out of bed I sat on the floor resting my head on her knees,

"Please tell me you understand and forgive me, I am so sorry I didn't tell you I felt so ashamed at what I was prepared to do for him. I just didn't know which way to turn."

Minutes passed and my mother never moved or responded. She just remained silent her eyes closed, her face ashen. What was I going to do if my mother turned against me too? I lifted my head to look at her, but she never responded when I pleaded with her to talk to me.

"Mum if you want me to leave I'll go, I am so sorry, believe me I never meant to hurt you or dad."

I rested my head back against her knees praying silently she would understand. Tears ran down my face, why had I done it, why had I let Dylan do that to me?

Sensing my mother's legs tense as if she wanted to pull herself away from me

I stood up my limbs as heavy as my heart. My feet were like lead as I walked towards the bedroom door. If I left this house under this black cloud, it would be impossible to come back knowing how my mother felt about her religious beliefs, and the unforgivable sin I had nearly committed. I looked at her once more willing her to say something, do something to let me know I was still her daughter and that she loved me, but she remained motionless.

The bedroom door closed behind me, my life in shreds as I descended the stairs slowly. I didn't look for my father who was probably in the garden; some-how I just couldn't face him, to see the shame in his eyes too. It was more than I could bear at that moment. I was at the front door my hand poised on the door handle to open it, never feeling more alone than I did at that moment. I had lost everything and everyone.

"Grace, stop"

I turned around slowly to see my mother standing at the top of the stairs her face heavily lined my confession adding years to her. Her feet carried her swiftly to me stopping as she reached me. My mother was a few inches shorter than my five-foot ten height so when she reached for me her arms outstretched I bent into them as she hugged me tightly. My tears now, were for my mother, to thank her for not letting me go. She had forgiven me for all I had done, for not listening when she had begged me not to marry Dylan, for lying to her when his harsh words had ripped me apart I just couldn't bear to prove her right. But, most off all I cried for my baby and my parent's grandchild.

"Grace my dearest child, stop your tears. You listen to me. You have been lied to, cheated and abused by a man who had the nerve to call himself your husband. You will survive this, YOU HAVE SURVIVED this Grace and you will hold your head up high. Remember this my darling girl."

Her hands gently lifted my head so I could look into her eyes.

"I am so proud of you for all that you have gone through alone, I love you very much and I am so sorry that I have let you down," her voice faltered.

"Mum…. You haven't" I stuttered between sobs.

"Hush Grace" my mother interrupted softly, "If I hadn't have been so judgemental and self -righteous at times you would have been able to come to me and perhaps…who knows life may have turned out differently. But for all our shortcomings I have never been so proud of you as I am at this moment. Darling, don't you ever give up in chasing your rainbows, one day you will find that special man who deserves you and your love. Who will give back your love a hundredfold and make you feel happy and whole again."

Chapter 9

I didn't return home that night, instead I stayed with my parents. My mother and I after my confession had become even closer than before. Though I realised there would be times in the future when today would not be uppermost in both our minds, the bridge we had crossed had had two profound effects on me. Firstly, I treasured and understood the true meaning of unconditional love. There were no boundaries or limitations like there had been in my marriage to Dylan. The support and belief though sometimes wavering in disagreement and misunderstanding were nevertheless strong and bent when needed. But, most importantly were always there regardless. My secondly, that I had been handed this god given gift of my baby and lost it through no fault of my own. The pain inside of me was so overwhelming that it hurt to breathe remembering if I hadn't lost the baby, I would have committed the most unforgivable act of my life.

"Grace, let it all come out. My dearest child let yourself grieve and over time the pain will ease."

"How…would you know that Mum?" I mumbled between sobs.

She went quiet for a long moment before replying taking my hand and leading me into the kitchen. She sat down opposite me taking my hands away from my face as we stared at each other across the kitchen table.

"Because once Grace I was in your shoes. I loved a man before your father. I was so convinced we were both on the same path, both making the same plans. But…" she stopped

Her eyes were no longer looking into mine but into someone else's. The smile that appeared briefly on her lips changed into the thinned line she often adopted now when things went drastically wrong. Looking back at me her eyes were sad as she continued,

"I didn't know, so when I found out I was accidentally with child I automatically assumed he would be as happy and we would get married sooner rather than later as planned. But…. When I told him about the baby, he couldn't run away from me fast enough, shouting at me for being so stupid and careless. That he could never marry me because he was already married. Back then Grace life was very different I had already committed three sins in the eyes of the church and my family. I had had sex before marriage and with a married man, and fallen pregnant as a result. My father condemned me for bringing shame to the family name and I was sent away to a mother and baby home to have the child, where it would be adopted soon after I gave birth. It was my punishment, my father had said for acting like a whore instead of the good catholic child they had raised me to be."

I opened my mouth to console her, but she shook her head silencing me.

"We had to work there to earn our keep. I was about five months when I had an accident, I was cleaning the stairs and I slipped. I lost the baby and when I was well enough to return home, my parents were no longer the same towards me. I found a job moved out and about a year later I met your father at a dance and well, the rest is history."

Holding her hands tightly my eyes met hers and for a moment our roles were reversed.

"Mum I am so sorry that's awful...."

Forcing a bright smile on her face she shook herself as if shrugging off the past like a cloak.

"That is why Gracie I am who I am sometimes. I don't mean to be and well your father knows why I am like it, yet for all that he has stoically loved me and stood by me, never letting me down."

By the time my dad had come in an hour later, my mother had adopted her daily role as if nothing had ever happened. As I set the table my eyes when they rested on my father held more love for him in that moment than ever before. When he looked up at me momentarily confused at my doting expression he cleared his throat before asking.

"You all right now Snicket, is anything the matter?"

My mother looked at me over his head her hands poised with the plate of sandwiches.

"No dad, I just love you that's all."

My mother smiled as she bustled past him putting the plate down on the table.

"I know that Snicket, I love you too."

"John, I hope you washed your hands before sitting down at my table."

Saved from replying by the front door bell ringing, we all looked at each other.

"Who can that be, we're not expecting anyone are we John?"

Before my father could reply I ran to the kitchen door shouting in my wake that I would go and find out.

Fingers crossed for good luck I prayed it wouldn't be Dylan. The amount of calls I had rejected that day from him could almost be classed as stalking. As I neared the front door my steps slowed. Slipping the security catch on the door as back up I opened the door peering round to see who the caller was.

"Jeremy" I exclaimed.

"Grace, are you ok. I told your father I would leave it a few days, but well...I was worried about you, and when I told Florrie she insisted I come round and see how you are. Not that I wouldn't have come around off my own back but well...I'm making a right hash of this aren't I?"

I smiled in return as I closed the door to unlatch the security latch before opening it wide. My smile faltered when I saw his accomplice sitting as good as gold on my mother's doorstep.

"What were you thinking bringing that reprobate with you?" I asked sternly, before smiling slightly at the woebegone expression on Jeremy's face.

"Hmmmm obviously I hadn't thought this through at all."

My father joined me at the door.

"Grace, don't leave our guests standing on the doorstep like Jehovah's witnesses come in."

"Dad, what will mum say"?

He looked at me momentarily confused. I beckoned with my head towards Buster.

"Let's find out" he grinned, as Buster bounded past with Jeremy in tow.
My mother's initial expression of the dog was scaringly evident. The whistling kettle was ignored as she watched him with narrowed eyes as Jeremy coaxed him to lie quietly under the table.

"Esther the kettle," my father gently reminded her as she looked at him before complying.

"Well, sit yourself down lad," my dad encouraged.

I looked at my mothers back so rigid as she poured water into the teapot. She was not happy, I looked at dad for guidance.

"It doesn't matter love" my father replied ignoring my questioning stare to sit opposite Jeremy.

Sitting down next to me my mother who looked accusingly under the table at the thick fur rug now lying quietly.

"So, Jeremy is it?" my father asked politely helping himself to one of the scones my mother had placed with jam and cream on the table. I looked at him in amazement. What was he doing eating scones before sandwiches. I looked at my mother who appeared not to notice. Where had all the strict protocol gone? I shook my head in confusion, even more so as dad always having problems with names, especially Dylan's had remembered Jeremy's sitting opposite him.

"Yes that's right." Jeremy replied smiling back at me warmly.

"So how is Florrie"?

"Is that your grandmother you were talking about earlier?" my father asked politely as I saw him take a small piece of buttered scone and slip it under the table.

"Um yes that's right."

The shifting of the body beneath the table confirmed my suspicions, as all you could hear was loud lavish licking of what I presumed was my dad's hand.

"Are you feeding that hound under the table?" my mother asked sternly, her eyes fixed on my father's.

"I may have dropped a crumb or two" my dad replied innocently.

My hunger had deserted me, as for the second time that day I felt like I was in a parallel universe. Jeremy was as comfortable here in my parent's home, like he belonged here. Dylan on the other hand had always suffered these visits with fortitude. I realised I was constantly comparing both of these men and why I didn't know. But what I had realised was that within a few hours of my life being in total tatters, it had swung itself around as if this scene before me was the norm and always had been. My mother must have sensed my distress for she looked at me enquiringly,

"Grace, is anything wrong?"

"Nothing I'm just fine" I replied easily.

"So, Jeremy" my mother enquired oh so politely.

He smiled warmly at her. I could see my mother was just about to question him further and before I could come to his rescue my dad intervened.

"So Jeremy you were saying earlier that you have moved into the next street, which house was it you bought?"

My mother at this unusual interruption of my fathers proceeded to offer the sandwiches around like nothing was amiss.

"65 Magnolia Road"

My dad paused between bites of the sandwiches mum had placed on his plate.

"Oh, wasn't that George Steins old place"?

"Yes, It was his daughter, who wanted a quick sale after her father went into a home."

127

"Hope you got a bargain then, the only reason she wanted him out of there sharpish is because that crafty old bugger never did a thing to that place in twenty years."

"John, really your language leaves a lot to be desired," my mother admonished.

"Are you offended Jeremy"? My father asked.

"Not at all."

I shot my dad a smile but my mother focused her attentions instead on our guest.

"So how do you know Grace? I don't ever recall her mentioning you before?"

"Mum seriously?" I interceded again.

"No Grace its fine, relax. No my grandmother and Buster had the pleasure of meeting your daughter first. We met for the first time today although I had heard a lot about her."

"You did" I replied surprised.

"Yes my grandmother really likes you Grace."

"What happened to her Jeremy?" my mother asked courteously.

"She fell at home. They are keeping her in for observation as she was pretty shaken and confused, hopefully she will be released soon."

"Oh" my mum replied interested, "How does she cope? Is she on her own?"

Jeremy winced, "She was but since the fall plans have changed. My old house needs a lot of work. I've been renovating the outhouse adjoined to the house so Florrie can live there with me."

"I take it your wife is happy with the arrangement. I mean sometimes in-laws don't get on," my mother continued purposely not looking at me.

"I'm not married, there's just me and buster."

I glanced at my mum knowing exactly what avenue she was going down. Ignoring me she smiled warmly at him. I froze. I knew exactly what that smile meant. It meant she liked him a lot. She also hadn't missed the singular 'me' either as she looked at me knowingly approving and smiling, before looking back at Jeremy.

"That's very kind of you to do that for your grandmother, don't you think Grace?"

I nodded not looking at either of them. My father not noticing my discomfort joined in the conversation.

"Those gardens are quite big aren't they?"

"They are sir, mine is a jungle at the moment, I've been meaning to get around to sorting it out but I am not green fingered and now with Florrie being poorly it will be awhile."

"Would you mind Jeremy if I popped around to see the garden?"

"Oh no, I wasn't insinuating sir."

"Call me John and I would be only too happy to help."

I looked at them in turn shaking my head in bewilderment. What the hell was going on here?

Buster as if sensing my predicament chose that moment to stand upright shaking the table alarmingly. My mother leant forward trying to stop her precious china from hitting the floor whilst my dad roared with laughter encouraging him further. I sat as if in slow motion as I watched Jeremy jump to his feet his voice authoritive in calling Buster to heel. The dog heedless of him continued his sprint round the kitchen before leaping on my dad almost knocking him of his chair, licking him furiously.

"John honestly" I heard my mother cry out as Jeremy tried frantically to pull Buster of him. The next few minutes were sheer mayhem as my mother tirelessly adamant about the table contents narrowly avoided the animal as he continued his hundred-lap race round the kitchen. My dad normally so quiet and heedful of my mother encouraged him further whilst Jeremy tried desperately to pacify my mother who having a hand to her heart flicked the air with her other hand as if for air. Meanwhile through all of this I watched silently detached. I couldn't believe what my eyes were seeing. Was I dreaming or was I having a mental breakdown. The scenario unfolding in front of me whirled around me like I was on a carousel looking in. If it weren't for the fact that I knew all the characters before me I wouldn't have believed it as my father roared with laughter.

What seemed an age but was only minutes later, I watched silently as my mother unable to deal with the hapless situation going on around her a moment longer, threw down the tea towel she had been holding and without further ado or consideration for anyone else in the room shouted out loudly, "Stop" at the top of her lungs.

Two things happened in very quick succession. All of us jumped but no one more than Buster who skidding to a halt upon the kitchen tiles looked frantically around for Jeremy before rapidly coming to heel by his side. The room was deathly quiet, each of us looking at my mother in awe. Jeremy stared at me cringing, mouthing sorry whilst I nodding my head looked stupidly first at my father then at my mother who giving all of us a fixed glare including the dog, stood up straightening her apron as she ran a hand gently over her hair and proceeded with filling the sink with hot water. As her back was turned to us we slowly looked at each other again, neither one of us daring to break the sudden silence that fell upon the room. Jeremy now having no more trouble with Buster who hanging his head flopped down on the floor spreading his legs wide resembling a multi coloured heap closed his eyes as he drifted to sleep. Jeremy unsure of what to do or say looked at my father and me. We in turn looked at each other shrugging our shoulders neither of us knowing what to do or say next.

"Well, one of you could pick up the tea towel and make yourselves useful" my mother's words rang out startling us. Standing up immediately I looked at the men who remaining where they were stared back at me blankly. Giving them both a withering look telling them to stay where they were, they nodded sheepishly much to my disgust.

"Well Grace" my mother said quietly her eyes fixed on the sink below, "Your new friends have definitely made an impression on us today."

I nodded bleakly looking back scowling at them, then at Buster who sensing he was being spoken about lifted a paw to cover his eyes.

"Mum about that I'm really sorry..."

She paused washing the plate she was holding to look at me, her next words astonishing me,

"Why are you apologising Grace, I rather enjoyed parts of it."

I had only just hung my coat up in the hall cupboard an hour later after waving goodbye to my parents with the promise of bringing both Jeremy and Buster again, when Dylan spying me from the lounge walked up to me blocking my way. His face was set in a serious uncompromising expression and as I gazed at him noticing his foul petulant mood. I realised with grim satisfaction that I didn't care. In fact I was glad he was in a bad place because after my discovery earlier that day when I had met with Zara I felt like hanging and quartering him very slowly.

"Where were you today Grace?" He demanded

"What's it to you, you're not my keeper," my voice just as churlish as his.

He grabbed my arm as I tried to push past him, forcing me to turn around and face him,

"What's your problem Dylan? Let go of me"

"Grace?" his eyes were filled with emotion.

Sighing deeply I replied, "What? "My voice purposely bland.

"I took this time off with you so I could be with you, and yet all you have managed to do is go out all the time and avoid being here with me."

"Look Dylan I don't know what's going on in that mind of yours and neither do I care. You are the one that decided to move back and to take time off. What I do with my time is my business not yours, so kindly let go of my arm so I can eat something."

"Does this mean your home for today?" His voice lighter and more hopeful.

Ignoring him I pulled my arm away and walked into the lounge, noticing that the telly wasn't on and neither was the stereo. He had obviously been laying in wait for me and the thought didn't thrill me like it would have done months before.

"I don't have time for this Dylan so just leave me alone and get on with your own evening."

I could hear him behind me as I walked into the kitchen. Opening the freezer door I pulled out the top drawer looking for a quick ready meal to eat instead of the omelette I had been planning to cook for myself. His aura was so charged I could feel the sparks enveloping me.

"What now?" I knew my voice sounded tense and I also realised I was being rude, but when he hounded me like he was doing now the only effect it had on me, was extreme irritation.

"I thought we could spend a night in with some wine and a movie."

Closing the drawer I took out a fork as I ripped off the packaging of sweet and sour chicken. Stabbing the bag of frozen meat and sauce trying desperately not to imagine Dylan's face being the bag I was holding I continued to ignore him, as I opened a cupboard taking out a dinner plate. Placing the sachet onto it I pushed past him and put it into the microwave pressing the stated number of minutes before flicking it on. Then I turned round to face him hoping he would notice the look of disbelief clearly displayed on my face.

"There's nothing stopping you watching it Dylan is there?"

He stepped closer to me his mouth set in a firm grim line.

"That's not what I meant and you know it."

"I realised what you meant Dylan. I have spent time today eating more than my fair share of humble pie thanks to you. My mother was extremely hurt and put out by your behaviour or have you forgotten that. So with that in mind you are the last person I want to spend time with now, or ever."

"Grace I have already apologised for that, I even offered to come with you to make things right."

Placing my hands on my hips I faced him squarely, "Wow that's big of you Dylan, but...no as you can imagine you are the last individual my mother wants to see."

Leaning against the worktop his arms folded he stared long and hard at me as I stared unflinchingly back at him.

"You have something else to say," my tone was mocking.

"What's happened today Grace, you've come home in a right bitchy mood"

"You Dylan have put me in a bitchy mood, so do me a favour and just leave me the hell alone."

Saved by the bell as the microwave pinged I walked past him careful our bodies didn't touch as I wrenched open the door placing the bag of rice inside before drumming out the minutes with my forefinger. I had thought long and hard when I had left Zara in how to play this out. So many emotions and information were being tossed around in my head I knew any decision I made now would be irrational and foolish before I fully thought it through. So I had decided to absorb what I had learned and act accordingly after that. But Dylan had other ideas being totally unaware of my afternoon rendezvous with his lover continued in his sickening way trying to brow beat me down till I acquiesced to whatever he had planned.

"If I've seemed a little heavy Grace it's because we don't seem to be making much headway, I realise you may need more time..."

"I'm sorry" I interrupted "We seem to be at cross purposes here. I moved back, you followed, if you think last nights sex is going to change the outcome of our situation you are sorely mistaken."

"You're obviously not in the right frame of mind to discuss this, so until you have calmed down I'll leave you alone," his tone sulky and final.

"By the way" he paused "have you seen my mobile, I can't find it anywhere"

"Nope" I kept my back turned from him. Mum had given it back to me and it was still lying in my coat pocket waiting to be slid down the side of the sofa cushion.

"No matter just as well I have two."

I looked at his retreating back with a mixture of disbelief and strong resistant urges to physically slap him. I wasn't normally in constant bitch mode but since returning with him in tow I had changed from a normal human being to one with constant conflicting emotions and behaviour. I felt sickened to my core recalling what he had done to me. The man was crazy and irrational his recent declaration of starting again, to

132

start a family together was abhorrent to me after what I had discovered that afternoon. I shook my head disgustedly thinking how sad, sick and selfish he had become. I wondered how I had let myself become so consumed and used by someone like him. Why had I never seen all these bad traits earlier? Love is blind, I could hear my mother say, but how had I not noticed the dominance and self-control he always had to have regardless of anyone else's feelings. I refused to believe he had been that way in the beginning for no matter how trusting and blind I might have been I would have seen that surely? The microwave pinged wakening me from my reverie. I took out the scalding plate cursing silently to myself as my fingers dropped the hot plate onto the counter. Carefully snipping of the corners I arranged my food now no longer hungry.

Managing to finish my meal I put the plate in the sink as my thoughts drifted back to Jeremy. I looked at my watch he would be seeing Florrie soon in the hospital. He had given me his home number almost shyly when he had given me a lift to the end of my road. I had pointed out my house to him but sensing my anxiety he had just smiled and said that he would be in touch. I pulled out my mobile smiling as I flicked hastily through the contacts. Then I paused. What the hell was I doing? My life was so fragmented and here I was complicating it even further with a wonderful guy I didn't even really know.

After Zara had shown me the nursery where I had collapsed into the rocking chair she had told me how Dylan had purchased the apartment for them both to live in. They had lived there for months unbeknownst to me and as I looked around me as I silently listened to her a lot of realisations hit me all at once. That now explained his absences and dark moods. I shook my head as to how naive I had been. She continued unaware of my musings. He hadn't been happy about the pregnancy at first when she had revealed it to him. In fact similar to my own experience when he had discovered I was pregnant, he had yelled and threatened to leave her and it was then it came to me why I had been the one he discarded. It was the timing. Zara had fallen pregnant and unlike me could not be coerced into getting rid of the baby. Therefore leaving him no option but to deliver his cold announcement to me that we were over. Now knowing the reasons it allayed a lot of unanswered questions, but what I couldn't understand were his reasons for his actions towards me now. I reluctantly thought about him now wondering what ledge he was clinging too, when the world of his own creation seemed to be coming away at the seams. What had he been thinking when he had run from me to her and then back to me. It had become so clear to me and though I didn't support his actions or deceit I couldn't help but think that he deserved every miserable minute of his comeuppance. Zara was obviously mentally stronger than I and that is what Dylan needed in a relationship no matter how hard he tried to convince himself otherwise. All I was to him now was a diversion, another direction he could run too, all the while keeping his little world safely intact.

He closed the front door quietly behind him when he returned. I had gone to bed by then. I had taken a pad and pen busy writing out a list of things I had to do the next day. My holiday was disappearing fast and though I had over a week left I didn't have much time to do what needed to be done.

The conversation with Zara revealed that during my marriage Dylan had been making some serious money. Our home bought before his success though not outstanding was very much a beautiful and above average home. The flat he had bought on the other hand made our home look paltry and though I wasn't quite ready to believe he had bought it outright I did intend to find out. His plan was becoming clear and I could kick myself for having been so trusting towards him. The bastard was trying to rip me off. Our savings though not stupendous were acceptable and if I hadn't had known about him and Zara I would have happily accepted the paltry thousands offered to me from the sale of the house. It made me wonder in what light Dylan actually saw me. Zara was now the crowning princess living in the castle whilst I had always been happy with the small handouts he had so lovingly dished out to little grateful old me. But, as I pondered more on it I realised one thing about me had definitely changed. I wasn't going to take this lying down, not anymore. His treatment and betrayal towards me no longer seemed so important, it was Zara and the baby growing inside her. Perhaps because I had nearly been that person I empathised with her predicament but couldn't help but feel that both had gotten what they justly deserved and that, was each other.

It was apparent Dylan was having second thoughts and he had been an A plus bastard using each of us in turn, but remembering his reaction to me when he had discovered I had come off the pill was now understandable and made me realise why he was behaving like he was. It must feel to him like his whole world was falling in on him and though I now felt no pity for him I did for Zara. I was lucky I reminded myself that I had escaped, whereas she had not. She knew what he was like and she would have to be the one to live with that everyday, wondering whether he would be hers for keeps. I thought of her now lonely and pregnant, yet so much in love with him she was willing to accept him for all his shortfalls of which I realised were many. I also knew now with certainty, in her shoes I would not have felt so fortunate and for that I thanked my lucky stars. I had every intention the following day to inform my solicitor of Dylan's deceit. It wasn't for the money that I was doing it. It was to make him hate me. I knew unless I did something drastic he would never let go, his coming back and those nights we shared proved that. I couldn't make him stay forever with Zara but I sure as hell could take away his other options, hoping that would suffice to make him commit to her. I put away the pad and turned off the light. He had gone to bed nearly an hour before and though he had not paused at my bedroom door I knew that tomorrow he would be demanding answers.

Chapter 10

It was nearly nine when I woke the next morning. Cursing myself for sleeping in so long again I shot out of bed and into the shower. As I entered the kitchen twenty minutes later clad now in my familiar jeans and shirt, my hair still wet was tied into a bun at the nape of my neck. There was no sign of Dylan and I wondered whether he was still sleeping. Making a quick cup of coffee I pondered my plan from the night before. I hoped Zara would ring me if she heard from him, which if everything went according to plan would be later today. I knew Dylan once confronted with the truth would try everything in his power to convince me to change my mind in proceeding any further. I was so deep in thought that when he entered the kitchen clad only in a towel tucked tightly round his waist he made me jump.

"Hi kitten"

I turned away from him rinsing my mug out. He stood in the doorway his eyes watching me closely as I continued to look away.

"Did you sleep well last night?" his voice, low and husky.

I shrugged my shoulders answering him without bothering to turn around.

"I did."

I could smell the strong scent of his aftershave as he watched me silently lounging against the door frame, which seemed to be his latest thing.

"How's your mood today?"

I bit my lip refusing to let him see he was irking me. I had devised a plan the day before and I was determined to carry it through. So forcing a smile on my lips I looked at him briefly answering as lightly as I was able,

"Fine, and you?"

He seemed pleased as he continued to watch me silently as I frittered around the kitchen unnecessarily doing things to keep my hands busy.

"Will you have any free time today?"

I paused before turning round to face him asking innocently, "Why?"

He smirked his lopsided grin before his eyes met mine.

"We need to discuss the house etc."

Feeling relieved at his remark I nodded before replying that I could be available later on that afternoon.

"Are you going out this morning again?" he seemed suddenly fractious.

"I am going out with my dad this morning." Ok a little white lie.

I could see he wasn't happy with my reply but as lies went it was a good one.

"Oh...well what time do you think you will be back?"

I shrugged my shoulders purposely being vague, as I didn't know how long my solicitor's appointment would last.

"I couldn't tell you as long as it takes I suppose."

He took my noncommittal response with a deep sigh and shrug of his shoulders.

"Fine."

He walked away from me his bare back glistening with water droplets from his recent shower. Whatever he had been meaning to say was obviously important enough for him to have come down so hastily when he had heard me downstairs. My eyes watched him walk away as I chewed my bottom lip determined to stay one step ahead of him.

I parked my car in the multi storey in town for two reasons. Firstly and most important it would remain hidden if Dylan had any designs on going into town himself, and two, I had decided to take some time out for retail therapy figuring I deserved a little treat. I was hesitant about going to the solicitor so quickly after my discussion with Zara. But after the initial shock she had been more than forthcoming in supplying me with concrete evidence to prove Dylan was trying to diddle me out of money. I wondered at her intentions for doing this, but recalling her harsh words earlier, she had for a while appeared embarrassed and remorseful, when she had seen my reaction to her devastating news, contradicting Dylan's version of events.

"Grace, I know we have been friends for such a long time and I know after all this our friendship is over, but regardless of Dylan I owe you an explanation and my help if you need it."

"And why would you do that" I had replied not trusting her words.

She looked down at her hands for a moment before taking a deep breath and looking me in the eyes said,

"I know how I would feel if the shoe had been on the other foot."

I didn't reply to that taking the option instead to get up and walk away from her towards the large paned window. My sight was blank as I stared out not focusing on anything in particular. I needed time to think, to sort things through but being here with her did not allow me that courtesy. So I replied coolly loud enough for her to hear,

"Why are you telling me now?"

She remained silent for a while before answering. I had turned to look at her wondering whether she had heard me. Her eyes met mine before she hastily looked away.

"Does he want to come back to you?"

"Yes" I answered matter of factly, not caring as I saw her cringe at my words.

She hung her head and I tried to ignore her sudden sobbing, but as I continued to watch her, I remembered how I had felt months before.

"Don't worry Zara, he may want me but I definitely don't want him."

She looked at me then her tears running down her face streaking her makeup.

"Why" was all she could mumble, wiping her face with her hands.

I remained staring at her for a long moment wondering what I could say. A part of me wanted to yell at her for betraying me for betraying our longstanding friendship, but as I stood watching her I realised none of it mattered anymore. Zara like myself had just been a pawn, the real perpetrator in this being Dylan. He was the one that should suffer for not caring how he trampled over the people closest to him.

"Zara are you sure you want to be with Dylan?" as soon as I uttered the words her head snapped up and looked at me with distrust. Realising she had misunderstood my words I shook my head.

"No, I don't mean it like that. I meant everything I said about him, but how can you be with him when you know what he has done, what he's still doing?"

"You mean him running back to the house he shares with you?"

I nodded not fully comprehending the even tone of her voice.

"I told you we were having some bad times. Being pregnant doesn't help," she paused as her hand caressed her stomach, "But I haven't been the easiest person to live with of late. My hormones are all over the place. One moment I'm happy, the next I'm crying."

I looked at her appalled realising what she was saying.

"And you're blaming that for the reason he left you?" I muttered shocked.

She nodded "I understand Dylan. He has needs; he doesn't handle my tantrums and mood swings. He works hard Grace and I can understand that when he comes home the last thing he wants is a hormonal woman screaming at him one minute and crying the next."

I found myself walking towards her hoping my face didn't show the abhorrence I was feeling at her words. She looked at me as I sat down beside her, her face adamant in her belief.

"Zara he made you pregnant. Just because his home life isn't perfect doesn't mean it's your fault. Dylan has to understand, has to accommodate your feelings in all of this. If he doesn't what will happen when the baby comes along?"

She stood up then her head high, "Grace you needn't concern yourself with that. He's mine, I love him and we're suited whereas you two never were."

I remained seated refusing to acknowledge the painful words she tossed my way.

"That's not fair you know nothing of our life together."

"You don't think he told me. Grace why do you think he left you. He left you because in his words you were boring. Everything about your life was constant and habitual."

I couldn't help myself. I stood up facing her head on, my face stern and unrelenting.

"And what do you think normal married life is Zara. It's not a bed of roses as you have recently found out. You are a fool to stand there blaming yourself, blaming me when you know deep down he is the one with issues."

She turned away from me her back rigid as she walked towards a glossy white cupboard by the fireplace.

"I didn't agree for you to come here Grace to argue and dissect Dylan."

"Then why did you?"

She closed the cupboard door holding papers tightly in her hand.

"I realise Dylan still has a soft spot for you Grace. You can't be married for over five years and not feel anything towards the other person afterwards. But..." she hesitated her eyes clear and coldly focused on mine, "I want you to send him home to me where he belongs. It was too easy for him to stay with you after our row, but he won't even talk to me now and I need him here with me. Our baby needs him. Why did you let him come back?"

"What makes you think I did?"

"You must have invited him back otherwise he would be here with me. If you hadn't pulled that stunt of moving back he would be here now, not telling me he needs space to think, to re-evaluate."

I stood for a long moment thinking about what she had just said. The girl was blinkered just like I had been all that time ago.

"He told me you had finished," my voice was low.

"No" she cried out grabbing the back of the sofa for support. I rushed towards her but she shrugged me off throwing the pile of papers at me.

"That Grace should satisfy you. You don't need him for his money anymore."

I looked down at the paperwork strewn at my feet.

"You're only after him for what he can give you; he always said that about you. That paperwork shows money that Dylan had to hide from you in case your got your hands on it and spent it doing up that stupid house you love so much. I would rather you take that, then take him."

I looked at her in amazement not believing what I was hearing.

"Zara none of what Dylan said was true. You must know yourself with this place how everything in it is what Dylan wants without anyone else's consideration or choice. I was never like that my god you must believe me, you know me, you've known me since we were small. How can you say these things to me and believe it?"

"Dylan is not a liar."

I looked at her for a long moment before picking up the papers putting them into the inside pocket of my coat.

"I feel sorry for you Zara. But you're right in one respect. He does belong to you. You're so well suited."

She remained silent her eyes hateful as she watched me walk towards the door. My heart was hammering, my eyes welling up from tears at the harsh words she had thrown at me believing every rotten thing she had said.

Now here I was fidgeting from nerves as I sat in the small stuffy waiting room with the paperwork poking out of my bag. Regardless of the interesting reading it made, it had shocked me to discover just how much money Dylan had hidden away during our marriage. Even now as I looked down at the bag lying at my feet, I wondered just how far I was prepared to go. It left me now with many options one of which was that I could now leave where I worked therefore cutting another tie with Dylan. As much as I had loved my job it now like my divorce didn't matter anymore. I had come a long way in a few weeks and it would still be awhile before I was able to say I was fully healed, but I was getting there and getting there fast.

"Mrs Hunt, the solicitor will see you now." My head still humming with thoughts of the day before, I smiled sadly as I was welcomed into the office the door closing silently behind me.

When I returned home Dylan's car was parked in front of the house. He hadn't gone out and as I picked up my shopping bags from my shopping spree I cringed inwardly as seeing me walk down the path laden with bags he opened the front door with a smile.

"Well you've been busy where exactly did you and your father go?"

"He didn't need me after all so I decided to go into town instead."

He said nothing as he followed me into the lounge, his eyes watching me as I left the bags to one side of the dining table.

"Fancy a glass of white?"

I looked at him then before nodding my head as I took off my coat. He was back so quickly he took me by surprise. I took the wine glass off him noticing as I tasted, that it was a chardonnay. It brought memories reeling back to me of the evening at the wine bar when he had called it quits on our marriage. I sat down on the armchair forcing him to choose the sofa. I looked out through the window at the sunshine hopelessly trying to break through the clouds. My meeting had been successful and although I didn't as urged by my solicitor go for the full whack I had opted for what I wanted. So as I looked at him now I wondered how to play out the news I had to tell him. He smiled back warmly at me mistaking my glare for something else. I ignored him choosing to look away.

"I've missed you."

I looked back at him sighing quietly that he was still on the same old track. How many ways could I show him that I wasn't interested in playing his game, but regardless of my lack of interest or verbal commitment he just hammered on regardless. I felt, as I looked back at him looking at me that I despised him. His looks, which I had always associated with a Chippendale male stripper, he was that handsome and put together meant nothing to me anymore. In fact it was only as I was staring at him did I notice the flaw of his previously thought perfect face. His nose though defined was a little too big and I frowned wondering how I had never noticed that before. He smiled back at me his lips opening revealing his beautiful aligned white teeth. Granted they were good I thought reluctantly as I continued to stare.

"See anything you like?" he asked casually as he sipped his wine.

"Sorry?" my reaction was immediate therefore not picking up his innuendo.

He frowned shaking his head looking put out for a moment as he sipped his wine again.

"It doesn't matter Grace."

Sitting up I put my wine glass down on the nearby table, not caring that I had missed the coaster. His eyes watched me and I had to bite my tongue from stopping the laughter that threatened to erupt at his cold stare at my misdemeanour.

"You wanted to talk to me...about the house" I reminded him smiling falsely.

"Ah yes I'm glad you mentioned that. Being as this house is going through, how do you fancy buying a bigger one?"

I looked at him in total shock. He continued pleased at my stunned silence and reaction.

"Well being as we were discussing babies I thought a bigger house was called for. Then we could start trying straight away."

I couldn't reply because I couldn't breathe. I looked at him incredulously thinking I had misheard.

"Did you say what I think you just said?" I muttered weakly my head still disbelieving.

"Yes. Come on Grace we discussed this the other night and well I've managed to choose a few online and wondered whether you would be interested in having a look?"

"Dylan, are you stupid, or are you just doing a very good impression of it?"

He looked askance at me, words escaping him as he looked at me in horror.

"Grace, why for god's sake would you say that?"

"You know for days now I have been feeling like I have been shifting between two universes and the only reason I mention it is because I am feeling it again right now."

He put his glass down leaning forward looking at me intently,

"Grace are you alright. What the hell are you talking about?"

"I often wonder that myself" I muttered "Dylan when did I ever lead you to believe we were back together again?"

He frowned looking upwards towards the ceiling before he faced me again, "Well we haven't ardently discussed it because well damn it you're never here, but I've made my intentions quite plain to you Grace."

I rubbed my forehead with my hand wishing I could be anywhere else than here.

"Seriously Dylan I can't do this now, you're doing my head in."

I stood up to go but he forestalled me with his hand.

"Grace what the hell has gotten into you lately?"

"Well it definitely won't be you" I replied coldly narrowing my eyes at him.

"That could be remedied straightaway," he cooed at me as his eyes once more headed upwards.

"The other night Grace you were mind blowing, I can never forget that."

He stood up putting both his hands on my forearms forcing me to look at him.

"I love you Grace, how many times do I have to say it before you believe me?"

I remained silent as I looked at him itching to smack him, but instead I smiled.

"Oh Dylan I must be confused."

"Why" he muttered not understanding.

"Have you a twin, a clone, I don't know about?"

"Grace what the hell are you talking about?"

"I'll tell you shall I" I replied before releasing myself from his grasp.

"I was just wondering how you can be in two places at the same time?"

"Grace I think you better sit down, you're not making sense."

"It's you Dylan that's not making sense. You see I was wondering how you could be with me and Zara at the same time."

"Zara, why would you talk about her? I told you it was over."

"Did you tell her that or is she still thinking you're still taking time out to re-evaluate?"

His face paled slightly at my words, "I don't understand."

"I think you do" I replied nonchalantly "I think you know exactly what I mean. You've lied Dylan and now you have been found out. How stupid I was to pine over you for months when secretly behind my back you'd been screwing my best friend for over a year. And if that wasn't bad enough you had the stupidity to make her pregnant."

His face whitened even more, "Grace don't believe a word she says. Okay so she enticed me, lured me, and wouldn't give me a moment's peace. I made a mistake for which I will be eternally sorry. I will make this up to you."

"Dylan I always thought of you as something very special to me. You were my world and everything in it. I had put you on a pedestal; there was

143

nothing I wouldn't have done for you as I have proved when you forced me to nearly abort our baby, remember that do you?" I spat out. "And what did you do with my misguided love and loyalty. You threw it away for a piece of arse. My friend's piece of arse no less. I never want you back, you belong with Zara in fact you two are perfect together. More than we ever were."

His reaction was cool not fiery in denial, as I had expected.

"It makes no difference," he finally replied looking at me with pleading in his eyes. "I love you, it's you I want, not her."

"Then your love will remain unrequited Dylan"

"I won't give up on us Grace. Eventually you'll back down"

I could feel my body shaking at what he was saying. As I looked at him I realised Zara had known he would do this, which is why she had tried to buy me off.

"Stop it. There is nothing you can do or say that will make me change my mind. Believe me when I say let this go. If you don't, this will get sordid and dirty between us, with only the lawyers making the money. Go back to her; you have to go back to her. You have a child coming Dylan; this is not something you can run away from. What would that make you?"

He stood up hanging his head as he ran his fingers through his hair.

"It's so easy for you isn't it Grace. To stand there telling me what I should and shouldn't do. But I don't love her; she isn't for me like you are. God...I wish I could turn the clock back but I can't. Won't you reconsider Grace for me...for us?"

I wanted to storm out of the room, to get away from him, but I couldn't. All I could do was stand there looking at him like he had lost his mind.

He saw my momentary indecision and smiled. Walking over to me he placed his hands on my shoulders pulling me closer to him.

"Oh Grace if only you realised how much I love you and regret what I've done."

Chapter 11

It was raining the next day when my solicitor rang me on my mobile phone. At first still groggy from sleep I had to ask him to repeat himself. When he did, I sat bolt upright, my eyes wide open and my heart in my throat. After the previous day with Dylan's denials still reverberating in my head, I had had a restless night. He had coolly informed me that my husband's lawyer disputing all the facts I had handed over to him the day before, would be in discussion with my husband, to verify the information before proceeding any further. I looked at the wall dividing Dylan's room from mine, hoping he was still sleeping and hadn't as yet been contacted by his legal representative. Knowing the moment, he was aware of what I had done, all hell would break loose, I clamoured out of bed not bothering to shower. Grabbing the clothes nearest to me I put them on brushing my hair hurriedly before leaving the room.

I tiptoed to his door sighing gratefully when I heard him breathing peacefully. Not bothering with coffee or breakfast I grabbed my coat and bag and rushed towards the door. It was only when I had reached the safe confines of my car, did I realise I had left my mobile lying on my bed. I pondered for a moment whether to rush inside or just go, but sensing the mood he would be in when he learned of yesterday's escapade, I moaned outwardly, before grabbing my keys and getting out the car. The front door opened silently as I paused to hear for movement. Not hearing anything I left the door ajar before sprinting up the stairs. It was only with mobile in hand and reaching the bottom tread did I hear his bedroom door open. Not wasting another moment I walked hurriedly to the door when his voice stopped me.

"Grace?"

I had two choices both of which I had to decide quickly on. I could ignore him and run out or I could answer.

"Are you going out again?"

I turned slowly to see him standing at the top of the stairs clad only in his boxers looking down at me. His face was sleepy telling me he didn't know yet what had happened.

"I err...have to go out" I mumbled kicking myself for coming back in the house.

"Why?"

145

I shouldn't have paused for thought, for when his hand touched my shoulder I jumped making me stand back as I looked round horrified at him.

Immediate concern drifted over his face as he looked at me.

"Kitten, are you okay?"

I nodded quickly taking a step back from him. He noticed this with a frown as he too stepped forward his hands now resting heavily on my shoulders.

"Grace you seem jumpy this morning. Has this to do with what we discussed last night?"

If I hadn't been like a cat on a hot tin roof I would have replied back sharply in denial. After his confession the previous evening I had avoided him claiming a headache and gone to bed. So instead I just shook my head lowering it so he couldn't see my cheeks, which I felt colouring up. I knew I didn't have long to get out of the house before his own solicitor contacted him, so feigning a smile I hurriedly replied I had to go to the chemist.

"If you can wait till I get dressed I'll do it for you," he murmured running his finger down my cheek. I sighed realising he wasn't going to let me escape easily.

"Ok" I mumbled letting him lead me into the lounge.

"I won't be a moment, so stay where you are," his words were light but I sensed the steel behind them. I nodded dumbly in response lowering my head again rubbing my temples with my fingers.

When I heard his bedroom door close I shot out of the house leaving the front door ajar behind me. As I drove away I looked into my mirror seeing him standing there in the centre of the road, half dressed with hands on his hips and a scowl on his face. I laughed nervously to myself. Enjoy it while you can I thought because in an hour or less he would be wishing he had kept me prisoner.

I drove aimlessly around for a while my eyes constantly straying to my mobile lying on the passenger seat. I hadn't taken into account the day before what I would do when Dylan found out what Zara and I had done behind his back. It served him right I constantly repeated to myself, but it didn't make me feel any better knowing what was ahead of me when he discovered I had hit him where it hurt. His wallet. It wasn't until I had subconsciously stopped did I look around confused not recognising the street I had parked in. It was only when I saw Jeremy's car parked in front of me did I stifle a gasp wondering why I had driven here. My hands clenched the steering wheel as I leant down to stare at the house he had

CHASING RAINBOWS

taken me to the day before. I chewed my lip trying to figure out in my mind what to do next. I was in tatters I realised acting so irrationally as I picked up my mobile wondering what to do. It was then I thought of Zara. Knowing I wouldn't be the only one today to suffer Dylan's wrath, I pondered whether to contact her and warn her. I was musing on this when a light tap on the window had me crying out dropping my mobile, which landed with a thud on the floor.

Jeremy's face was staring at me with concern. I smiled apprehensively at him chewing my lip kicking myself for not driving on. I didn't want him to think I was stalking him. Knowing I just couldn't sit here smiling back at him like a loon I reluctantly opened my door and got out. He stood up to face me across the roof of the car as our eyes met.

"Hi Grace this is a surprise."

The statement hung in the air between us and I cringed inwardly of what he must be thinking of me right now.

"I'm sorry," I muttered before rapidly hanging my head, shocked at the tears spilling from my eyes. He was by my side in an instant his hand lying gently on my shaking shoulder.

"Grace what's the matter?"

I shook my head from side to side trying to stem my tears but to no avail.

"I shouldn't have come here, I don't know why I came...I think I should go."

His hand fell away from my shoulder as I turned from him to get back into the car. Before I could open the door he was in front of me both of his hands resting on mine forestalling me.

"Grace I can't let you drive off in this state. Come inside and have a coffee till you calm down."

I let myself be led, grateful when he took the keys from me locking the car. I stumbled along beside him too embarrassed to stare at him as I muttered thanks.

Buster was nowhere to be seen as I stepped apprehensively inside. Seeing me look warily around Jeremy smiled, "He's outside in the back garden with your dad."

My mouth dropped open my tears easing as I groaned.

"Oh no if my dad see's me like this..."

"Don't worry Grace I had just come in to make coffee."

"So how did you see me?"

He paused as he flicked on the kettle confusion briefly on his face,

147

"I don't know. I just felt like going outside...hmmm" he muttered pausing to look at me baffled.

We stood there for a moment looking at each other. His eyes soft and gentle caressed my face his hand wiping away a stray tear that had escaped.

"Would you like a coffee?" he asked softly smiling down at me

I nodded unable to speak. He took my coat from my shoulders and laid it on the table. His hands cool and comforting propelled me to a chair making me sit down.

"I bet you haven't eaten anything either," he asked looking at me.

"Didn't have time," I muttered feeling foolish looking away.

His eyes had been questioning as he dropped two slices of bread into the toaster I looked back at him.

"I'm sorry."

"Why. You don't have to apologise Grace. You're obviously upset I'm glad you thought to come here."

Knowing my intentions weren't exactly as he thought I just smiled back weakly not wanting to shatter his illusion of me.

"I'm not usually like this, but living with Dylan, it's wearing..." my voice faded realising what I had said.

Jeremy remained quiet for a moment as he placed the steaming mug of coffee in front of me,

"Your dad has been telling me a little of your situation."

My head snapped up, "He has" I mumbled shocked.

"He worries about you Grace, he loves you very much."

I nodded dumbly as my eyes strayed to the window overlooking the jungle beyond.

"You surprise me, he doesn't normally talk to people about me, he's quite a private man."

"I can understand that. I was quite shocked to see him at my door this morning, he's pretty keen on us combating that wilderness commonly known as my back garden."

His words stunned me for I was pretty shocked too. Placing the plate down in front of me he smiled at me murmuring quietly,

"Eat whilst I try and find your dad and Buster out back."

I watched him leave glad for the few moments alone. Life was definitely throwing me some curve balls at the moment and I wondered how in less than the blink of an eye my father and Jeremy had formed such a bond. My dad when he entered the kitchen smiled widely when he saw

148

me as brushing his cap full of grass against his trouser leg hurried over to me kissing me loudly on the top of my head.

"Snicket well this is a lovely surprise."

"Likewise" I managed to utter my mouth full of toast.

"Well after Jeremy telling me about his garden and with your mother in one of her spring cleaning moods, I thought I'd come along and see if I could help."

"I'm glad you're here dad."

He sensed immediately the break in my voice. Looking at Jeremy and then back at me he sat down on the stool beside me his arm resting casually along my shoulders.

"What's happened snicket?"

I didn't mean to tell him or want to but before I realised everything came tumbling out, as the tears once more cascaded down my face.

"Baby girl it will be all right don't you worry about that," my father uttered soothingly as I let my head rest against him as he stroked my hair.

"I don't think it will dad, Dylan will go mad."

My father harrumphed as he continued to cuddle me. His eyes met Jeremy's who also grimaced.

"You should come home today with me. I'll go and get your clothes Grace; you don't have to put up with the likes of him anymore."

"No" I cried out grabbing his hand.

"Dad don't, this is my doing I have to sort it out."

"Your mother may have brought you up most of the time Grace, but I'm your dad and there are times when dad's come in useful."

"No dad seriously, I don't want to involve you and I don't want mum knowing about this yet, promise me."

He looked doubtfully at me for a moment before resignedly nodding.

"If that's how you want to play it, but Gracie what are you going to do?"

I shrugged my shoulders biting into my toast. Jeremy sitting opposite watched both of us closely.

"Well for a start you can spend the day with us and then if you like come with me this evening to see Florrie."

"Sounds like a plan" my father decided smiling at me as I continued to nibble at my toast. I looked at Jeremy his smile was warm as his eyes glinted amusedly at me.

"You'll be ok Grace trust me."

His hand large and warm covered mine. I stared down at it then back up at his face.

"Ok" I mumbled smiling back.

When Buster two hours later ran off with the spare spade trying to bury it, my father amused ran after him mockingly shaking his fist. Watching through the kitchen window both Jeremy and my father had hacked away at the waist high grass till is was easily visible to see them now. I smiled as I watched them pondering what a lovely scene it made. During my years with Dylan scenes like this had never been created, with him always feigning work or other things more important for both of us to do. I had accepted it then but as I looked out now through the window watching them bemusedly, I realised what I had been missing. I put my hand into my jean pocket for my mobile to take a picture of them realising it wasn't there. I frowned trying desperately to think of where I had left it when suddenly I remembered. Looking back once more I walked away with a smile grabbing my keys off the table. It was sunny outside even though the early November weather was freezing. I shivered hugging myself wishing I had put my coat on. Pressing the remote I opened the door leaning in to retrieve my mobile. The light was flashing manically at me telling me I had missed calls. I frowned for a moment wondering whether to ignore them. I walked back into the house closing the door behind me. I was still frowning when I entered the kitchen not noticing Jeremy standing at the sink filling the kettle.

"Oh" I mumbled, "I can do that, sorry I was just outside fetching my mobile, I had forgotten it earlier"

"Grace relax and stop apologising ok."

His smile was easy and genuine and I felt the warmth emanating from him fill my insides making me glow. I looked down at the mobile still in my hand before laying it on the table continuing to stare at it. I felt suddenly so lonely and nervous, I didn't notice Jeremy till he was standing beside me.

"In two minds eh," he whispered smiling down at me as I looked up at him. I nodded silently my mouth set in a grim line before my eyes strayed back to the phone.

"You can always just ignore it Grace"

I looked up at him before replying," I know, I just wish he had never made me resort to it."

"Dylan. Would he ever hurt you Grace?"

"No not physically it's all mental with him."

"Look I know you don't know me but I don't like the thought of what he's doing to you. If you don't want to go home tonight and you don't want to go to your parent's then you can always stay here Grace. It's safe here you have nothing to fear from me."

Time stood still for me as I stared at him. This man who I had known for just days was staring back at me with genuine concern and sincerity in his eyes. He smiled at me as I smiled back both of our eyes locked in each other's.

"Thank you for the offer," I whispered lowering my head.

Dad left a few hours later his smile lingering on mine as he waved Jeremy goodbye.

"Snicket, will you be alright?"

I nodded quickly ashamed to have him worrying about me.

"Yes dad, don't worry. I'm going with Jeremy tonight to see his grandmother."

"And after that?" my dad asked softly.

I shrugged my shoulders not sure what to say. "I don't know Jeremy offered for me to stay here but...I don't know dad."

"He's a good sort Grace, kind of heart and spirit. Just do what you have to do, and snicket..."

I looked up at him with loving eyes.

"Be careful," his eyes lingered on mine for a moment before tenderly rubbing my chin with his thumb smiling as he blew me a kiss and left. I stood at the door a long time after he had gone wondering how I got so lucky to have the parents and the people I had around me. Buster seeing me for the first time raced through the kitchen signalling me he was on his way. Shutting the door quickly I braced myself against it as he leapt up washing my face avidly with his tongue.

"Oh..." I muttered my eyes still shut, "I don't think I will ever get used to this"

The hospital car park was quite busy when we arrived a couple of hours later. Looking aimlessly around for a space it was with relief when eventually we managed to find one close to the entrance. Picking up the bouquet of flowers I had insisted on buying, Jeremy just smiled as he took my hand and we walked slowly towards the entrance. I felt very conspicuous as we entered the hospital knowing to anyone else bothering to look at us we looked like a happy couple. It wasn't that I was against the image we presented but purely because it wasn't true. I looked at him shyly as we walked up the corridor following the line to the Geriatric ward.

"Grace are you ok, you're very quiet."

I smiled briefly more so at his tightened grasp than at his words. I was more than fine I was ecstatic. But I still had to pinch myself to make sure it wasn't all a dream.

"I'm just a little nervous, are you sure Florrie won't mind that I came with you?"

"Are you kidding" he replied stopping and pulling me gently to the side of the long corridor out of the way of the pedestrians behind us.

"She has done nothing but talk about you ever since I mentioned meeting you in the park."

"Oh" I mumbled trying to ignore the thrill that ran through me. He looked down at me smiling as he looked into my eyes.

"You still want to see her don't you" he asked gently his eyes surveying mine.

"Of course," I uttered trying to ignore the butterflies flying full throttle inside my stomach.

"Good, that's all that matters then."

I followed him almost in a haze his steps growing slower as we neared a set of double doors wedged open for visitors.

"We're here," he smiled down at me as I nervously licked my lips, suddenly wishing I hadn't come.

"Great," I whispered as we headed onto the ward. Great I thought to myself, couldn't I have come up with something better than that? My life had gone from one end of the scale to the other in a matter of weeks, and hard as I tried, I still found myself thinking and acting like a teenager on her first date.

The ward where Florrie was, housed eight beds, four on each side facing each other. In front of us at the end of the room stood a large basin with a mirror attached above. Higher up a television was bolted to the wall its screen staring blankly at me. Each bed was filled with patients, their cubicles laden with cards and flowers. So busy was I looking around me I didn't notice we had stopped till I heard Florrie call my name.

"Grace, oh I am so glad you came."

I looked at her and smiled shyly as I stood at the end of the bed whilst Jeremy having kissed her was busy rearranging her pillows. I chewed my lip nervously as her arm raised her hand outstretched to take mine. I walked slowly around the opposite side of the bed to where he now stood smiling at me. I knew that he could sense I was nervous by the wicked gleam in his eye.

"Jerry why don't you go and get a couple of chairs."

"Ok I won't be a moment."

I must have looked horrified at his leaving because as he went to pass me he stopped and whispered gently.

"Grace?"

I nodded smiling weakly as he lightly touched my hand in comfort before leaving the ward.

"I see you and Jeremy have got to know each other rather well," Florrie said her faded blue eyes twinkling at me.

"Oh no" I hastened to add but she just waved my denial away and tapped the side of her bed for me to sit down. I complied remembering the flowers I held in my hand.

"I hope you like these Florrie."

"Why thank you Grace how lovely they are, and how sweet of you to bring them."

I didn't know he had returned till I heard him cough, as I turned round quickly he passed me a chair.

"Thank you I mumbled avoiding his gaze feeling my cheeks colouring up.

"How's Buster?" the old lady asked as he sat down looking at her, taking her hand gently in his.

"Missing you."

She smiled back, "Well the feeling is mutual, but it will be awhile, till I'm fit and able to take him for walks again."

"About that" Jeremy interceded, "He's too big and boisterous for you, gran I really don't think it's a good idea."

She cut in her voice adamant, "You're the grandson remember and I, young man, do what I can to help."

He looked at her silently for a moment his eyes narrowing reprimanding her, but she only winked at him before turning her attention back to me.

"So Grace, are you back at work yet?"

I was surprised she had remembered our previous conversation on our initial meeting.

"No, and to be honest, I'm thinking of handing my notice in."

"Oh," Florrie replied, a little surprised whilst Jeremy looked at me closer.

I began to feel uncomfortable but with a tight grin I shook my shoulders before replying.

"Well I've been doing a lot of thinking and I want to make a clean break across the board before I start my new life."

I felt his eyes intent on me as I continued looking at his grandmother.

"Have you thought about what you would like to do Grace?" He asked quietly.

I looked at him then, unable to answer. I hadn't. It had literally escaped my mouth before I had given it any serious consideration.

"No, not as yet."

Florrie resting her head back against the pillows smiled bemusedly as she watched us.

"Jeremy, would you mind fetching a vase for these beautiful flowers Grace brought me?"

"Of course" he grinned at me knowing I was dreading him leaving me alone again.

When he had disappeared, I looked back at Florrie forcing myself to smile and relax.

"So, tell me Grace, how is life treating you?"

"Well," I stumbled not knowing what to say.

"Are your troubles over now?" She enquired, not giving me time to answer her first question.

I chewed my lip before answering, trying to think what to say. I already knew Dylan had been to see his solicitor, by the blasphemous messages he had sent me throughout the day.

"It's getting there" I replied cringing at the thought of going back home later that evening.

She rested a veined wrinkled hand on mine, "Grace, it always gets worse before it gets better."

I nodded blindly as Jeremy returned with a thick square vase half filled with water.

"Shall I?" I offered standing up the bouquet of flowers resting on my arm.

"Thanks" his reply was brief, but regardless of that it still didn't stop my hands shaking when they touched his, as he placed the vase on the table at the end of Florrie's bed.

Thankful for the distraction no matter how short, I spent longer than usual arranging the assorted brightly coloured flowers.

Clasping her hands together Florrie smiled widely as I stood back, so she could admire them.

"Grace you've done me proud, how beautiful they look, don't you think Jeremy?"

He nodded bemused, his eyes never leaving mine till I lowered my head for a moment overcome with her enthusiasm.

"Gran, Grace and I are going to get a drink from the café, would you like anything?"

"No, you two go off. I'm a little tired; I'll just grab a nap whilst you're gone."

"I figured you needed a breather," he whispered to me conspiratorially as he led me back out into the corridor.

"Thanks, I'm just not used to all this" I faltered, not wanting to explain further.

"Don't worry, she's not as scary as she appears."

I laughed with him feeling the tension ease out of me as we followed the sign for the cafeteria. I noticed his hand was holding mine again and it made me smile as we walked slowly down the stairs together. The cafe was half filled with people. Some were patients clad in their bedtime garb, the others like us were visitors with only a handful of staff taking time out on their break.

"Cake and coffee ok with you" he asked ignoring me when I mentioned I had forgotten my bag. Whilst Jeremy queued up behind a few others waiting for tea, I meandered to the nearest table and sat down. I was deep in thought thinking about what was ahead of me that evening when I returned back home. The thought of coming face to face with Dylan still in full stride from this morning's news, was something I was dreading. I dug in my pocket for my mobile hesitating, wondering whether it was such a good idea I read what he had sent. It was then I heard the voice and froze. My head began to swim, my eyesight blurred as I looked stupidly down at my mobile. The voice was cool and frigidly polite as I continued to keep my head low so as not to be observed. My hands had begun to shake, whilst my stomach churned making me feel queasy. I took in a deep breath before looking sideways, my thick hair acting as a curtain. He was walking in front of Jeremy, his face firmly set as he walked brusquely to the exit. Jeremy noticing my pale face when he reached the table looked down at me with concern.

"Grace, my god what's the matter, you look like you've seen a ghost."

I couldn't move not even to acknowledge I had heard him. It was all I could I do to stop myself falling apart as he sat next to me clasping my cold hands.

"What's happened?" Jeremy asked firmly, his face worrisome.

I wanted to reply, but nothing came out. I swallowed deeply before inhaling sharply and exhaling slowly.

"I just saw Dylan."

He looked at me in puzzlement, before slowly his face registered as to whom I had been referring to.

"He was here?" he questioned looking around him.

"He was in front of you in the queue. How he never saw me." my voice trailed off as I shivered, imagining the consequences if he had.

"Grace, don't worry I'm here you'll be fine."

I looked at him then wishing I could feel as confident as Jeremy apparently did.

"You don't know him," I whispered cringing now at the tea and sponge cake he placed in front of me.

"That's true I don't, but there's nothing to worry about Grace. Is this how he makes you feel all the time?"

His question didn't register with me. I was too busy wallowing in the aftermath of Dylan's appearance. Was it because of the messages he had been busy sending to me all day, or was it because I was with Jeremy. I had come on in leaps and bounds over the last few weeks and now, I felt like I had reverted back to square one. That one thought alone, had me feeling so at odds with myself, that I bit my lip trying desperately to focus on something else other than the fear Dylan had instilled in me when I had unexpectedly seen him.

"Grace, did you hear me sweetheart?"

I looked up at him my eyes and face blank.

"Do you want to go?" he asked gently.

I nodded quickly, my appetite and happiness now gone. We stood up, my senses affecting my awareness so intensely, that I stumbled making Jeremy take my arm firmly as he guided me towards the exit. The first thing I did was check the corridor in both directions before fully stepping out. I could feel him looking at me, which in return made my embarrassment more acute. So holding my hand in his, we proceeded back to Florrie's ward.

"I don't think I can do this," I mumbled as our feet slowed.

He looked down at me for a long moment saying nothing, before raising his face to look into the ward where his grandmother lay. Already clutching my hand, he squeezed it tighter before slowly releasing it whispering,

CHASING RAINBOWS

"I won't be a moment."

I felt such an idiot as I leant against the wall of the corridor for support. The smell of disinfectant infused with other odours I couldn't put a name to, only increased my feeling of nausea as I looked pathetically down at my feet, trying to ignore the verbal humming surrounding me created by chatter from other visitors and staff. I couldn't blame him I thought, as I watched him tenderly leaning in, whispering into his grandmother's ear. He must think I was a complete and utter head case as I fully expected him to whisk me out of the ward and into the psychiatric unit near-by. But he didn't. Instead he kissed Florrie gently on the forehead, making her smile wiping away the anxiousness her face had assumed when he must have explained my sudden absence. She smiled saying something to him as I hung my head trying to appear unobtrusive.

"Grace are you ready to go?" his voice was soft and unassuming making the relief spread throughout my body in gratitude. We reached the entrance to the hospital in silence, the coldness of the air making me gasp realising I had left my coat in the car. Jeremy noticing this said nothing as he wrapped his arm around me pulling me close as we walked slowly back to the car. I felt comforted and safe and realised unashamedly, I wanted to stay exactly where I was forever.

Leaning out of the car window paying the fee at the machine situated at the exit of the car park, I leaned back in my seat wondering how I would begin to apologise.

"Grace, do you feel up to telling me what happened in there?"

I sighed deeply before looking at his darkened image as he manoeuvred the car through the traffic.

"I don't know what happened,"

I innocently replied as he looked at me briefly.

He said nothing for a long moment as I turned away to look out of the window.

"I'm taking you to your parent's Grace."

His words hurt me as I hung my head, understanding his sudden need to be rid of me. I remained silent. He was probably right and I could understand why he had said it. I had completely fallen to pieces in the cafeteria when I had seen Dylan. So instead of agreeing I lifted my head, staring straight ahead as I heard my voice reply coldly,

"Just take me home."

It took only twenty minutes before his car pulled into the kerb outside the dark exterior of my house. None of the lights were on indicating Dylan was still out. I wondered then, why had he been at the hospital? I must have frowned as I sat there deep in my own thoughts. Had something happened to Zara and the baby? But, before my mind could delve any further, Jeremy's voice broke into my musing making me reluctantly look at him with absent eyes.

"Will you be ok?" he asked.

I looked at him my eyes vacant. I could understand why he felt the need to expel me as quickly as possible from his car, but as I continued to stare I felt such a rush of disappointment that after a mild hiccup of behaviour on my part, he wanted me to leave. The thought had me feeing so lost and misunderstood, that without another word I grabbed my coat and bag from the back and hastily opened the car door.

"Grace."

I ignored him, I was angry at his shallowness. I had, since I met him felt he was a man of kindness and loyalty, but as I slammed his car door behind me and walked towards the house, I was re-evaluating my obvious misconception of him. He continued to call my name regardless of my determined doggedness to ignore him. I shuffled around in my bag hunting desperately for the keys, not wanting to continue being a sideshow for him, when I felt his hand on mine forestalling me as I tried to insert the key into the lock.

"Grace, stop! What is happening here?"

"You tell me" I replied my voice cold.

He shook his head slowly as he ran his fingers through his blonde hair glinting in the glow from the streetlight.

"What did I say or do to make you act like this?"

"Like what?"

"Like you can't wait to get away from me. Look I know you are going through a divorce but after seeing Dylan today, if something has changed, or you don't want to see me anymore then please tell me now."

I looked at him like he had grown two heads. What the hell had he digested from this evening's events?

"Why would you think that?" I cried out, "I hate Dylan."

Jeremy stepped in closer as my back turned to lean against the front door.

"Are you sure that you guys are over? Because Grace if you are, then I very much want to be in the picture. I care for you Grace, a hell of a lot."

His lips when they touched mine were gentle, his hands gently cradling my face like he was holding something precious. I felt like internally combusting with the sudden heat that begun coursing through me, making me tremble. My only reply was a moan as I leaned into him feeling him lean more into me. When we pulled apart I was glad to be leaning against the door, for I desperately needed the support to keep me upright.

Breathing heavily, he looked into my eyes,

"Grace, get inside now, before I take you home with me."

I did and as the door closed behind me, the temptation to run after him was so strong I almost opened the door when I heard his car pull away.

Chapter 12

"Where are you, you lying conniving bitch?"

I was in my bedroom packing the last of my clothes when I heard the front door slam and Dylan's raised words floating up the stairs to my room.

Shit I thought as I stuffed the remaining clothes into my bag zipped it up and shoved it quickly under the bed. I looked around hurriedly groaning as I noticed the wardrobe door wide open displaying its emptiness. I raced to it shutting it in time before my bedroom door was flung open as a dishevelled Dylan stood in the doorway. His eyes quickly found me as he paced hurriedly in my direction his face contorted with anger.

"What the fuck have you done Grace, I could kill you for this."

Without replying, I looked hurriedly towards the bathroom door hoping I could make it in time to lock myself in. My eyes had alerted him to my intentions and before I could reach it his arms grabbed me swinging me around, making him the wall I had to break through to make myself safe.

"Let me go Dylan, take your bloody hands off me."

"My bloody hands, Christ Grace do you know what you have done?"

Breathing heavily from the exertion of breaking free I stood there staring back at him.

"I don't know what the hell you are talking about." Okay I was lying, but I had to buy time to get away. I started reversing, never before had I seen him so outraged. His eyes focused solely on me, as slowly he took a few steps forward

"You lying bitch, you know exactly what you have done. You have no idea the consequences of your actions Grace, but do you know what, I am going to make it my sole responsibility to put you straight. You think, you can take everything away from me and that I was just going to let you. Well wrong," he spat out as his hands grabbed me again.

The weight of him took me off balance and I screamed as I fell onto the bed with him falling across me winding me. Without hesitation I pushed him off as he fell to the floor. Swinging my legs round to the other side of the bed I had nearly made it when he threw himself across the bed, his hands catching my shoulders pulling me back down. I screamed again as I fought to break away, but his strength mixed with adrenalin had hauled me onto the bed with him kneeling over me. His face was white from anger and exertion, his chest heaving as he sat astride me, his hands resting on his thighs. One of my arms was trapped beneath his left leg. The pain was excruciating as I struggled to free myself. Grabbing my free arm, he pinned me down to the mattress, whilst his other leg leaned more heavily onto my numbing arm. I yelled out in agony trying to buck, to get him off me, but instead it only aided him in getting closer. I could feel his breath on my face as his eyes scanned mine.

"Not so fucking clever now, are you Grace? If you think, for one minute, you are going to rob me of all I have worked for, then you can fucking think again."

"You, are the robbing bastard" I hissed turning my head away, "Did you honestly think I wouldn't find out about your secret hoard. We are married Dylan, fuck you for thinking you could rob me."

He growled as he leant in closer, "Don't remind me that we're married. I should have realised what a twisted scheming bitch you really are."

"Dylan that's the pot calling the kettle black, you are hurting me, get off my arm before I have you for fucking assault."

He stopped then, staring at me silently, before lifting his leg releasing my arm. The pins and needles that shot through me made me wince. I could almost have cried with pain as the blood coursed back through my arm. His hand shot out to grab it, but instinct had me pushing violently at his chest knocking him off balance as he fell sideways. Seizing my only opportunity to get away I sat up frustrated my feet weren't touching the ground giving me any leverage. I felt his body move to grab me and with a scream I twisted round fisting my hand. My fist connected with his groin making him yell out. Falling back, he rocked on his side cradled in the foetal position. Standing up I went to run to the door, when my toe caught on the handle of my bag hidden under the bed. I fell heavily onto the carpet groaning as the air left me. Dylan's moans had lessened but he was still incapacitated, I lunged back to grab my bag and ran for the door.

"Come back you bitch" I heard him yell as I almost threw myself down the stairs, the bag hanging over the bannister giving me a little stability as I nearly fell. Grabbing my purse from the hall table I flung open the door and ran into the street. Where had I parked my car? I couldn't remember in my hurry to get away. Delving in my purse I got my keys and pressed the fob. My car alerted me four cars up and I ran to it, like my life depended on it, looking over my shoulder as I heard him scream out my name. I jumped into the car flinging my bag onto the passenger seat before starting the engine. The gap was small as I grabbed the wheel and turned it cursing. I had to reverse so as not to hit the parked car in front. As I slowly edged backwards I saw him in the mirror running up the street to where I was.

Shit I cried out as I put the car into first gear, hoping I could manoeuvre the car out before he caught up with me. But I didn't. He stood in front of my car his hands on the bonnet stopping me from leaving. At this moment I was sorely tempted just to accelerate and to hell with him, but as calmness slowly settled within me I knew I couldn't do it. No matter how angry or scared I was right now I couldn't make the situation worse. So instead, I put my handbrake on and locked all the doors before I slowly looked at him through the misty windscreen. He was breathing heavily but it still didn't annihilate the angry expression on his face. When he was sure I wasn't going anywhere he held his hands up.

"Grace, don't run I need to talk to you. Forget what happened back there, I don't know what came over me. Will you please come back inside?"

I clasped my hands together on my lap to stop them shaking not sure what to do next. Sensing my uncertainty, he spoke again.

"Please Grace."

I started the car which had stalled when he had waylaid me, his eyes looked into mine intensely as he ran his fingers through his tousled hair.

"Grace?"

"Get away from my car Dylan" I shouted, still unsure of my next move.

"Only, if you promise to come inside and sort this out."

My lips thinned at him as I shook my head in disbelief. Even now he still couldn't bow down. Why did he always have to be this way? Letting out a long sigh, I hung my head in defeat. One of two consequences would arise out of this. Either I would run and he most probably would chase me in the mood he was in, which meant if I went to my parents as previously intended, then all hell would break loose and I couldn't do that to them. So slowly I nodded as he stepped back onto the pavement whilst I re-parked my car. I switched off the engine, grabbing only my handbag slipping my phone into it, I slowly and very reluctantly opened the car door and got out. He was standing on the kerb watching me, his face stern and unrelenting. I looked away hoping I wasn't making a big mistake.

I walked a little behind him, not trusting him fully as I once had. He looked back stepping aside when he reached our garden gate. I stopped too, not wanting to go inside.

"After you Grace" he beckoned with his arm for me to move forward. Instead I shook my head standing firm.

"I don't think I can do that."

CHASING RAINBOWS

He inhaled deeply before giving me a slight nod and going ahead of me. I paused on the pavement not sure whether to follow or just remain where I was.

He stood staring at me from the threshold of what was once our home, yet now, it was beginning to feel like a prison to me, with him as my jailer.

"I promise I won't touch you Grace, if that's what you're worried about."

"You need to stay away from me Dylan. The moment you get too close, I am gone."

He walked away as if he hadn't heard me and with heavy steps I followed closing the front door reluctantly behind me. When I entered the lounge he was sitting on the armchair nearest the fireplace. His head was in his hands.

"You can sit down, I won't bite Grace."

"Here is fine."

He raised his head looking at me standing in the doorway. He shook his head

"Grace, sit the fuck down, please." the last word coming out almost like a plea.

I did without a word, knowing from this moment on, both Dylan and I were entering new territory. I held on tight to my handbag, just in case I needed to flee.

"How, Grace did you find out?"

I gulped, silently realising in the first sentence he had trapped me. If I was completely honest, I would tell him that Zara had told me and I knew that would not bode well and would be a deal breaker for him and her. Which then meant, as I knew about the funds, that he would reiterate how much he wanted us to be together. Then all would be perfect again in Dylan's little world with all monies intact, so I lied.

"I had you investigated."

His head shot up nailing me with narrowed eyes, but I showed no sign of fear, knowing how much everything depended on my performance.

"Really Grace, I hardly believe that."

"Oh well you should, otherwise how would I know. You are not the only cunning player in this sham of a marriage."

He remained silent as he stared at me, his expression telling me he wasn't sure whether to believe me or not. I returned his stare with conviction.

"If that is the case then, why return here if you were so sure. There would be no need would there?"

Shit I thought, so instead I smiled thinking quickly.

"On the contrary Dylan, I had to keep an eye on my investment. To make sure you had nothing else up your sleeve. What better way, than to move back here and like a sheep, you followed. If you had something to hide, you would keep a close eye on it, which meant you would be back, to keep a close eye on me."

He stared at me and I wasn't sure whether it was with amazement or contempt. He got up his gaze never wavering and for a moment I wasn't sure whether to stay or leave.

"You know what Grace, I have never, until now, seen you in this light. I almost want to feel proud. I can't believe how I got so bored with you." His eyes slanted sideways at me, a smile lurking on his lips.

"I can answer that one for you. You see now I am free of you, I no longer have to hide, to pander to your every need, to make you happy, so you would make me happy in return. I gave up everything for you, I was even willing to give up my baby because you made me believe we could only be happy with each other."

His mouth tightened as he sat down again,

"I didn't want to share you Grace, can't you understand that?"

"No, I can't" I spat back. "You speak in riddles. One moment I am boring you to tears, the next you can't share me with our own child." I broke off as tears threatened to fall.

"For fuck sake Grace, I don't know what the hell I want, anymore."

"Then let me make it easy for you, you can't have me. Just share equally what's owed and move on with Zara and the baby."

"Is that all you're interested in, the money?"

I flinched, "Dylan, after all that's happened, it's the only thing I have left. You lied and cheated and wanted to take away the most precious thing you ever could have given me. You saw it as an ending, when in reality, it was a new beginning for us. When you destroyed that, you destroyed us. You ripped out my soul because you already had made the same fucking mistake with Zara. Why was it me that had to suffer, if you loved me so much?"

"Grace, stop what's the point. We can never have that baby back. If it helps I am sorry, I just couldn't deal, either way I would have lost you when you found out about Zara."

CHASING RAINBOWS

He looked at me then "Admit it, if you hadn't miscarried and you found out about Zara, you would have left me. I had to push you into the abortion, I had to keep you. Without the baby you were broken and lost. You needed me. I didn't want two separate lives with two separate families."

I shrivelled in front of his eyes. I couldn't believe what he was saying. How could a man be so cold and ruthless? How could I have loved someone so much, that he would do that to me?

"I have to go," I cried just wanting to get as far away from him as I possibly could.

"Grace, if it means anything to you, I am sorry, and I still love you."

Chapter 13

Six days had passed since I saw Dylan. My parents never questioned me when I moved back in, neither did they ask me about why I was so distressed. My mother had brought up meals, which I never ate, only picked at, she took calls when Jeremy rang or called by and never once did she push me as she usually would about why I had become so withdrawn and reclusive.

I can't recall those last days for I had wallowed so deep in my own despair and misery that my mind had obliterated it and for that I was truly thankful. Even breathing was difficult, the need to wake up every morning and for that one split second before memory returned I was Grace before returning to the zombie I had become. But that was then and this is now.

Two weeks after returning home I emerged from my bedroom. Washed for the first time in ages and dressed. I had lost weight again, my skin was sallow from my induced imprisonment and my eyes framed by dark circles, but for all that I was alive and breathing. The grief eating me from the inside out was gone now. There was nothing I could do except move on and most of all avoid shithead at all cost. That is what I called him now because to call him by his given name only brought back the months of grief I had fought so hard to forget. As I entered the kitchen my mother paused in her washing up and without a word made me a hot cup of tea and two slices of buttered toast. I was suddenly starving and half a loaf later I felt full.

"Well its good to see you up and around at last Gracie" my mother said as she stroked my head on her way past.

I knew she was itching to know but this burial was mine and mine alone. I looked at her the sorrow reflecting in my eyes and she just nodded as she got on with preparing lunch.

I had thought long and hard about what I was going to do. My job had granted me garden leave as shithead's protégé was so involved with the publishing house they didn't want a conflict of interests. It suited me fine and with wages paid and what I was owed from my divorce, which would be finalised in a couple of weeks I could take the time out that I needed. The house sale was proceeding well and with that all in hand everything was progressing, as it should.

So when I woke the following morning I smiled for the first time in ages, as the sun filtered through the curtains. After breakfast and with my parents out food shopping I flicked through the local newspapers, which had accumulated and looked for somewhere to live. Mum was always a few steps ahead of me and as I looked more closely she had ringed a few she thought might be of interest. After making a few calls and with viewings lined up for that day I had my second cup of coffee.

The first apartment although nice was too close to Zara's for me to feel comfortable, so with a reluctant shake of my head I left hoping the rest of the flats would be more suitable. As I drove to the next property I noticed for the first time how great the day was. The sun was still out welcoming me and as I took a long inhale of breath everything was right with the world.

The second flat was on the fifth floor small with an odour to it I didn't even want to think about. By this time I was beginning to feel despondent. I was happy staying with my parents my mother attending to my every need no matter how often I told her not to. I knew it wouldn't be long before eventually it would get on my nerves. I parked up at my last appointment looking at the semi-detached building that had been converted into two flats. The one I was looking at was on the first floor and was classed as a maisonette. The letting agent, young, suited and freshly faced welcomed me as I followed him into the building.

It was Victorian with high ceilings and large rooms with three bedrooms, a massive kitchen and a garden on the ground floor. All the wood was antique pine and I loved it on sight. I knew it was too big for me but that didn't matter. I could put my own stamp on it and being on the first floor did make me feel safer in case shithead once more decided to make me the object of his attention. An hour later I left the letting office after signing the lease for six months and paying the deposits.

My mobile phone, which I had carelessly discarded days before, was as dead as a dodo. Connecting it to my charger I got on with my morning. It felt so good to be alive and as I looked back at my reflection in the bathroom mirror after my shower, I knew the only way for me was up. I had languished under the hot water using it all, which meant my mother would be on my back about the wastefulness but I didn't care, not today. When I eventually had gone downstairs to the kitchen all was quiet, neat and tidy. I frowned momentarily at the quiet eeriness of it all, where was my mother who was always preparing and cooking food at this time. Then the light bulb in my head went off reminding me that both of them had gone out for the day.

So I had the house to myself.   This rare occurrence I was thoroughly going to enjoy. The evening before my parents had asked casually whether I wanted to tag along, but I had just shook my head and neither of them had pressed me further, though the silent glances shared between them spoke volumes. I opened the fridge door as my stomach began to rumble and as if by telepathy there on the middle shelf was a dinner plate cling filmed over with a note from my mother.

Gracie, heat this up in the microwave for five minutes, let it stand for two minutes before eating it. I don't know what time we will be back and dad and I are dining out. Be good and wash up after. Love mum xxx

I raised my eyes to the heavens in silent recrimination. I had been married for over five years and heedless of my mother's thoughts had cooked and yes reheated. I looked more closely at the cottage pie. It did look appetising and I was hungry so as instructed in the microwave it went in for the allocated time. I half filled the kettle putting it on for my first cup of tea of the day.

Minutes later sitting at the table with my food and brewed mug of char I sighed feeling all was right with the world. The house being so deathly silent alerted me in high volume when my mobile started ringing from my bedroom I paused in my eating and looked up. Should I answer or just leave it. Whoever it was would ring back if it was important. But, the niggly little voice inside my head had me standing up and running out into the hallway. Of course when I reached the phone it was silent and for a moment I pondered ignoring it. But then the light was flashing telling me you've got a message. Open me it pleaded so I did.

I was amazed at the amount of messages on there from Jeremy. Mum must have given him my number and added him to my phone, so much for not interfering I thought. I looked at them long and hard musing whether to read them or leave them till later when I felt ready. I know I was being a coward but I hadn't seen or spoken to him for a few weeks now. I just didn't know what to say to him or how to apologise. Time had healed me in the aftermath of shithead, but at the same time had made it more difficult where Jeremy was concerned. He was a nice decent guy and I had treated him like dirt. It was easier to let sleeping dogs lie I thought.

I was about to put the phone down when Zara's message caught my eye. Now I froze wondering what the hell she wanted. As far as I was concerned everything between us had been said at our last meeting at her place, so this was probably a ploy on shitheads behalf when he couldn't get hold of me. Before pressing the delete button I scrolled down the list of messages surprised to see none from him. Frowning I returned back to the message from Zara. Heading back downstairs to the kitchen it wasn't until I was sitting down picking up my fork to finish my dinner when I looked again at the screen flashing on my phone. I finished my meal, washed up and put away before returning to the table to drink the cool dregs of my tea. As I put the mug down on the table I looked once more at my mobile. Chewing my bottom lip I eyed it like it was about to scarper. I picked it up then put it down again still in two minds whether I wanted to put my curiosity at rest and maybe ruin my day or just simply ignore it. Yet for all that I knew I wouldn't be able to avoid it knowing it would bug me, so with a deep sigh I picked it up and opened it.

A few words were all she had texted me but it sent me reeling.

In hospital, in labour please can you come.

I read and re read in seconds my mind reeling from her message. I jumped up putting my mug in the sink all the time looking at the screen. When did this happen and why did she need me? Where was shithead when the chips were down? Oh yes that's right doing his own thing. Then it hit me. He had been in the hospital cafeteria when I had been there with Jeremy visiting Florrie all those weeks ago. Florrie her name slipped out of my mouth making me stop on my way to the hallway. I had left her along with Jeremy all those weeks ago without a word or a care. I felt ashamed and for a brief moment considered retracing my steps back to the kitchen to hide away. I needed to think, to breathe. I sat down on the hall bench the mobile beside me. I hung my head between my knees trying to overcome the dizziness that followed. Come on Grace you can do this I kept repeating to myself, all the time concentrating on my breathing until it became shallow again. What had happened to the new me, the new resilient, reborn Grace? I was in there I was just having a problem reaching the surface. Minutes ticked by and when the dizziness had subsided I had come to a decision.

Dropping my mobile into my bag, grabbing my coat I headed towards the front door. It was time for me to come back and come back I would. I had nothing to feel afraid of, I had achieved so much in the last six months I almost didn't recognize myself. Starting up my car I hunted for my phone sending Zara a quick message

'Are you ok are you still in hospital?'

Her response was immediate *'I am in the apartment, come round'*

This time when I pressed the buzzer for entry into the complex I was thinking of the last time I was here when Jeremy had brought me. Taking a deep breath as the gates opened I walked briskly up the drive not as slowly as before only looking round to see if shithead's BMW was parked up. It wasn't, so with renewed confidence I pressed the buzzer again and walked into the foyer straight towards the lift. This time the grand surroundings did not daunt me and as I stared back at my reflection in the lift mirrors, I found myself smiling back. When I entered the hallway the door opposite me was still closed. I frowned momentarily knowing that Zara was expecting me. Ringing the bell it was a few moments before she opened the door. The previous image of her on my last visit had vanished and in its place stood my ex friend with tousled hair an unmade face wearing jogging bottoms and a sweatshirt. The shock must have been evident on my face as she let me in I noticed her trying to tidy her hair.

"Grace, better late than never"

"I just read your message what's happened" as the words left my mouth my eyes glanced down to her stomach which was no longer swollen with pregnancy.

She looked down following my gaze wincing a little.

"I had to have an emergency caesarean."

My eyes followed her to the kitchen my steps slow

"Zara are you all right, is the baby ok?"

"Grace is that why you've come, I sent that message weeks ago"

Her voice wasn't condemning but her eyes carried a clear statement. *Where were you when I needed you?*

"I err... haven't been well?"

Zara never replied she just nodded as she lifted the instant coffee jar nodding in my direction whether I wanted one. I nodded back still trying to work out why I was here.

"So what happened Zara, where's Dylan?"

She put down the kettle her hands holding onto the worktop for support.

"He's gone back to work. He was there for me when I needed him in the hospital and he keeps in touch daily always wanting to know about Matthew. I think it's going to be ok with us."

I looked at her in bewilderment. Who was this woman and where was Zara?

"So are you going to tell me what happened then?"

She looked at me sorrowfully.

"Grace, I'm sorry you know for...everything. I miss you, you know."

I remained silent as she mumbled follow me. I did so my heart felt like stone her words failing to have impact. The sitting room was messy nothing orderly like on my previous visit. Before I could summarise further she indicated for me to sit down. I did so looking confusedly at her back.

"I would like you to meet Matthew Tobias Hunt."

I sat rigid as my eyes watched her closely. In her arms lay this little bundle of white blanket with a dark curl of hair protruding out the top. I caught my breath unable to move as she stepped closer. I leant back in the chair to put distance between us, but whether Zara noticed or not she continued towards me, until gently beckoning me to open my arms she laid the sleeping baby into them. I couldn't move as I stared stonily back at her.

"What the hell do you think you are doing? Do you think this is funny Zara are you trying to hurt me?"

She stood momentarily her face blank at my reaction.

"Grace I didn't do this to hurt you, I just wanted you to meet him. I'm sorry"

I was so rigid that the baby stirred in my arms. I couldn't bring myself to look at him knowing if I did all the resolve, the soul searching I had gone through, could so easily undo me.

"Please take him off me" I cried wanting to get as far away from her and the baby as I could.

Reaching for her son she cooed to him gently as she laid him back in his crib before turning to look at me again.

"Grace...please don't go I just wanted..."

I rounded on her as I reached the door.

"Wanted what, to gloat Zara is that it. As if what you have done already isn't enough. You wanted to ram it home that you have what I always wanted, perhaps even point out that it's because you were pregnant that he tried to coerce me into aborting mine before I lost it anyway."

She looked at me her eyes blurring as she reached me.

"Grace...What are you talking about. I am so sorry. Believe me I didn't know."

I looked at her with unshed tears. She was too close for comfort all I wanted to do was push her away and get out of there.

"Grace...please don't go. I wouldn't have done this if I knew."

I looked at her with disbelieving eyes

"Really, I find that so hard to believe"

"You have to believe me... he never told me about your baby."

When I thought he couldn't have stooped any lower I shook my head as I stared back at her coldly.

"Well now you know."

The baby started to cry I looked over in his direction watching his little fists waving as he wailed for attention.

"Grace I understand how you must hate me but can you wait I don't want to leave him alone and I must go to the bathroom."

I stared at her, "Have you gone mad he's your son you deal with him." I turned and opened the door. As I did I looked back once more my eyes straying to where the baby lay. Zara had disappeared I had to get out of there but as my feet crossed the threshold I stopped as his cries grew louder. I looked back again for her but she hadn't reappeared. Tears ran down my face my body shaking as his cries increased. Without thinking I ran back into the apartment to where the baby, red in the face now wailed like his life depended on it.

"Hush now" leaning forward I picked him up and held him close to me, rocking him gently as his cries lessened. My tears fell onto his head as he nuzzled in closer.

Sitting down in the nearest chair with him in my arms, I looked through my tears inhaling his sweet baby scent, stroking the fine strands of his hair as he gradually calmed. I stroked my forefinger over his face all the time gently rocking wondering whether my baby would have been this perfect. His face was cherubic, he had Dylan's eyes a deep blue as he stared up at me and my heart wrenched over at the loss I had suffered. Holding him closer I whispered into his ear how he could have been mine and how much I would have loved him. I didn't realise until holding him how much I missed not being a mother. When I looked down at him again his mouth opened in a yawn.

"Would you mind if I held you a little longer till the pain goes away?"

His eyes closed and I hugged him closer.

I looked around for Zara but she still hadn't returned and as much as I wanted to carry on holding this precious little boy in my arms, he didn't and never would belong to me. I stood up slowly and laid him in his crib looking down at him for a long moment before whispering goodbye. Zara called out my name I paused as I walked towards the door and opened it.

"Goodbye" I muttered as I closed it quietly behind me.

Zara watched from the hallway her breathing slowing as she watched her friend leave for the last time. Stepping quietly towards the crib she smiled at her son. Looking towards the door, she hoped she hadn't done more harm than good.

Chapter 14

"Grace how did your interview go?"

I had just hung my coat up in the hall and looked at the closed kitchen door in disbelief. How did my mother do that? Walking in she smiled briefly at me as she placed the sponge fresh from the oven onto a cooling rack.

"It went fine I should be hearing from them in a week with a decision.

My mother sniffed "You are more than qualified for that position, they would be stupid not to employ you."

I smiled at her as I sat down at the kitchen table.

"You mum are biased.'

She huffed in response as she put the kettle on for tea.

'Did I mention your dad and I are out again tomorrow?'

"You are... that's twice in two weeks, what are you two up to or is dad courting you all over again."

She looked at me sternly hands on hips.

"Grace really the nonsense that comes out of your mouth sometimes."

Now I knew something was adrift. That was it that was all the explanation I was going to get. No there was something definitely afoot.

"Shall I come with you tomorrow," I asked remembering the last time I had refused them.

"As nice as that would be, you young lady have much better things to do with your time."

I nodded frowning. Okay she didn't want to tell me that was, fine.

The telephone call from the solicitor notified me not only had we exchanged contracts on the house but also I was finally Ms Fairfax again instead of Mrs Hunt. I took this news rather well I thought and ignored the strangeness of my new name as I mumbled it quietly to myself. Now all I had to do was check all my belongings at the house were in order before having them sent to the flat, which in a fortnight would become my new home.

"Mum I am going out for awhile just remembered something I haven't done."

"Okay Grace be good see you later."

Not quite sure how to take that I shook my head at my mother's new behavioural skills.

Life had definitely changed in all directions and it made me smile as getting into my car I started it and drove towards my old home.

CHASING RAINBOWS

Shithead's car wasn't there so parking in front of the house I got out and walked towards the house. As I entered the hallway I noticed how empty it looked now. Dylan had been busy whilst I had been away and for that I was thankful, as he had left me alone. What Dylan hadn't wanted he had left in fact he had left more than I was entitled to but what I didn't want the charity shops were more than welcome to have.

A couple of hours had passed and so engrossed was I in labelling what was mine and what was going to charity, I didn't hear Dylan arriving until he stood in the lounge coughing gently to get my attention. I started when I realised and looked at him with wariness bracing myself for another round of head crunching. He looked tired and somehow different. He remained quiet whilst I took in his appearance. His clothes were not as pristine and his face unshaven made him look rugged and older.

"Hi Grace. I am glad to see you."

"I wish I could say the same " I replied focusing again at my task at hand.

"How are you?" he said

I looked up from my work shrugging my shoulders

"Fine"

"Good I have already sorted out my stuff."

"Yes I noticed " interrupting him,

"We have to arrange a date for completion. Have you any thoughts on that?"

I sighed and put down my sticky pad,

"As soon as possible for me, I just need a couple of weeks to get in to my new place for somewhere to put all of this, save on storage fees."

"Ok two weeks then, I'll let the solicitor know."?

I nodded folding my arms as he turned to go.

"You all right?" I asked wondering why I had.

He stopped in the doorway,

"Yeah just tired"

"A baby will do that to you," I replied.

"You know about Matthew then," he enquired walking back into the room. He stopped a distance opposite me and for a moment we just stared at each other.

"Yes he's a beautiful little boy Dylan look after him won't you"

Although I hadn't voiced the words (like you didn't with our baby) he picked up on them and just nodded his head down.

"When did you see him?"

"Why will you bitch Zara for it?"

"No Grace."

I remained silent suddenly feeling very awkward in the room alone with him. It wasn't like before, something was missing and I couldn't quite put my finger on what it was.

I walked into the dining room and sat down at the table.

"This hasn't got a marker on it."

He looked confused for a moment before he noticed me looking at the table.

"No the new owners are buying it along with a few other things"

"Ok"

We both were silent for a time both immersed in our own thoughts.

"Dylan, I need to talk to you. After all that has happened will you stay with Zara and Matthew?"

"Why what does my future have to do with you Grace?"

"Can't you for once just answer instead of replying with another question."

He looked down at his hands letting out a long sigh before looking up.

"You have no idea Grace, what I have gone through in the last few weeks. Whilst you were out living it up I went to hell and back," he ran his hands hurriedly through his hair.

I let that jibe slide, "Why don't you tell me"?

He looked at me for a long time before he reluctantly nodded.

"Well after the last time that I saw you, work kicked off and suddenly I didn't have time for anything. Then I get a phone call from Zara saying she was bleeding and had gone called an ambulance. By the time I got to the hospital she had been rushed into theatre. When Matt was born he was rushed to intensive care and Zara... well they didn't know if she was going to make it. Eventually they stopped the haemorrhaging but for awhile I thought I was going to lose them both."

"But everything is ok now?"

"Yes. Even now just being away with work. Its all I can think about hoping they are both ok."

"Dylan can you do me a favour"

He looked at me questiongly.

"Thank Zara for me"

"For what?"

CHASING RAINBOWS

"For doing something very special and selfless. Just tell her thank you for those precious moments she gave me. She will know what I mean. If she wants to tell you that's fine with me."

He stared at me before nodding his head and getting up.

"I have to get back."

I stood too nodding in understanding,

"Well its time for goodbyes. I hope you guys will be happy"

He walked over to me then his eyes searching my face.

"Grace,"

I returned his stare "What Dylan"

"I was a prized bastard... I'm sorry for that. Matthew may only be two weeks old but God he's already taught me a lot."

"I know what you mean."

I held out my hand in farewell, "Goodbye."

He looked at my outstretched hand and shook his head. Without hesitation he pulled me into his arms and hugged me tight.

"Oh Grace I will miss you."

I hugged him briefly back without answering. After he left I took one long last stroll around the house committing everything to memory. Then grabbing my bag I left the house locking the door behind me.

It was great having my parent's home all to myself for the second time in as many weeks but by lunch I was bored to tears. I put on the radio trying to get into the beat and that didn't work. Sat down in the lounge with a book I had wanted to read for forever and that didn't work. By one o'clock I was at my wits end and looking out of the window seeing how sunny and mild it was I decided to go out. Slipping my bag over my shoulder I tucked my hands into my coat pockets and huddled into the deep collar of my coat. Mum had knitted me a red beanie hat and I wore it now thankful for its warmth. Although sunny it was very cold. I walked for a while avoiding the street where Jeremy lived. My thoughts on him though sad could not entice me to walk to his door and knock. I was too shy and too embarrassed and I wouldn't have blamed him for shutting the door in my face. So without any other destination in mind I headed for the park. Christmas was around the corner and by New Year hopefully I would have settled into my new home along with the new job I had been offered.

I entered the park enjoying the peace and quiet. The early afternoon on this sunny weekday brought me internal peace, as my surroundings were mostly empty of other people. I smiled to myself as I walked the grounds remembering the last time I was there. My life had been so different then so upside down and now all was as it should be. Noticing after a time dusk was beginning to fall I turned round to walk back the way I had come to the entrance. Deep in thought I hung my head with only my imaginings for company.

"Hey watch where your going," a voice said as arms came around me to stop me from falling as I lost my balance.

"Oh I'm sorry," I muttered the words dying on my lips when the familiar blue eyes and warm smile greeted me

"Hey Grace fancy seeing you here."

Jeremy was as warm as ever and seemed genuinely pleased to see me. I felt so embarrassed by my lack of consideration towards him my face coloured and I stepped back from his embrace.

"Sorry I have to go."

He didn't come after me and I never looked back.

I missed him after seeing him briefly that day in the park. I felt miserable and that didn't go unnoticed by my mother.

"Whatever is the matter with you Grace?"

I shrugged my shoulders in response as my eyes stared fixedly at the tv programme my father was avidly watching. The clicking of her knitting needles stopped.

"Well."

"Well what," I replied my voice rising knowing she was going to question me.

"Sssh" my father interrupted giving us both a stern look, "I am trying to listen."

My mother flicked my fathers words away as with a harrumph he turned up the volume.

"Grace into the kitchen with me I cant hear myself think."

Begrudgingly I followed noticing immediately after vacating the lounge the volume returned to normal.

"Well what's bitten your bum and made it fester" my mother demanded the moment I entered.

"Nothing," I replied sulkily sitting on the nearest chair available.

Looking at me sternly waiting for more information I looked down my arms folded tightly across my chest.

"I can see this calls for cocoa it looks like it's going to be a long night."

I groaned, "Mum just let me take the cocoa and then I will go upstairs and be out of your hair."

CHASING RAINBOWS

"Stop behaving like a moody teenager. I haven't got you for much longer Grace before you'll be moving out and starting your new job, so humour me ok."

Fair dues I thought. I sighed and looked up at her as she looked down at me,

"What on gods green earth has happened today?" Mum demanded seeing she had my full attention.

"Nothing."

Placing the hot cocoa in front of me she sat down opposite waiting for me to explain.

"I saw Jeremy today in the park."

She nodded saying nothing. I watched her but the words of wisdom never came.

"And," she eventually said looking intently at me.

"And... I felt embarrassed so when I realised who I bumped into I did the fastest disappearing act in history' I groaned.

"Oh Grace"

"I know... I know I didn't think it through. I felt so bad for not staying in contact with him when he was so nice to me after the Dylan fiasco, and I did think of contacting him when I felt better but by that time weeks had gone by and well... I decided to leave it as it was."

"You know when you were poorly shall we say, he came around everyday to see you."

"He did but why didn't you tell me?"

"Because you were in no fit state and your dad and I didn't want to put any more pressure on you, and neither may I add did Jeremy."

"But Mum come on I have been fine for a while why didn't you tell me then?"

She looked at me intently sipping at her cocoa before replying.

"Well I figured if you were interested you would have asked me."

"Since when has that ever stopped you Mum."

"True, but your dad thought as you were getting better it was best to give you some time."

"Since when have you listened to anything dad has to say?"

"Now come on Grace that's hardly fair, I admit", she added reluctantly. "That mostly I tend to heed my own advice, but on this occasion, I try to do what's best and even that's wrong."

At that moment Dad came into the room noticing the cocoa and looked at my mother enquiringly.

"Yours is in the microwave a minute or two should be enough."

He sat down "So what have you two been talking about?"

Mum shook her head in despair as she got up and switched on the microwave.

"Whatever will you do John if I die before you?"

"Probably starve my darling," he replied smiling at her.

Placing the steaming mug of cocoa in front of him she returned to her seat.

"Gracie did you get any messages from Jeremy I'm sure he told me he sent some."

My eyes opened in alarm.

"Messages" I yelled out as I ran out of the room "I had forgotten all about them."

When I returned both parents were waiting patiently looking up at me.

"Well snicket?"

"Dad why have you taken a sudden interest?"

"Because I like him. I have spent a lot of time with him helping him in that garden and now that Florrie has moved in we are trying to make it nice for next summer..."

"Florrie has moved in...you have been there, often" I cried.

My dad looked taken aback at my verbal onslaught.

"Well yes snicket your mother and I were there last week getting her room ready."

"You were" I exclaimed my eyes focused intently on my mother. She stared right back at me.

"You didn't think for one moment we weren't going to offer. You should know us better than that Grace." Her tone was indignant, like I was the one in the wrong.

"Were you ever going to tell me"?

"Yes..." my dad, stammered looking at my mother for back up.

"Oh grow up Grace. He's a lovely man and that is the one you should have married instead of that Dylan character."

Her words offended me, where was the loyalty I wanted to yell. You're my parents not his, how could you do this to me. I remained silent giving them both the evil eye. My mother's reaction to this was to beckon to dad to go into the lounge with her.

"Come on John, Grace has some reading to do."

I sat there for a while listening to the drone of the telly in the other room.

180

CHASING RAINBOWS

Chapter 15

I didn't read the messages until I was lying on my bed. My parents looked enquiringly up at me from the sofa when I announced I was having an early night.

"Sleep well snicket see you in the morning."

My mother opened her mouth to add her two pennies worth but a nudge from dad had her wishing me good night.

Propping up my pillows I looked at the mobile phone in my hand. Chewing my bottom lip I flicked to the messages counting all ten from Jeremy. Opening the first one at the bottom of the screen it read.

1.   *Grace its Jeremy your mum gave me your number. Are you ok? xx (sad face emoticon)*

2.   *Your mum says you are still unwell. Wish I were there to make you feel better. Xx (big heart emoticon)*

3.   *Miss you Grace Buster says Hi. Here if you need me xx (2 hearts emoticon)*

4.   *Grace it's been a week please let me know you're ok cant stop thinking about you. Xx (lips emoticon)*

5.   *Came round today saw you sleeping. Nearly woke you with a kiss my sleeping beauty. Xx (two faces with heart in centre emoticon)*

6.   *Grace this is an insanity plea I am going out of my mind worrying about you. Xx (crazy face emoticon)*

7.   *Thinking if I don't hear from you soon I will start walking the park aimlessly hoping to see you there. Xx (smiley face emoticon and lips emoticon)*

8.   *Your parents have been great helping me with Florrie still missing you though xx (2 sad face emoticons)*

9.   *Great news your parents tell me you are up and well. Can't wait to see you. Xxxxxxxxxxxxxxxxxxxxxxxxx oooooooooooo*

10.   *Saw you today in the park I could hardly believe it. What happened Grace?*

My eyes had blurred by the time I had read the last message sent earlier today. How could I have been so stupid? Looking at the clock it was just after eight. I read and re-read the messages again. Some making me smile the last making me sad. Without further hesitation and phone in hand I ran out of my room and into the hall pulling on my coat. My mother opened the door a smile on her face.

CHASING RAINBOWS

"Gracie don't forget your key and love... say hi to Jeremy and Florrie"

I kissed her hugging her quickly as I shouted before closing the front door, "love you."

I was shivering it was so cold outside. The car took three turns before the engine kicked in. By the time I reached his road the car hadn't even had time to warm up. I parked up close to his house suddenly feeling too shy to go any further. Taking out my phone I pressed reply to his last message

Grace: Hi I'm sorry I don't know what came over me today. Just read your messages xx (smiley face emoticon)

Jeremy: Grace hi you ok?

Grace: Fine now, how's Buster and Florrie?

Jeremy: They're great, both missing you.

Grace: Can you ever forgive me for how I have treated you lately?

A few minutes passed before his reply

Jeremy: Sorry Grace but I'm feeling very confused after what happened earlier today?

Grace: Jeremy I can understand that, but cant we just forget everything that has happened before and start again???? (Smiley face emoticon) x

Jeremy: *Is this for real Grace? I'm not the kind of guy that plays the field I like you too much to be messed around. X (sad face emoticon)*

I paused momentarily as I read his last words. I wanted so much to go forward with him but he didn't sound so sure and the way I had been of late I honestly couldn't blame him for his reluctance. I had two choices now. Either take the easy way out apologise for wasting his time and leave, or go for it and let fate decide.

Grace: *Can we start from message 5 and go on from there?????(Heart emoticon) xx*

His reply wasn't instant but I refused to run

Jeremy: *I would need you here to do that. Xx (2 heart emoticon)*

Grace: *Then your wish is my command xx (happy face emoticon)*

Jeremy: *Grace what does that mean exactly? Xx*

I got out of the car locking it dropping my keys in my pocket. I walked towards his house and stopped as I began to text.

Grace: *Go to your front door but not Buster only you xx (big heart emoticon)*

I stepped onto the path as the front door opened. Jeremy stood there his hair a golden halo from the porch light beyond.

"Hi" I greeted him nervously.

"Grace, come inside you must be freezing."

He stood aside for me to pass our bodies not touching. My heart sank the tepid welcome not what I was hoping for after our recent texting. I turned around to take off my coat when I felt his hands on my shoulders stopping me.

"Grace, I need to know one thing."

I looked at him then my heart swelling at the sight of him.

"What do you need to know?"

"I need to know if you mean this, or do you still need time?"

I moved closer into him his eyes filling with concern.

"I don't blame you if you're unsure if you've changed your mind, I can go, but I don't want to. I am so embarrassed about how I have reacted towards you lately that it was easier to avoid you than face you."

I turned to go when he didn't reply.

"Grace, can you wait here a minute?"

I nodded suddenly feeling very dejected. What was going on? My phone buzzed in my pocket. Not seeing any sign of his return I heaved a long sigh thinking it was best I go before it got any worse. He was obviously too nice to say no to my face. I took my phone out of my pocket noticing the new message. It was probably mum wanting to know how things were going. I put it back in my pocket without reading it as my hand turned the lock to open the door and leave.

"Grace, where are you going?"

I reluctantly turned around confused

"What?"

"Look at your message Grace" he added patiently watching me.

I did as he asked looking up at him when I saw it was from him.

"What's this... I don't understand?" I asked more confused than before.

He stepped closer to me

"Read your message Grace."

I took one long look at him frowning before I opened the message. It read,

Grace if it's too early to say this I apologise but I've missed you so much. I wanted you to have this in writing so you will always know how much I care for you. The future for us if you are willing starts with a (kiss emoticon) and in time when we are sure I will give you this (a ring emoticon). I will never leave you and I promise to love you everyday. When we have our ups and downs I will always be there. I want forever with you. I want this (mum, dad and children emoticon) What do you say? Xx.

CHASING RAINBOWS

My eyes blurred at the sight of him now hazy. I nodded my head without hesitation. He took me in his arms wiping away my tears.

"Do I take it that's a yes Grace?"

I smiled unable to speak. His arms came around me pulling me so close as he kissed me gently on the lips.

Ooophh the air left us both as Buster careered into us knocking us off balance. Jeremy steadied us against the porch door frame.

"Grace I forgot to mention we come as a package can you handle that?"

I was so choked all I could do was nod.

"Welcome home Grace."

Chapter 16

March the eighth two years later.

"Grace darling you can do this"

I stared at Jeremy the sweat beading on my forehead my breath laboured as another gripping pain had me yelling as grabbing his hand tightly I pushed as if my life depended on it. My husband cringed as my fingernails dug deeper into his hand.

"That's it Grace you're nearly there c'mon one more good push and it will all be over."

The midwife smiled at me between my legs as the pain eased temporarily. Jeremy smiled down at me his eyes full of pride. Love you he mouthed silently as before, I couldn't respond as another gripping pain had me yelling as red faced I pushed down for all I was worth. I felt a burning sensation below as with a smile the midwife looked up at me.

"Grace the head is out, now one more deep push and you will have your baby.

I looked at her like she had been sent from hell to torture me.

"I cant" I managed to utter before falling back against the pillows.

"Take a moment," the midwife instructed.

Jeremy looked down at the small head now lying there between my legs before looking back at me. His grin was wide as he leant in to kiss me.

"Oh noooooo..." I yelled as one more deep contraction took hold of me forcing me with all my might to expel my firstborn from my body. In one swift movement the body of our child slipped out covered in blood and white goo.

"Good girl Grace," the midwife smiled as quickly wiping our child's face our infant began to whimper.

"You'll have baby back shortly."

My eyes followed the bundle I had just delivered as it was handed to another nurse for cleaning and inspection. I fell back on the pillows exhausted yet elated. Jeremy wiping the damp hair back from my forehead leant in whispering.

"Grace the baby is beautiful."

I smiled back at him without words as the nurse returned handing me a small bundle wrapped up in a white towel.

Two little eyes of blue blinked rapidly up at me, as a surge of emotion inside of me erupted.

CHASING RAINBOWS

"What do we have?" I enquired looking at Jeremy who shrugged looking at the midwife for an answer.

"Take a peek" she replied.

We looked at each other before gently I lifted one side of the towel. This made our daughter Scarlet cry out in disgust.

"Grace we have a girl."

Jeremy's voice trembled as I handed her to him.

"Right Grace, we just have to deliver the afterbirth and then we can get you cleaned up" The midwife leaned over Jeremy now sitting in the chair a look of wonderment on his face.

"She's a pretty little thing. Looks like she has daddy's fair hair."

I had been home for a couple of days, and still between four hourly feeds and night duty I was exhausted. I turned over, my arm reaching out for Jeremy but his space was empty and cold. He had been gone awhile. Blinking trying to wake up, I heaved myself up and fell back against the pillows. It was then the bedroom door opened and my mother in all her elated grandmotherly glory swept through the door with my daughter in her arms.

"It's a lovely day Grace," my mother informed me opening the curtains before I could stop her.

"Our little princess is living up to her name, look at the colour of her face she's hungry again and letting us all know about it."

Tiredly I sat up as mum plumped up my pillows before placing a yelling, red-faced, hands fisted Scarlet in my arms.

Sitting down beside me she smiled as the baby now placating herself with breast milk, lay peacefully in my arms.

"Mum, was I ever this demanding?"

Sitting back her arms folded in front of her she smiled and nodded in answer.

"Oh yes you were more of a handful where feeding was concerned than your brother Andrew ever was."

"Where's Jeremy?"

My mother's face changed into indignation before replying.

"With your father in the garden. Buster has been up to his old tricks again and ruined the honeysuckle your dad fixed to the trellis yesterday by Florrie's window. When I catch that hound what I will do to him is nobody's business."

"What?" I interrupted trying not to laugh.

My mother, all pretence of fury vanishing from her face just shook her head. "I'll give him another bone maybe that will stop him."

"And how many bones will that be so far?" I questioned trying to keep a straight face.

"About a hundred. Your dad will have a fine old time trying to hunt that lot down."

"It doesn't matter Buster will dig them up when he wants one."

"Exactly" my mother replied her stern expression back, "Only this time I will not sit around listening to your father harping on how that dog has ruined another flowerbed."

Scarlet now full made a little pop as her mouth released and she stretched.

"Do you feel rested enough Grace to get up and have a bath?" My mother enquired taking my sleeping daughter from me and winding her over her shoulder.

"Oh yes that sounds wonderful."

"Wait there I'll just go check Florrie has run it."

I sat up my legs dangling over the edge of the bed,

"Really, you know I only had a baby not open heart surgery" I replied shaking my head.

My mother stopped on her way to the door looking back at me with raised eyebrows.

"Grace, let us spoil you."

Jeremy when he came into the kitchen smiled as he saw me, quickly ignoring the protests from my mother of muddy feet on her clean floor.

"Hey darling how you feeling?"

I looked at him inhaling the fresh air he 'd brought in with him.

"Better, found the bones yet?"

Jeremy's brows drew together before grinning.

"Nope but your dad's still out there refusing to give up. He's determined to find them all before Buster starts digging them up again."

Hearing his name the dog loped into the kitchen my mother protesting loudly again as the freshly wiped floor just finished after Jeremy's entrance was muddied again with paw prints.

"My God how do you cope with this hound?" My mother's raised voice was indignant once more.

Jeremy and I shared a secret smile before he stood up his face straightening.

"Esther, don't worry its only mud," he replied lightly, trying to placate her with a smile.

Receiving the same critical eye as the dog beside him, with her arm outstretched her forefinger pointing towards the back door they both left without a word.

I smiled loving my life and loving him. As always when I felt especially blessed I picked up my phone to read the message I had saved such a long time ago. His oath to me still gave me that thrill and I revelled in the happiness he had, as promised, bestowed upon me. I looked up to see my mother and Florrie in quiet consultation, as stopping their conversation they both looked enquiringly at me.

"Grace, are you ok?" My mother asked gently.

"Couldn't be better," I replied smiling at them my eyes resting on my daughter happily sleeping in her crib beside my chair. Resting back in the armchair I looked around my large kitchen/diner come snug. We still lived in the house Jeremy bought only now instead of a building site promising us years of commitment and blood sweat and tears to complete it I had used Dylan's secret funds to hurry it to the finish line.

Jeremy on the other hand had stood proud and was totally against the idea

"No Grace, no way will a penny of that man's money ever find a place in my home."

"Is that your final word?" I demanded my anger threatening to spill.

"Grace, I love you this is our home. I made a promise to you and I will keep it. I will get it done but it will take time and a lot of money, but we'll do it."

I stood there my arms folded my eyes narrowing at him.

"But that will take years. Why does it matter so much to you where the money comes from to finish it? Sooner rather than later, right!"

He looked at me dejectedly.

"Because it just does. Dylan was a bastard to you Grace, I just cant bear the thought of anything of him in here in our home, our life."

Feeling the tears gather in my eyes I sat down on the nearest chair, my arms folded tightly across my chest.

"I earn't that money fair and square. I don't want to have it just sitting there in the bank doing nothing when all it's achieving is zeros. I love you, my god you love me, you gave me an engagement ring to prove it," I cried holding up my left hand in evidence. It's just so stupid not to use it, to put it to good use. I've done my time please let me do this so I can replace the pain with our memories and our happiness."

He sat down silently, his elbows resting on the kitchen table, his head resting on his arms. A few minutes passed before I got up and went over to him bending down to hug him.

"Its money, that's all it is, please understand that."

Jeremy didn't reply, feeling annoyed at his pride I walked out of the room and upstairs to our bedroom where I just lay on the bed to angry to cry.

Florrie hearing the sudden quiet got up from her armchair in her lounge and walked over to the door opening it. Jeremy sat unmoving at the table not stirring when she entered the kitchen. Buster lifting his paw up that had covered his eyes when the voices had raised looked at her as he lumbered over to the back door to be released into the garden.

"There you go boy," Florrie muttered handing him a treat as he ambled outside.

"Would you like a cup of tea?"

Jeremy lifted his head, his face sad. "That would be great gran."

Whilst the kettle boiled she wondered if she should intervene, no interfere. That was what was needed. Finishing the drinks she placed Jeremy's in front of him.

"I couldn't help but hear your conversation with Grace."

Her grandson sighed looking at her with eyes of defeat.

"Sure why not."

Florrie took a sip of her tea before looking directly at him.

"Do you remember when you bought this house? How it took every last penny you had."

He nodded in silence, so Florrie continued.

"Do you also remember how proud I was of you, that you had managed alone without any other financial help to buy it?"

He nodded again.

She sipped her tea again.

"Because, if I remember correctly, when I offered financial help to get you started on the renovations you adamantly refused that too. Quite heatedly too if I remember rightly."

Folding his arms across his chest and with a sigh he answered.

"Gran, your point is?"

CHASING RAINBOWS

"Pride comes before a fall Jeremy. That wonderful girl of yours has fought long and hard to get where she is now. Ah ah, ah... don't interrupt me" she continued as Jeremy opened his mouth to intervene.

"What I am trying to say, is cant you see what she is trying to say without being direct and hurting your feelings?"

Jeremy looked more confused.

"This house belongs to you nobody else. When you and Grace get married and start a family she also wants to feel as though she belongs here."

"But Gran she does, this is our house."

"In your head maybe but not in hers. Her mother told me how her life had been with Dylan. How he had manipulated her and belittled her, everything being on his own terms."

She paused whilst it sank in.

"Now do you catch my drift. If you can find it in yourself to get of that high horse and let her contribute, everyone will benefit from it. The house will be finished and then perhaps we can start with the wedding arrangements. So do I take it it's a yes to the house fund?"

Jeremy looked back at her with seeing eyes. Standing up he smiled at her before heading for the stairs.

A year later on a sunny June day Grace took a deep breath not believing that today was her wedding day. Her mother, dressed in a deep shade of lilac flustered around her, as she stood upright in front of the full-length mirror staring at her reflection. This time round she had chosen a simple gown in ivory satin. It hung to the floor in gently folds, catching the rays from the window. Her hair left long had been interwoven with an ivory band of real flowers and when she looked back at herself, all she could see was a young woman so happy her eyes shone.

"Snicket, are you ready?" My dad asked gently his eyes caressing my face as the wedding march began to play.

"I am." Looking straight ahead to see my fiancé turning to look back at me I let myself be led forward. His smile was beaming as I neared him kissing my dad on the cheek he handed me over with moistened eyes. Jeremy took my right hand holding it gently in his own. Looking down at me he smiled.

I love you he mouthed; I love you back I whispered.
THE END

46181863R00113

Printed in Poland
by Amazon Fulfillment
Poland Sp. z o.o., Wrocław